Eyes round, both her hands now on the door for balance, Kate tipped her head, trying to see what Ian was about and inadvertently gave him access to her long neck. He brushed his lips across the smooth white flesh just beneath her jaw and she gasped.

Inhaling the scent of rose and woman, he murmured, "'Tis petal soft, Kate, just as I imagined."

"Cease imagining!"

A Thief in a Kilt

Sandy Blair

ZEBRA BOOKS
Kensington Publishing Corp.
www.kensingtonbooks.com

ZEBRA BOOKS are published by

Kensington Publishing Corp.
850 Third Avenue
New York, NY 10022

All Kensington titles, imprints, and distributed lines are available at special quantity discounts for bulk purchases for sales promotion, premiums, fund-raising, educational, or institutional use.

Special book excerpts or customized printings can also be created to fit specific needs. For details, write or phone the office of the Kensington Special Sales Manager: Attn. Special Sales Department. Kensington Publishing Corp., 850 Third Avenue, New York, NY 10022. Phone: 1-800-221-2647.

Zebra and the Z logo Reg. U.S. Pat. & TM Off.

First Printing: November 2006
10 9 8 7 6 5 4 3 2 1

Printed in the United States of America

To Suzy, my dear friend and critique partner.
For laughing in the right places,
For getting misty-eyed where I'd hoped you would,
And for all your invaluable support.

ACKNOWLEDGMENTS

The author would like to thank:

Hilary Sares, editor par excellence, whose steadfast encouragement and support turned this fourth dream into a reality bound between two beautiful covers;

Paige Wheeler, agent extraordinaire, for her invaluable advice and enthusiasm;

Nancy Berland, publicist without peer, whose magic I couldn't do without;

Scott Blair, husband and lover, who took me from castle to castle and carried mountains of research books up winding staircases with a minimal amount of *humphing;*

Alex Blair, son and computer wizard, for keeping a straight face every time I misplaced the manuscript in my computer;

Dearest friends Suzuanne Welsh, Julie Benson, Jane Graves, Lorelle Marinello, Kandy Tobin and Dianna Love Snell, whose enthusiastic support and goading keeps me going;

My dear friends in DARA who taught me how to write;

The Wet Noodle Posse for being the shoulder I lean on;

The brilliant Billie Jo Case for creating the Fan Club, and all the wonderful readers who come there each morning to visit with me;

Avid romance reader Kim J. for solidifying this heroine in my mind;

And lastly, my heartfelt thanks to the incomparable and gracious *New York Times* bestselling author Lorraine Heath for providing the wonderful quote on the cover.

Chapter 1

Late spring, 1411
Stirling Castle, Scotland

While smoke from a dozen rush torches wafted about the rafters like worried ghosts, Ian MacKay studied the men and women milling before him in Stirling's great hall. Each, he'd decided long ago, was either flint or kindling. Each, whether they kenned it or not, had the capacity to turn Scotland into a raging inferno.

Something he'd willingly die to prevent.

His attention shifted slowly from one chieftain to another but never lingered. Should he focus too long on one man, he could inadvertently set rival tongues to wagging. He served, after all, as Albany's eyes and ears within the realm. Their regent's spy. Not a position he relished—in fact, he loathed it—but that couldna alter his determination to maintain his position. 'Twas his only hope for seeing his rightful king on the throne and for keeping his kith and kin secure in their northwest Highland home.

Nay easy task, given the MacKays were a querulous

lot forever at odds with their neighbors, the more powerful Sutherlands to their south and the St. Clairs to their east. Worse, his liege lord was now the hot-blooded Black Angus. Worse still, the man was his brother-by-marriage.

Aye, for his clan and king he would remain, suppressing his longing for a family of his own, more often garbed in silk instead of his *breachen feile,* suffering ridiculous shoes when he much preferred going barefoot, traveling hither and yon at Albany's whim, all in the name of Scotland.

He heaved a resigned sigh as a harassed-looking warrior shouldered his way through the crowd and approached the cluster of Campbells.

God's teeth, now what?

He tried to read the agitated man's lips as John Campbell, a barrel-chested chieftain normally of good humor, narrowed his eyes and then scowled. A heartbeat later the warrior rushed off.

"What has the auld man scowling?"

Ian glanced at his younger brother, Shamus, and again mentally cursed the pox that had ruined the lad's once-handsome countenance. Thank God their sister had been spared.

"The Campbells are at odds with the Stewarts of Appin again. Not wise, given the Stewart's marriage alliance."

Shamus grunted. "Aye, and their powerful Douglas allies."

"Aye." But then the Campbell had a few allies of his own. Duncan MacDougall of Drasmoor, for one.

A strong liege lord in his own right, the laird of Castle Blackstone could bring nine hundred battle-tested warriors onto a field of battle if need be. Duncan's entry into battle would doubtless suck

Angus the Blood of Donaleigh in; the men had fought shoulder to shoulder for decades. Sensing a possible Stewart defeat, the Douglas—having signed a secret pledge with Albany—would have nay choice but to call forth his five thousand men. The earl of Sutherland, loathing Douglas, would then enter the battle, and Ian had little doubt *his* liege would use Sutherland's entrance as an excuse to summon his four thousand warriors with the lift of his beefy hand.

Then, God help them all.

Meanwhile, the loathsome English would be watching and grinning into their cups, waiting for Scotland to self-destruct.

Which, given the current tensions, was altogether possible.

That Scotland should be so easily torn asunder— that matters could so easily get out of hand by a simple reiving or misunderstanding—made Ian's blood boil.

"Shamus, ye will have to excuse me. I fear I have work to do else all hell breaks loose." Without waiting for a response, he strode toward the Campbells.

"Brother, before ye go!"

Ian turned to find Shamus shouldering his way through the crowd. Finally at his side and grinning, Shamus murmured, "'Pride. Envy. Avarice. These are the sparks have set on fire the hearts of all men.'"

Ian laughed. "*Inferno* and sadly too true. Ye now owe me L700 and sixpence."

"Shit. How could ye have read it already? Ye just purchased it."

Ian winked. "I had plenty of time on the way back from France."

Shamus made a derisive sound at the back of his throat. "One of these days . . ."

"Aye, one of these days ye will best me. Now be off with ye. We both have work to do."

Ian grinned as Shamus, muttering, his back hunched, walked away. They'd played this game for nigh on to a decade now and his having a prodigious memory did have its advantages. Ian's repetitive winning kept his brother reading. An imperative, given he fully expected to die without issue, leaving Shamus to take control of Seabhagnead, his beloved mountain keep . . . should he ever finish it. And to be an effective laird, his brother would need more than his engaging smile and strong arm; he'd need the insight and resourcefulness he'd glean through the books Ian deliberately left hanging about.

But enough of this. He had a war to prevent.

With his gaze on the Campbell, Ian nearly trampled Lady Mary MacKinnon when she stepped into his path. Forcing a smile he murmured, "My pardon, my lady."

The raven-haired chatelaine of Brittle Moor placed her hand on his arm. "Ian, dearest, I've missed ye."

"Ah, I have thought of ye often as well."

Mary tipped her head and studied him through thick black lashes, a charming pout gracing her bowed lips. "Then why am I seeking ye out instead of whithershins? Ye have been home for nearly a week, yet my bed remains cold. Hmmm?"

He sighed. On Albany's orders he'd gone to Brittle Moor to offer the crown's reassurances that the lady and her clan would continue to have protection after her husband died. She, in turn, had spilled her tears and fears all over his chest, as many a lady tended to do. Being a gentleman and having

a weakness for bonnie brunettes, he'd naturally offered comfort. But like the seasons, each had its
own time and theirs had passed.

"Now, Mary, ye ken I canna be tupping another
man's wife. I do have some scruples." Not many when
it came to bedding luscious wenches, but a few.

Glancing about, she whispered, "I'm no man's
wife for a fortnight yet and well you ken it." She
shuddered in delicate fashion. "Oh, to be man . . .
or a wealthy woman who could buy her way free."

Ian patted the delicately boned hand, which had
brought him a good deal of pleasure some three
moons past, before easing it off his arm.

Mary had been sold into marriage at the age of
fourteen to a sickly man thrice her age and was now
pledged to an apparently viral chieftain who had
sired five daughters and desperately needed a son.
Her bed wouldna be cold for long. "If ye find
MacLeod so loathsome, ye should have taken my
advice and pledged yerself to the church, become a
voweress."

Mary snorted derisively. "Now? After ye introduced me to the delicious—ah, my lord MacLeod!"

Ian glanced left to find Mary's burly fiancé bearing
down on them. He acknowledged the ruddy-faced
Lord of the Isle of Lewis with a nod and raised his
voice to normal volume. "I'll keep an eye out for a
suitable palfrey, my lady. Docile, black and no more
than thirteen hands high, as ye lust."

Bright pink spots bloomed on Mary's cheeks. "Perfect." She beamed up at MacLeod, who looked none
too pleased to find Ian at his betrothed's side. "My
lord, I was just telling Sir MacKay that my ancient
mare willna be able to handle yer Isle's rugged terrain, and he graciously offered to find me another."

MacLeod wrapped a possessive arm around Mary's waist and pulled her to his side. Locking gazes with Ian he muttered, "We have cattle aplenty, my lady. No need to bother MacKay with such trivial matters, now is there?"

Mary patted MacLeod's mail-clad chest and sighed. "Of course, my lord. How thoughtless of me. My apologies, Sir MacKay."

Ah, as he suspected. The lady wasna as opposed to this new union as she would have him believe.

Ian bowed. "As ye lust, my lady. I shall forget the matter entirely." To MacLeod he said, "Good eve, MacLeod, and my best wishes on your upcoming nuptials."

As he strode away, MacLeod growled "bastard" under his breath, and Ian sighed. Mary played a dangerous game. Thank heaven he had had the wisdom to ignore her last missive summoning him to her chambers. He wouldna be the least surprised to learn her betrothed had secreted a number of spies about her. 'Twas one thing to have half of Scotland calling him the Thief of Hearts. 'Twas quite another to be caught at it.

He shuddered and quickened his pace, again focused on forestalling a conflict between the Campbells and Stewarts.

As if sensing his approach, the seafaring Campbells of Dunstaffnage parted, and Ian caught sight of an extraordinarily tall woman in widow's garb on the far side of the hall. The hairs on the back of his neck bristled and he slowed to study the stranger silhouetted by a full moon.

Humph!

Albany had been explicit when he had summoned the chieftains to the General Council. Each was to have no more than ten in their party and those were to be kin. He kenned every leader within the realm and none had married or produced such a tall and . . . *plush* lass.

An angry shout jerked his attention back to the Campbells. Ack. The mystery of the stranger would have to wait. But not for long. He wouldna put it past the bloody English to put a Trojan horse amongst them. Were he in their position, he most certainly would.

Chapter 2

Oh, to be back in England where I belong. Aye, and with a substantial bowl of bread pudding before me at that.

Despite the evening chill racing through the open windows at her back, beads of sweat trickled between Katherine Templeton's breasts as she scanned Stirling Castle's crowded great hall for the one man who could be her undoing: Scotland's infamous Thief of Hearts, Ian MacKay.

"Should you find yourself in Stirling be on the watch for an extraordinarily tall and handsome man with flaxen hair, whose laugh sounds like thunder. Under no circumstances," Sir Gregory had warned, *"are you to engage this man's interest. He's Albany's man and therefore your enemy."*

Why King James's ancient guardian had felt compelled to say "engage the man's interest" was beyond understanding. Standing nearly six feet tall and weighing ten stones, Kate had never engaged a man's *interest*—much less that of a reputed rogue's—in all her four and twenty years. Well, perhaps more than a few men have stared—referred to her as "the cow" behind her back—but none had ever expressed an *interest.* Praise the saints none save her grandmother knew of her gift of sight or her life would truly prove unbearable.

Feeling a hand on her arm, Kate jerked and found her escort, Charles Fraser, frowning up at her. "Madame Campbell, are ye nay feeling well?"

Oh, mercy, how long had the old man been trying to get her attention? Calling her Madame Campbell? She really needed to pay more heed. "I am quite well, my lord, although a bit nervous, this being my first visit to your illustrious court."

Sir Charles, a balding, sallow-skinned man who had found her beating on his keep's door—looking for all the world like a drowned cat after she'd lost her map and thus her way in a torrential rain—chuckled in gravelly fashion. "'Tis a sight, I will grant ye. But then again, it canna be much different from the French court, now can it?"

Praying she had not been misinformed, Kate assured him, "Aye, but it is." According to her father, France's king had more dust in his coffers than gold thanks to his taste for war and opulence, whilst these Scots—particularly the Lowlanders Sir Douglas and Sir Donald—were hip-deep in obvious prosperity, which did not bode well for her mission: to find Lady Margaret Campbell, Sir Gregory's wife, and to learn why the Scots were allowing their king to languish in the Tower of London.

Hoping she sounded calmer than she felt, Kate murmured, "Truth to tell, Sir Charles, I find your ladies far fairer than mine. I fear Robbie's family will find me quite lacking." Sir Gregory had insisted her gowns be altered so that they clung to her every abundant swell instead of hanging the way she liked them, all loose and comfy. Augh.

Sir Charles's watery gaze shifted from her face to her gown's scooped neckline. "Trust me, my lady, ye havena reason to fash on that account."

Oh, good heavens, she'd opened herself up for that observation, now hadn't she? Were she in London, she would have bristled like a hedgehog and stared the old man down. But she wasn't at home but deep within enemy territory, thanks to her blasted gift and conscience.

Hoping to redirect Fraser's gaze, Kate pointed to the large group to her right. "Who is the tall man dressed in black leather and plaid?" She had no idea who among the throng were her supposed relatives-by-marriage, and she had to find Lady Margaret Campbell as soon as possible.

It took an uncomfortable moment for her aging escort to pull his gaze from her overflowing décolleté and to look at the man she had indicated. "'Tis the MacDougall."

Not a Campbell. Oh, well. At least she had correctly assumed from his garb that the man was a Highlander. "And the lovely lady in green at his side?" There was something familiar about the woman, which of course there couldn't be—or rather shouldn't be.

Charles's brow furrowed. "That would be Lady Beth, the MacDougall's fourth wife."

"Fourth?" The poor man.

"Aye. His first—a distant cousin of yer dearly departed husband's—died in childbirth. The MacDougall's second wife committed suicide and the third died under mysterious circumstances."

Hmmm. Watching the MacDougall chieftain slip a protective arm around his new wife's waist, and then grinning, whisper in her ear, Kate nearly sighed. "A love match this time?"

Fraser snorted. "Kenning the MacDougall as I do, I doubt it, but then again they do appear quite taken with each other now that ye point it out."

A twinge of jealousy skittered across Kate's heart as Lady MacDougall, a willowy woman well into her third decade, suddenly blushed under her handsome husband's close scrutiny.

Would such a man ever look upon *her* in such fashion? Not likely, what with her standing a full head higher than most, her king included. Heaving a resigned sigh, Kate cursed her raiding Norse ancestor for the hundredth time and then her gift of sight, the very thing that had brought her here.

Some *gift*. Ugh.

Cursed since birth, she had quickly learned to keep her insights to herself. Her Norman-bred and deeply religious father had regularly chastised her gifted mother, the daughter of a Romany fortune-teller, until the day she told him that she would die on the morrow—and did, trampled by a team of runaway horses during a London food riot.

Now, should Kate happen to sniff the air and absently mutter, "Rain is coming," her father would question her to the point of madness. To her sorrow his inquisitions were usually the only attention he ever paid her.

As tutor to the imprisoned James I of Scotland, her father had been charged by King Henry five years ago with "correcting the Scottish brat's misconceptions." To instill the concept of feudal law and to make a proper English subject out of the boy or die trying. By default, she had become poor James's only female companion. Eight years his senior, she had initially provided comfort and distraction when the terrified eleven-year-old had arrived in the Tower. But as time passed and James matured, their relationship grew strained. Now sixteen years and nearly a man, James was decidedly distant and hostile.

So she had kept her concerns to herself until that dreadful day—King James's birthday—when she had visited him in the Tower. After a stilted greeting, he had reluctantly opened her gift, what she had hoped was an accurate rendering of his homeland. As he studied the details she had painstakingly created, images she had garnered from the stories he had related over the years, his eyes filled with tears. He then threw his arms about her. To her horror, the sudden image of her young friend as a ferocious and vengeful adult nearly blinded her. And the atrocities he would commit—

She shuddered, willing them away.

With absolute certainty she knew then that she could no longer keep her fears to herself. To save her friend from the man he would become, to save the innocent he would destroy as he sought revenge on those whom he believed had abandoned him, she had confided in the one closest to James, Sir Gregory, the old man who had been captured with him.

Which is how she came to be in Scotland, posing as the French widow of Sir Gregory's youngest son.

"Would you care to meet the MacDougall and his bride?"

Startled out of her reverie, Kate sputtered, "Yes, yes, my lord, I would indeed." The MacDougall was one of the men she very much needed to speak with. Alone.

As Fraser guided her through the throng, Kate again scanned the crowd for the Thief of Hearts.

Finding a tall blond man on the far side of the room, her steps faltered and her pulse quickened.

Oh, Lord, is that the Thief?

As if hearing her thoughts, the man standing before the enormous stone hearth glanced to his right, giving Kate a clear view of his profile: one ravaged by pox. Nay, that can't be him. Blast and the devil take it!

How could she avoid MacKay if she didn't know precisely where he was? Perhaps Albany had sent the letch on a distant mission. Could she be so fortunate?

Please, Lord, let the Thief be in Flanders or Rome, anywhere but here, so I might do what I came here to do and be gone, with Albany and MacKay none the wiser.

At her side Fraser murmured, "Laird and Lady MacDougall, may I introduce our guest Madame Katherine Campbell, the widow of Sir Robbie Campbell."

On shaking legs Kate managed a respectable curtsy before the handsome MacDougall liege lord and his lady. "My lord, my lady, 'tis a pleasure to make your acquaintance."

The MacDougall, a dark-haired man a full hand higher than she, grinned as he took her hand and helped her to rise. "Ah, another coigreach to our land like my Beth. Welcome to Scotland."

Coigreach? Ah, Sir Gregory had used the word as he taught Gael to James. It meant foreigner. Praying Lady MacDougall wasn't French, Kate murmured, "Thank you, my lord."

"May I be so rude as to ask to *which* Robbie Campbell you were married to? My apologies, but we have so many."

"To Sir Gregory Campbell's youngest son."

The MacDougall's eyebrows shot up. "Truly?"

Oh, dear! Why does he find this questionable?

"Yes, we met in Rhone and were married just three months prior to his being killed."

"My condolences on the match."

Huh?

He was offering his condolences not on her supposed loss but on the match? Her stomach quivered, wondering what on earth Sir Gregory had neglected to mention about his son.

Before she could form a probing question, Lady MacDougall murmured, "I apologize for my husband, Madame Campbell. I am sure he did not mean for his words to come . . . umm, as they did. My sympathy."

The woman then clasped both of Kate's hands. Before Kate could pull away, a formidable ache roared to life behind her eyes. With the pain came the sounds of battle and the image of Lady MacDougall, keening and covered in soot, clutching four terrified children to her breast as flames crackled and shot up all about them.

Oh, dear God. No wonder I thought the lady familiar. I have glimpsed some of this before in dreams.

Hoping she viewed a moment from Lady Mac-Dougall's past, but suspecting it was a flash of the lady's morrow, Kate battled the pain and tried to memorize every detail before the image faded.

Before she could glean the location, Lady Beth let go of her hands and the troubling vision evaporated. She then heard Lady Beth murmur, "Oh, Duncan, now look what you've done. You've made Madame Campbell cry."

Kate blinked and felt tears slip down her cheeks. Embarrassed, she dashed them away. "Please pardon me. I fear I am easily discomposed of late."

The MacDougall, looking totally contrite, muttered, "My apologies, Madame Campbell, I didna mean to upset ye, but what with Robbie Campbell having a hairlip, a bald pate and the temper of a wild boar, I had simply assumed ye might be happier now than before . . . if ye catch my meaning."

What?

Looking as appalled as Kate felt, Lady Beth slapped the back of her hand against her handsome husband's middle. "Duncan! For God's sake—"

The blood drained from Kate's head.

Lady Beth had spoken in English—oddly accented to be sure, but still English! Bile rose in Kate's throat.

Oh, Lord have mercy! I never should have agreed to come here. She was either losing her mind or these people were already aware of who she really was and were merely toying with her.

Before she could utter a word, inexplicable heat infused her back from nape to buttocks and a warm, deep-throated murmur—one carrying the scent of mint and heady male musk—asked, "Now who have we here?"

Kate's heart slammed against her ribs and her knees buckled. Without turning her head she had no doubt who stood so close that she could hear his heart. Or was that hers?

As if to confirm her worst fears, Lady Beth exclaimed, "Ian! How wonderful to see you again."

Wishing with all her might that she was truly in her grandmother's Salisbury cottage where her father thought her to be, Kate slowly turned her head.

Chapter 3

Oh. My. Word!

The man staring down at her was . . . magnificent.

Not only did the Thief of Hearts stand a full hand higher than she and have the widest shoulders she had ever beheld, but he appeared to be made of gold.

Golden, shoulder-length hair swung in wavy profusion around a striking chiseled countenance highlighted by gold-flecked eyes rimmed by gold-tipped lashes, above which lay thick, dark gold eyebrows on a broad, intelligent-looking forehead. Even his sun-darkened skin carried a decided golden hue. The wide, hammered brass cuff encircling his left wrist and the matching belt girdling his narrow hips only added to the illusion. As she stared, double dimples suddenly carved great channels into his cheeks, making him appear years younger and very approachable were she of the mind.

Suddenly realizing she gawked, stood not on her own two feet but leaned against him, she yelped, "Unhand me."

MacKay chuckled. "I would, my dear, but note, *ye* are holding me."

Brow furrowing, Kate looked down and saw that her left hand did indeed clutch the Thief's heavily muscled forearm. She squeaked and let go as if burnt, wobbled, and then hurriedly stepped away.

Good graces! Nothing was going according to Sir Gregory's plan. And why was MacKay still grinning at her?

Thankfully, Laird MacDougall asked, "Ian, how goes it in Edinburgh?"

MacKay's gaze regrettably remained on her as he responded, "Growing by leaps and bounds. The burghers have taken over. 'Twill look like London or Paris in another decade."

Lady Beth sighed. "About time. I am weary of waiting for foreign shipments that fail to meet even my low expectations."

MacKay flashed his dimples again. "Nonsense, my lady. You, as always, outshine the sun."

Lady Beth tsked. "You, Ian, are incorrigible and in sore need of a wife." Moving to Kate's side, she said, "Madame Campbell, may I properly introduce Sir Ian MacKay, counsel to our regent and all-round scoundrel of the heart."

Eyes flashing, crinkling at the corners, MacKay pressed a hand to his heart. "Ack, Beth, ye wound me."

MacDougall's wife rolled her eyes and leaned toward Kate. "Never say I didna warn ye."

Oh, dear. Apparently Sir Gregory hadn't exaggerated. Feeling a burst of color blooming in her cheeks, Kate managed to curtsey. "Sir MacKay, it's a . . . pleasure. I have heard much."

He held out a long-fingered, calloused hand as Laird MacDougall had. Reluctantly she placed her hand in his. Heat surged through her as he helped her to rise. Studying her from beneath partially low-

ered eyelids, he assured her, "Nay, my lady, the pleasure is all mine, and I pray the gossips have been
kind."

Hoping she appeared somewhat composed and
experienced, Kate tilted her head and studied him
in turn. "Kind? Perhaps *truthful* would better suit."

Ha! He blinked. Perhaps this wouldn't prove so
difficult after all.

"My lady, seeking the truth is my mission in life."

"Oh." Not what she wanted to hear.

"So, what brings you to our humble shores?"

Her hand now shaking, Kate reached into her
gown's deep pocket. From its black-velvet depths, she
pulled forth the swatch of Campbell tartan that Sir
Gregory had given her. Upon it was pinned his intri-
cate bronze brooch. "This belonged to my husband."
Praying she lied with some credibility, she ran a shaking finger around the brooch's large center amethyst.
"I thought Robbie's family would like it returned. He
said it once belonged to his father."

Sir Fraser cleared his throat and Kate jumped.
She had completely forgotten her escort stood
beside her.

"Madame Katherine, here," Fraser told them, "re-
cently lost her husband, Robbie Campbell. Going to
meet his family she was when she got lost in a
bleedin' storm. I took her in. As I was coming this
way for the Council, I brought her along. From here
'twill only be a few days' ride to Castle Bovane, where
Maggie's sister abides. Ye will recall Maggie was a
MacNab back in '70." Fraser hesitated and his brow
furrowed. "Nay . . . mayhap 'twas '68 when she and
Greg wed. In any event, 'twas a grand *an roic,* with
mountains of venison and mead enough to drown a
man. And the pipes and dancing, the likes—"

MacKay placed a hand on Fraser's shoulder. "Thank ye, Fraser." Turning his attention back to her, MacKay murmured, "My condolences. May I be so rude as to ask when Robbie passed?"

"Umm, last November."

She had almost forgotten, so disconcerting was MacKay's unwavering perusal.

Mercy.

MacKay arched a golden eyebrow. "And for how long will we have your delightful company?"

Kate swallowed the thickness in her throat. "I, um, do not know. I have yet to find his mother."

Frowning now, MacKay turned to the MacDougalls and murmured in Gael, "Has no one told her?"

Old man Fraser asked, "Tell her what?"

Warned not to alert anyone to the fact that she understood Gael, it took all Kate's willpower to keep from stridently reiterating her escort's question.

Duncan MacDougall shook his head. "I was about to tell her when ye arrived."

To Kate's shock the Thief of Hearts took her hand in his and gently stroked a calloused thumb across her palm. "I am sorry, Lady Campbell, but Sir Gregory's ladywife passed just a fortnight ago. Some say from a broken heart."

The blood drained from Kate's head once again and she snatched her hand from MacKay's. "Nay!"

Poor Sir Gregory. He had spoken so often and lovingly of Lady Margaret that Kate felt she already knew the woman. He would be heartbroken hearing of this.

And what was she to do now? Only Lady Margaret had the information she needed. Knew which liege lords were still loyal to James, which ones had provided coins for James and her husband's ransom. Worse, Sir

Gregory had said that Lady Margaret was the only person within this hostile place she should trust.

I need air. More, I need time to think. Alone.

Her palms sweaty, her middle roiling, Kate looked about for a means of escape. She had come in over there by the third large arch, yes? No?

So many people were now milling about that she couldn't be sure. But arches usually indicated doors and she headed toward the nearest one. Muttering *"Excuse-moi"* repeatedly, she wove her way through the boisterous crowd until she could see that there was indeed a door beneath the arch. Greatly relieved, she pressed through another group.

Just feet from her goal, the heavy door suddenly swung inward and a large, beefy man bellowed, "Robert, Duke of Albany, governor of Scotland!"

Kate froze as Albany, a man of perhaps seventy years, strode in, his finery as opulent as any she had seen.

Merciful mother of God, she couldn't breathe. The two men she had been warned to avoid had her trapped. Like mortar betwixt stone, she stood paralyzed, one nemesis before her and the other behind.

A strong arm suddenly wrapped around her waist. A powerful hand grasped her wrist and the scent of male and mint wafted across her cheek.

Before she could yelp in alarm, the Thief of Hearts whispered, "This way," and guided her to the left.

Keeping to the wall, he whispered, "Trust me. We'll be out of here in just a moment."

Wide-eyed, she nodded, no longer jerking back but willingly following. He stopped at the edge of a large tapestry and glanced around. She did as well.

Seeing that all eyes were on Albany, MacKay lifted the heavy wall hanging and slipped into a darkened passageway, pulling her in behind him.

It took but a moment for her eyes to adjust to the reduced light and to see that she stood in a short hallway with circular stairs to her left leading down and straight steps to her right leading up. Before her stood a partially open door and beyond it what appeared to be a well-lit receiving room with tables and low backless couches. She turned toward the richly appointed room, only to feel a tug on her hand.

She looked over her shoulder and found MacKay heading down the stone stairwell, his left hand holding a safety rope.

Oh, dear God! MacKay was hauling her to the donjon!

Frozen on the top step, Kate jerked back, trying to free her hand. There was absolutely no way she would go to her death . . . not without a fight. He tugged on her hand and, frantic—her eyes no doubt the size of copper pence—she tried to pry his fingers loose.

MacKay looked up at her, a question etched on his face. "My lady, these stairs only lead to the scullery and beyond that to the outer bailey where ye will find some much-needed air. Come."

Without waiting for a response he started down the stairs again. Too terrified to speak, she repeatedly tugged to free her hand but he proved stronger and heavier and down she went, tripping and stumbling.

At the bottom, he pushed on a plank door and she was assailed by heat, chatter, the clanging of pots, and the scents of roasting partridge, venison and freshly baked bread. With tears threatening to spill, she heaved a heady sigh of relief. MacKay hadn't lied. She was, in fact, in a scullery.

A dozen sweating, red-faced women, seeing he held her hand, stopped their work to gawk or hoot.

A fulsome woman of about forty—one Kate assumed, from her tall, colorful hat, to be Albany's head cook—gleefully warned as they passed, "Take care, mistress, he's a handful!"

Grinning, MacKay countered, "Behave yeself, Bridie. Ye are a married woman!"

Bridie laughed and blew him a kiss.

MacKay murmured over his shoulder, "By the saints I swear Bridie is the finest cook in all of Christendom." As if to prove the point, he snatched one of the plump apple tarts cooling on a nearby table and then winked at her as it disappeared into his furry sporran. Oh, but that she could steal a tart. She hadn't eaten in hours.

He tugged on her hand again. "This way."

MacKay pushed on another, heavier door, and she found herself in a walled, half acre of budding plants that would, no doubt, soon infuse the air with the heady scents of rosemary, basil and thyme.

He led her through rows and vaulted a low stone wall. To her amazement he then turned and reached for her waist. Oh, nay! He was going to try and lift her. No one had even attempted the feat in more than a decade. "Nay! 'Tis quite gallant of you, but truly I can—*EEEK!*"

She was airborne. Instinctively she threw her arms about his neck, realizing too late what she had done.

The Thief of Hearts' perfectly carved lips were moving, possibly saying she'd broken his back, but she heard naught save hot blood bounding in her ears.

Searing pain flashed to life behind her eyes, followed by the image of Ian MacKay lying upon her, his weight nestled between her thighs, his heavily muscled arms and chest glowing like polished brass by the light of a fire. Her heart thudded painfully. They were alone in a low, dark place. His incredibly handsome face was too near, his golden gaze intense, focused on her lips, as he whispered, "Tell me the truth, lass. Now, or—"

Oh, no! No, no, no!

The image faded, and Kate found herself, still held by the hand, in a large, open bailey, the few trees surrounding them stunted for lack of purchase on the granite hillock, their fragile arms reaching for the full moon high above the rampart walk. She jerked free of the Thief's hold.

Good Lord and the saints preserve her! She rarely experienced insight into her own life and those few usually proved false, but then again one had come to pass with—

She *had* to get away. Aye, this very minute.

"My lady, are ye nay feeling well?"

Why on earth was everyone asking her that?

She clenched her jaw to keep from shouting, *No, I am not the least well, thank you very much, what with my only ally being dead and you hauling me about like a rangy mutt you, you . . . seducer!*

What was she to do now? She couldn't run home. If she did, then all she feared would come to pass. James would become a murderer, women like Lady Beth and her children would be slain, castles would be set afire and razed, cattle slaughtered, men decapitated—all in the name of vengeance.

No, she could not leave without learning who within this gathering wanted their king released, who—if any—had put forth hard-earned coins for his ransom, for surely there had to be some. It was imperative that at least those families be spared James's wrath.

Feeling strangled, unable to breathe, Kate yanked on the stiff muslin cowl wrapped about her chin and neck, signifying her supposed widowhood. Still unable to breathe, she reached with both hands beneath her veil. One hard tug and the offending cowl fluttered to the ground, a stark white slash on the brittle grass at her feet. She took great gulping breaths, but still feeling stifled she reached for the starched brow band holding her veil.

MacKay startled her by taking a gentle hold of her wrists. "Allow me."

He released her wrists and then startled her further by running a thumb along her now-exposed jaw. "Lass, ye have a nasty red grove here." Almost as an afterthought he added, "And ye have nay reason to fear me."

Oh, she most certainly did, but didn't dare blink in response, as pins eased out of her hair and her black headdress went the way of her cowl.

Happy to have the weight off but anxious to get away, she murmured, "Thank you," and started to bend to pick up her headdress, but he stilled her with a hand to her chin.

"Nay, not yet."

Augh! Now what?

He pulled more pins, and she felt the weight of her hair being lifted; a decidedly curious sensation, given they stood almost breast to breast, hip to hip.

Acutely aware of the odd stirring in her middle that MacKay's nearness was causing, Kate stood silent, her heart beating a frantic tattoo against her ribs as her waist-length hair flowed through his hands.

"Ah, 'tis as I imagined. Black as a raven's wing and glimmers like Loch Meadie on a clear night under a full moon."

Her hair?

He continued to stare as if truly fascinated while the heavy strands spilled over her shoulders and settled around her ample hips. With an odd gleam in his eye, he whispered, "Were ye mine, ye would wear naught but this."

Kate snorted and spoke the truth for the first time in days. *"Bullocks."*

Chapter 4

Bullocks?

Had Madame Katherine Campbell just slapped his face Ian wouldna have been taken more off guard. First, because he hadna meant to speak aloud but had—in Gael—and she had obviously understood. And secondly, because women simply didna say *bullocks* when he made amorous overtures. They swooned or batted their eyelashes, mayhap even came back with a saucy comment, but never, ever did they snort and say *bullocks!*

"Humph!"

The woman was really beginning to try his patience. She'd caught his undivided attention when she'd blanched to the color of whey at the news of Lady Margaret's passing. In his experience, few wives even liked their mothers-by-marriage, much less nearly fainted hearing that they had died. When she bolted like a hare with a hawk on her tail, he instinctively followed.

And for some reason, she feared rather than sought his attention. Humph!

He stooped to pick up her headdress. When he

straightened he found her some twenty feet away and strode after her.

She apparently heard his footsteps for she spun and faced him, her hands on her hips. "What do you want?"

He stopped a mere foot from her. With his gaze locked on hers, he pulled on the lace that held his voluminous silk shirt closed and rolled his sleeves to above his elbows. Feeling a good deal better for having released the bloody stranglehold the garment had on his body, he crossed his arms over what he kenned to be his very impressive chest and took his time taking her measure.

The lady definitely lacked the soft oval countenance required for beauty. Her cheekbones were too prominent, her lips too wide and full, her eyebrows—left unplucked—made dark slashes across a lower-than-fashionable forehead, but those eyes . . . blaver blue, as intense in color as a fine, midsummer sky and so thickly lashed. Beautiful, and the total amounted to . . . *unique.*

"Ye, wee vixen, ye ken Gael."

At his words, she blanched and looked away. "What of it? My husband was a Highlander."

Hoping to rattle her, he said, "'Tis just odd given ye had only been married three months."

"We spoke much before we married."

Kenning Robbie Campbell as he did, Ian seriously doubted they'd spoken at all. "And when were ye going to mention ye kenned our language?"

She bit into her lower lip and shrugged. "When I saw the need."

Humph. He then heard her stomach rumble. A nasty mix; fear and hunger. Well, never let it be said that Ian MacKay was above taking advantage or using bribery.

Some might say all Scottish food was based on a dare, but not so Bridie's tarts. They amounted to love in yer hand. He opened his sporran, pulled out the still-warm apple tart and held it out. "Want some?"

She eyed the tart—he could almost hear her mouth watering, did hear her stomach rumble yet again—but instead of taking it, she crossed her arms at her waist and narrowed her eyes at him.

He sighed. "If ye dinna want it, then I will eat it."

He broke the tart in half and took his time savoring his first bite. "Mmm."

In response, she backed up a step. "Why do you still follow me?"

Humph! Stubborn. Hearing her stomach rumble a third time he held out the last half of the tart to her. "'Death is hateful to an unhappy man, but worse is death from hunger.'"

She scowled and snatched the tart from his hand. "Favor Homer, do you? Though why that should come as any surprise . . ."

Well, she'd certainly caught him by surprise. She was obviously lettered. And being so, what on earth had she seen in Robbie Campbell?

As she caught the dripping juice with the tip of her tongue, he admitted, "Ye, my dear, are an enigma."

Her back stiffened, her tart apparently forgotten. "Sir MacKay, I assure you there is—"

"Ian. Please call me Ian."

"Augh. Sir Ian, there is nothing about me the least mysterious. I am—"

"Just Ian. No 'sir.'"

She huffed then, making him grin.

"Ian . . . I am naught but a simple widow, who

came here to return a brooch to her husband's mother. Nothing more."

Nay, she was a good deal more. But just what, he wasna sure. He tipped his head and asked, "And now that ye ken yer mother-by-marriage has passed?"

She nibbled at the edge of her lower lip. "Truth to tell, I have yet to decide."

Ah, finally the truth. He watched as her gaze darted about the battlements. She then turned away and studied the castle bastion. He stepped to the left and saw that a wee wrinkle had formed between her slashing eyebrows and that her magnificent eyes had grown glassy. Ah. She might fear him but she feared something else far more. Then it hit him.

"Ye havena anyone left who cares for ye."

Apparently he'd hit the mark, because it took too long for her to face him, then look him in the eye. "For your information I do have some who care. I have Nana, my father and . . . and Monsieur Bottes."

"Monsieur Bottes." What kind of a name for a man was Mister Boots? A cobbler nay doubt.

"Oui, Monsieur Bottes."

He found it curious that a new widow would even consider admitting to having a lover, much less appear pleased that she did. "And for how long have ye had Monsieur Bottes's affection?"

She lifted her chin in haughty fashion. "Three, mayhap four years, not that it's any of your concern."

Humph! No great surprise, he supposed, given how unfortunate her dearly departed husband looked. Still he decided to goad her. He arched his left eyebrow and grinned. "Tsk, tsk, and ye a married woman at the time."

To his surprise, she gasped, her eyes growing as round as a pair of tankard tops. "Augh! You atrocious man, get your mind out of the slew! I will have you know Monsieur Bottes is . . . a companion, quite ancient and gray."

Ho! Listen to her.

Only a handful of men had the balls to speak to him in such fashion. Despite his reservations his respect for the lady grew. Taking her measure again, his gaze slid slowly over her hourglass figure from eyes to toes. Aye, he could still recall the feel of her pressed against him as he lifted her over the stone wall. Just a hand shorter than he and albeit robust, she'd still felt soft in all the right places and better yet, as they stood toe to toe, her burgundy lips had been a mere four inches below his. Normally, he had to fold in half to kiss a lass. And her breasts . . . God's teeth, a man could use them for pillows, so full and round were they. Imagining her heart-shaped hurdies pressed against the bastion wall at her back, her long legs wrapped around him, her opulent breasts overflowing his han—

"Ah-hum!"

The irritated throat-clearing evaporated the image, and he found the Widow Campbell thumping her foot, her hands once again on her hips, her gaze centered on his groin.

He grinned, suspecting she kenned precisely where his mind had wandered. "My apologies. You were saying?"

Her gaze flew to his. "And," she growled, continuing the conversation he'd apparently missed, "you really should"—she pointed to his chest—"dress more appropriately . . . for the weather."

He couldna help himself. He roared with laughter, the sound echoing off the castle walls, nearly startling her out of her slippers.

He caught her waist with one hand to steady her and tipped her chin with a finger so he could better look into her eyes. Aye, clever and a bit fractious, the lady would likely prove a hard nut to crack, but crack this gilpie he would and dine on the succulent and saucy meat therein.

Chapter 5

Good heavens above!

Had Kate not witnessed the thunder rolling out of MacKay's mouth, she would have looked to the sky, expecting black-bellied clouds and lighting. Never in her life had she heard a man laugh so.

And why had he laughed? She'd said nothing in the least humorous. In fact, she'd done her utmost to insult the man.

If you were mine ye would wear naught but this.

Ha! Did he take her for a fool? Men like MacKay never wooed the likes of her, not without an underlying purpose. Mayhap, to gain her confidence. Something she had absolutely no intention of giving.

Feeling a hand settle at the nape of her neck, she yelped and slammed her hands against MacKay's chest, alarmed to find it unshakable. A lesser man would have stumbled, if not toppled, backward. "What on earth do—"

His lips settled on hers, shutting off her words. A mere heartbeat later his tongue slid, satin on silk, through her open lips. She gasped as it gently stroked her tongue.

Oh, my word! Her heart fluttered like a bird with a broken wing. Never had she been kissed in such fashion. Augh, what was she thinking? She'd never been kissed . . . ever.

As his thumb stroked her neck and eased down to her jaw, her mind shouted a warning, shouted *kick him,* but instead she sighed, giving in to the delicious heat and intoxicating scent of a man for the first time, to the feel of his powerful muscles moving like waves beneath her fingertips. Oh, kissing was far grander than anything she had ever imagined while lying, lonely and aching, upon her straw pallet. Far grander.

Her legs, normally as stout as pier supports, inexplicably wavered and felt like strawberry jam. She really needed to lie down. Mmm, down—

"Yoo-hoo! Madame Campbell! Are ye out here, my lady?"

Cold air immediately replaced the delicious warmth of Ian MacKay's lips. Why had he pulled away?

And had somebody called her name?

"I say, Madame Campbell! Are ye out here, lass?"

Oh no! There was no mistaking Sir Charles Fraser's rusty bark. Kate stumbled backward. MacKay, in turn, just grinned. The beast.

She spun and saw the old man's shadow within an octagonal splash of light coming from the open kitchen doorway. Her host was, thank God, still within the garden walls and had not seen her making a bloody fool of herself.

Her hands flew to her tousled hair. "Oh, he can't find me like—where's my headdress?"

As if by magic the offensive muslin suddenly appeared in MacKay's hand. "Shhhh. Just turn and I will have ye to rights in a heartbeat."

Having no choice, she did as she was told, her eyes locked on Sir Fraser's approaching shadow. She felt MacKay gather her hair. After a quick twist, she felt a tug, another, a scrape against her skull, and then the starched headdress with its requisite neck covering settled into place. Truly amazing, given it had taken her the better part of the afternoon to accomplish the same feat.

Wanting to know the secret, wanting to thank him, although why she could not say, she glanced over her shoulder, only to find the Thief gone.

Augh! So she was good enough to kiss in the dark but not to be seen with, huh?

The stupidity of that thought came crashing in as Sir Fraser came into view.

Dolt. Why was she so upset? She'd wanted MacKay gone, had she not? And now he was. Well, good riddance. Yes. Yet the feeling of somehow being betrayed persisted, which made no sense at all.

Sir Fraser waved as he shuffled on stork-thin legs toward her. "Ah, there ye are. I have been searching for ye high and low."

Kate ran a shaking hand down the front of her bodice and stepped forward to greet Fraser, only to feel something squish beneath her slipper.

"Augh!" Picturing Albany's hounds running loose, fearing the worst, she lifted her skirt with both hands and cautiously stepped back. Her forgotten half of the apple tart lay flattened beyond recognition on the brittle grass and the toe of her lambskin slipper dripped. She huffed. Yet another reason to dislike Ian MacKay. She had only two pairs of slippers to her name and those on her feet were her newest and most comfortable. And now one was stained.

Eyes narrowed, teeth bared, she cast another glance around for MacKay. Oow, when next she saw him—

"Lady Campbell, what are ye about, out here all alone?"

Kate spun. "Oh, Sir Fraser, my apologies if I caused you distress. I simply stepped out for a breath of fresh air."

"Ah, and so ye found it." He took several deep breaths and sighed. "Frightfully hot in there, I agree." He then clasped his hands behind his back and looked about as if viewing the dark bailey was his sole intent for coming. "Lovely reiver's moon. Lovely night, come to think on it. 'Twas on such a night as this that I handfast to my dear departed Peg. Aye, she's gone now, but oh, what a lass she was. Had hair as bright as a Yule log aflame, she did. And eyes the color . . ."

As Fraser waxed on about his lost love, Kate mentally shook her head. The poor man reminded her of Nana. Kate had not lied when she'd told MacKay that she had some who cared. Her grandmother did care very much . . . on those rare occasions when she could recall who Kate was.

Poor Nana.

At Sir Gregory's insistence Kate had traveled by sea to Scotland and been warned to return the same way, but she could not. No, she would be going home by land so she could go by way of Salisbury, Nana's home. She patted her pocket, again reassured by the feel of the copper and silver coins secreted there.

Knowing her father had neither the coins nor inclination to provide her with a dowry, Kate had been saving a penny here and a penny there for well over a decade in the hope that a man might someday ask for her hand. Finally seeing the futility in that, she decided to use her coins to buy a horse. Yes, a grand steed. One who could carry her weight without buckling, one she could pat and brush, one she could love and call her own. The fact that she had not saddled or ridden a horse since childhood mattered not. There was ground aplenty betwixt here and London. They could learn each other's ways as they went.

Yes, and too many hours to think about MacKay and his kiss.

Realizing Sir Fraser had finally gone silent, she asked, "Did you seek me out to tell me something?"

His brow furrowed. "Well, umm . . ." It took a moment before he brightened. "Aye, I did indeed! What a clever lass ye are."

Not feeling the least clever, not with the taste of the Thief still on her lips, she murmured, "Thank you, and what might that something be?"

He clapped his hands. "I have good news."

Smiling, for he looked like an exuberant youth seeing his first pig race, she said, "Splendid. Do tell."

"Alistair is here! And most anxious he is to meet ye."

Alistair? The name resonated like a clanging fire bell within her mind. Sir Gregory had warned about an Alistair, but what precisely had he said? She gave herself a mental shake. MacKay's kiss had obviously disturbed more than her heart and middle.

Hoping to jog her memory, Kate asked, "Alistair who?"

Eyes twinkling, Fraser chuckled in gravely fashion. "Why Alistair Campbell, of course. Yer brother-by-marriage."

Her brother-by-marriage.

The air froze in Kate's chest as she again heard Sir Gregory warn, *And for the love of God, stay away from Ardkinglas, me home. Alistair would sooner see ye dead as look at ye.*

Charles Fraser scratched at the gray thatch encircling his head and stared at the prostrate figure of Madame Campbell on the receiving room's velvet couch. "I say, MacKay, 'twas a stroke of luck that ye happened by when ye did. Nay way could I have lifted the lass on me own." He heaved a weary-sounding sigh as his gaze ran along the widow's imposing length. "Well, mayhap I coulda in my younger days, but nay now, that's for damn sure."

Kneeling at the lady's side, Ian placed a cold cloth on the egg-sized lump on her right temple. "Aye, mayhap in yon days. In any event she's here now and before a warming fire."

And looking none the better for it, which was proving worrisome.

Ian had been lurking within the bastion shadows when Kate Campbell toppled. Had stood listening, ready to intercede should the auld man comment on the widow's kiss-swollen lips or her too-red countenance, but Fraser hadna. He'd merely addled on as was his way these days. That the pair remained where Ian had left Kate—where he could easily overhear their conversation—had simply been a boon.

Which called to mind a most pressing question.

Why would the news of Alistair Campbell's presence in Stirling cause the lady to faint? Alistair was, after all, the acting laird of the very family she sought.

Humph.

And not for a minute did he believe she had anyone in France awaiting her return. Had she, they would have insisted she simply pay someone to bring the brooch and plaid back to the family. 'Twere Scots aplenty roaming about Burgundy and Normandy these days who would have gladly done it. Or had she proved stubborn and insisted on returning the brooch herself, someone——the incomparable Monsieur Bottes, nay doubt——would surely have accompanied her to Scotland, not let her go wandering about like some will-o'-the-wisp.

He shuddered, thinking of the fate that could have befallen her. Thank God, she'd wandered onto Fraser land and not onto the Gunn's, a liege lord renowned for taking what and when he wanted it, be it his to take or not.

Auld Fraser muttered, "Hey, she's finally stirrin'."

"Aye." Madame Campbell's pink tongue again flickered across her still kiss-puffed lower lip. Feeling a rush of relief, a sensation he had no intention of examining, Ian took her cool hand in his. "Madame Campbell, can ye hear me?"

Her brow crinkled. "Augh." Her free hand moved toward the cold compress.

"Take care, ye have a nasty bump there."

Apparently not heeding, she yelped when her fingers found the knot and her eyelids fluttered open.

Feeling an inordinate amount of relief, he brought her hand to his lips. "Welcome back."

She didna smile as he'd expected. Instead, her

lovely eyes grew wide and then just as quickly narrowed into slits. *"You."*

Humph. *She's apparently still in a pique because I left her alone to face Fraser.*

Had he the choice he would have remained, but the lady had been widowed less than a year, a strict mourning period he had yet to fathom, and his presence would have only set Fraser's tongue to wagging. And the last thing she, a coigreach, needed as she tried to establish a new life were rumors regarding her character. There would be speculation enough about her as it was.

Fearing she'd say something to embarrass herself, he warned, "Aye, 'tis, and we have company."

Brow furrowed, she looked over his shoulder. Finding Fraser grinning at her, she groaned and struggled to sit.

"Allow me." He placed an arm about her shoulders, only to have her push it away.

Not to be thwarted, since he acted in her best interests, he took a firm hold on her elbow and leaned over her. Cheek to cheek, he whispered, "Behave or the next time I find ye alone I will kiss ye senseless."

Blue flames sparked from beneath thick, sooty lashes as she glared back. "In that unlikely event, you had best find a priest."

He arched an eyebrow. "Is that a proposal? For if it is I must warn ye—"

"For your *last rites,* you idiot."

Grinning, he tweaked her nose and then straightened. "How are ye feeling?"

"My head aches."

"And well it should," Fraser muttered as he pressed forward to squint at her. "Ye keeled over, topsail over tailfin, like a galleon in a hard blow. Bloody alarming, let me tell ye. Aye, fell like a pine before the ax. Landed flat on yer face like a beached sper—"

"Fraser!" God's teeth, the man was a bloody nuisance. "Fetch some mead for the lady, will ye?"

"Oh, of course."

As Fraser shuffled toward the fireside table where a veritable feast awaited Albany and his guests, Kate assured him, "He means nay harm."

"That I ken, but he's just as likely to say the wrong thing to the wrong person and ruin yer reputation for all time."

She made a derisive sound in her throat. "Ruin *my* reputation?" She shook her head, then turned her attention to the room. Her eyebrows tented and her teeth caught her lower lip as her gaze shifted from the stenciled ceiling to the tapestries. "Where am I, and how did I come to be here?"

"Ye are in the receiving room, and I carried ye here."

"You carried . . ."

Kate groaned. Picturing MacKay struggling up the circular staircase, with her limp in his arms—no, likely thrown over his broad shoulder like a sack of wheat, her buttocks in the air—she buried her face in her hands. Feeling hair slide, she opened her eyes and found a puddle of black in her lap. Good graces, could matters deteriorate any further? And where was her headdress?

"My lady, here's yer mead."

Using both hands, she raked the black waterfall off her face and found Fraser standing before her, holding a hammered goblet bedecked with amber cabochons. "Thank you."

She brought the fermented-honey concoction to her lips. Finding it warm but not hot, she took a much-needed gulp.

MacKay squatted and rested a hand on her arm. "Easy, lass, 'tis potent."

Fraser, a goblet in his hand, smacked his lips. "Aye, has a wee bit of the *visgebaugh* in it."

The water of life? Oh, splendid. The duke had watered down his drink. No surprise, she supposed, given the number within the castle. Well, she'd just have to drink all the more. With any luck she'd fall into a stupor before dying of shame.

She looked about again, this time noticing a large desk and behind it a partially opened door. "What is through there?"

MacKay looked to where she pointed. "The king's chamber. Now Albany's."

She was in the *Albany's suite?* Oh . . . She had to get out, go, be gone.

Yes, but before she did she needed more mead. As she took another healthy gulp she heard the door creak and craned her neck to look over MacKay's shoulder.

A stout man of about forty years stood frowning in the doorway. As he thumped toward her on long-toed shoes, the tiny brass bells attached to his red and green tunic tinkled in counterpoint. Thinking the man looked like a Harlequin egg, Kate asked, "Who on earth is that?"

MacKay, his face an expressionless mask, muttered, "Alistair Campbell, yer husband's elder brother."

"Ah, my brother-by-marriage. Why ever not." Kate brought the goblet to her lips and this time drained it.

Using the back of her hand, she wiped a drip

from the corner of her mouth, then took a deep breath, relishing the fire searing her gullet. Hmmm, mayhap the cook hadn't added all that much water after all. Campbell came to a stop before her just as the mead landed like a hot coal in her middle, its heat radiating like the sun.

MacKay murmured, "Fraser, please fetch the lady some meat."

"Certainly."

As Fraser shuffled off toward the banquet table, the laird of Ardkinglas crossed his arms over his chest. "So, ye found her."

"Aye." MacKay took the goblet from her hands and again examined the goose egg–sized knot on her noggin. Frowning, he told her, "'Twill be sore for another day or two."

She nodded but kept her gaze locked on the man who would do her the most harm.

Alistair will just as soon kill ye as look at ye, Sir Gregory had said. Precisely *why* Alistair would like to kill her, he had conveniently neglected to mention.

Her brother-by-marriage scowled. "What happened to her?"

"She fainted. Hasna partaken since her arrival this morn.'"

Campbell humphed. "If any should ken such, 'twould be ye."

Eyes narrowing, Ian rose to his impressive height. "And why would ye be saying that?"

Campbell snorted but backed up a step. "Ye ken well my meaning, MacKay."

Kate huffed. "Sirs, *please* cease speaking as if I were not here." She glared at each man in turn while her fingers struggled to braid her hair.

What bloody chaos her day had become. Worse even than her ragged appearance.

MacKay murmured, "My apologies. Madame Katherine Campbell, may I introduce Sir Alistair Campbell, yer husband's elder brother. Sir Campbell, your sister-by-marriage, Madame Katherine Campbell."

Campbell executed a jerky bow. "My honor, and now I lust a word, my lady." He cast a narrowed glance at MacKay. *"Privately."*

MacKay snorted. "Why? So ye can talk her out of her inheritance?"

"Whoa." Kate held up her hand. "What inheritance?" She would definitely kill Sir Gregory when next she saw him. First he neglects to tell her that his son—her supposed husband—was an ugly brute and now this?

MacKay's lips quirked up on one side. "My dear, ye now hold one-third of all which Robbie Campbell once held near and dear."

"I do?"

"Aye, my lady, ye most certainly do."

Oh, merciful mother Mary. No small wonder the egg man before her wanted her dead.

Her throat suddenly felt like parchment. "But . . . But Robbie was a second son. Simply a knight."

Everyone knew second sons were merely spares. 'Twas why so many became priests and soldiers.

Campbell, apparently losing patience, growled, "Leave us, MacKay. What we need discuss is sept business and nay concern of yours."

MacKay remained rooted in place, only tipping his head in question. "My lady?"

She had little doubt MacKay would stay if asked, but it might prove wiser to learn what Campbell

had to say. What had Livy written about enemies?
Ah: "The evil best known is the most tolerable."
Aye, that and something else quite profound but
what precisely escaped her. Augh, her ears buzzed.
Mayhap she had taken in too much mead.

Kate signaled MacKay closer with the crook of a
finger. When he leaned forward, she whispered, "I
seem to have misplaced my headdress. Would ye be
so kind as to loan me your lace?"

"Lace?"

She pointed to his chest. Seeing the golden froth
her fingers had grazed in the bailey, she sighed.

*Hmmm, I wonder if that lovely golden thatch goes all
the way to his waist?*

Years ago she'd seen a smithy with a black hairy
mat that went from shoulders to waist both front and
back. Reminded her of a bear. Disgusting, really.

MacKay's lovely chest suddenly disappeared from
view and was replaced by his almost-straight nose. A
nice-enough nose, to be sure, but she much preferred his chest. Or eyes. Ah, there they are. Such
lovely eyes, dark and light, flecked with gold and
amber, ringed by dark sable, with little crinkles at
the corners.

"Kate? Lass!"

Fingers snapped before her eyes, startling her.

Why was he staring so?

"Lass, are ye nay feeling well?"

Good graces, she'd been woolgathering. She
gave herself a good shake, trying to recall what
she'd last said. She looked down and saw that she
still clutched her braid in her left hand. Ah, she
had asked for the leather lace in his shirt. "I just
need your shirt lace to hold my hair else it comes

undone again." She waggled the braid's tip so he might see.

"Of course."

Before her tongue could manage a thank you, the leather strip was out of his shirt and wrapped around her braid.

She studied the pretty bow. My word, the man had fast hands. Something she might be wise to remember.

MacKay patted her hand, then straightened. With his gaze on Campbell, he murmured, "My lady, should ye need me I will be on the other side of the door."

"All right."

As soon as MacKay disappeared, Campbell stepped to within a foot of her. Placing his hands on his eggy hips, he growled, "So where is the bairn?"

Bairn? Oh, *child*. "I have none."

"None?" Campbell snorted. "Lady, I kenned my bastard brother well. No decent woman would lay with him, much less wed him. He either got ye with child against yer will or ye be a whore. So which is it?"

Why, the insufferable man! "I told you I have no child. I will also have you know that I am the daughter of a learned man, and I will thank you to keep a civil tongue in your head."

"Oh, ye will, huh?" He eyed her warily for a moment. "So if ye havena a bairn, if ye truly didna ken that ye had a paltry inheritance due ye, then why have ye come?"

"I had hoped to return something to your mother." She reached into her pocket, brought out the Campbell brooch and held it out in her open palm. Candlelight bounced off the polished circles and center stone, sending a prism of purple into the air.

"That bitch?" Campbell snatched the brooch from Kate's hand. "She wasna a mother of mine."

Taken aback as much by his words as by his grabbing the brooch, Kate blustered, "If that be so, then give the brooch back. It must now belong to your father."

Campbell took his time examining the brooch, front and back. After a moment he asked, "Now what would ye be kenning of him?"

"Ummm . . ." Knowing she'd already made one tactical error in showing the brooch to Campbell, Kate hesitated. How much could she admit to knowing about Sir Gregory without causing more suspicion? Surely if she had really been wed to Robbie Campbell, he would have mentioned his father's imprisonment, if for no other reason than to brag about his connection to the crown, but then . . .

"Robbie said that his father had been captured by the English and placed in the Tower of London."

"Hmmm, and did he happen to say why?"

Kate nodded; her gaze locked on the brooch, the one proof of who she claimed to be and the only legitimate reason for her being in Scotland. "He said your father had been captured while escorting your King James to France."

Campbell murmured, "My King James. And last I saw this brooch it was on my father as he sailed away."

Kate struggled to keep the panic out of her voice. "No, he gave it to Robbie before he sailed."

He looked at her then, his gaze again assessing, narrow with obvious distrust. "So how *did* ye come to be wed to my dearly departed brother?"

"He . . . did a great service for my father." Surely that sounded plausible.

Campbell snorted and his lips curled but not in

a friendly way. "So ye were sold . . . like any whore on the ways."

Sold? A whore? *That does it.*

No one called her a whore—not once but twice, no less—and got away with it.

Jaws clenched, Kate stood for the first time in Campbell's presence and took great satisfaction in watching his jaw go slack. Yes, she could be quite imposing if it so suited her needs. And now it did most certainly suit her.

Hands on her hips, Kate leaned forward and glared at the man standing a good foot shorter than she. "You offensive little toad. I journeyed leagues above whales and God knows what other demons, trudged though mud and bog, climbed hillock and goat paths in a bloody storm—all in an effort to return a family treasure to Lady Margaret. And what do I receive for my efforts? Your respect? No. Your condolences? No! You accuse me of being a whore and then you all but accuse me of picking your pockets. And who is the thief here?"

She poked a firm finger into Campbell's chest. When he stumbled backward, she stepped forward and poked him again. "Now hand over"—she poked again—"that bloody brooch before I grab you by the ankles, turn you bottoms up and shake it loose."

Enthralled with her boldness, mesmerized by her own fury, Kate took no notice of anything save Campbell's shocked expression until searing pain suddenly pierced her breastbone.

Shocked silent, she looked down and could only gape at the foot-long blade pressing into her bodice. With effort she pulled her gaze from the double-edged dirk to the man holding it and found him sneering, hot rage making his mud-brown eyes black.

No.

Untimely though it was, her end had apparently come. Worse, at the hands of a foul-mouthed glutton. At least she'd die having been kissed. There was some consolation in that. Now she could only do the one thing worth doing.

Chapter 6

Madame Katherine's bloodcurdling scream jolted Ian out of his slouch against the passage's stones. "Shit!"

Calling himself every kind of fool for leaving her alone with Campbell, he reached for the sgian duhb secreted under his left arm as his shoulder slammed into the door.

Blood thundered into flexing muscle as the latch gave way and the door swung wide, then reverberated against immovable stone. His heart stuttered in kind finding Kate ashen-faced but blessedly upright. Given the piercing nature of her cry he'd fully expected to find her bleeding at Campbell's feet.

Glaring at Campbell, taking note that the man's hand rested on the hilt of his sheathed dirk, Ian strode into the room. "What the hell goes on here?"

Campbell, red-faced, looked at Ian's hand and eased his hand away from his sword. "*Naught* that is yer concern, MacKay."

Seriously doubting it, Ian shifted his gaze to Kate. "My lady?"

"I—" Kate cleared her throat and took a shaky

breath that did little to improve her pallor. "I believe I shall go to my room now."

Glaring again at Campbell, Ian stepped between the pair and held out his left hand, his sgian duhb palmed but handy in his right. "As ye lust, my lady."

Her hand, cold and damp, shook as it came to rest on his wrist. Deciding he would someday take great pleasure in gutting Campbell, Ian led Kate from the room.

As they stepped into the hall they were met by three guards, their claymores drawn and at the ready. Two obviously alarmed lasses huddled at their backs.

The captain looked from Kate to Ian. "What is amiss? We heard the lady scream."

Ian slipped an arm about Lady Katherine's waist. "A spider fell onto her lap. Took her by surprise."

The captain muttered, "Sounded more like the lady thought she was about to die." He then craned his neck to look into the room, where he doubtless saw Campbell.

Ian chuckled. "I expect she did."

Kate, still as pale as the moon, nodded like a sandpiper. "Terrible furry beast. Sir MacKay knocked it away, then squashed it. Very brave of him, would you not agree?"

"Humph." The captain shifted his gaze between them, then apparently deciding he had no role to play, motioned for his men to follow and strode away. To Ian's annoyance the curious lasses lingered.

"Have ye nay *darg* to do?"

The eldest, Albany's current bed warmer, if rumors were true, murmured, "Aye, my lord, there is work aplenty," and scooted away. The other, eyes cast down, immediately followed.

"Humph."

Ian sheathed his sgian duhb and reached for Kate's hand, which he was pleased to find decidedly warmer. Heading toward the stairwell, he whispered, "Ye did well, my lady."

She snorted. "And you have a glib tongue, Ian MacKay."

He stopped. Ah, she'd called him Ian again. He was making progress. He gazed at her plump, wide lips and grinned. "They're more than glib and well ye ken it."

When she blushed to a furious red, he chuckled and resumed walking. Aye, soon she would be where he wanted her. Beneath him. And in the afterglow she'd spill her secrets, as many before her had. His gift to the world. Ack.

Just once, he'd like to experience an honest relationship with a woman. To spill *his* secrets, *his* fears, and ken that they'd be in safekeeping. To ken to his marrow that her whispered "I love you" was heartfelt and soul deep, not simply words spoken in hopes of garnering protection or favor. Just once he'd like to utter the precious three words himself . . . for he had yet to do so, and he was already one and thirty. Already on the downward slide to his grave. And, alas, alone.

And matters would remain so for as long as Scotland and Albany needed him.

The raucous sounds of pipes and laughter from those in the hall followed them up the stairs.

Behind him, Kate asked, "What goes on below?"

He looked back to see her hand full of skirt. "They are celebrating the gathering."

But few would get deep into their cups this night. Come dawn the General Council would convene and more than a few had already heard that Albany was proposing a new tax.

Struggling with her skirts she muttered, "God, what a place. Smiths and armorers hammer all day, pigs squeal, carpenters saw and pound, men clang and bang at the lists, cattle low, and now you blow those ungodly pipes. Is this place never quiet?"

He laughed. "Nay, my lady. Never."

"Augh."

At the third landing, he turned left. Directly above the room they had just left, he stopped and pushed open a door.

He cast a quick glance about. Finding a fire in the hearth, the shutter closed, a flagon of mulled wine sitting on the brass-studded chest betwixt two sturdy, leather-slung chairs before the hearth—and most importantly his bed empty, he pulled Kate in and closed the door. "Be at yer ease, my lady. Ye are safe."

While the Widow Campbell looked about, a frown marring her brow, he hauled the sheath holding his weighty claymore over his head.

"Whose chamber is this?" Before he could respond, she held up a hand. "Never mind. It's yours." She huffed and reached for the door latch.

Ian tossed his broadsword onto the bed where it landed with a clang despite the deep furs, then he casually leaned, shoulder to wood, on the door.

He grinned and lifted a tendril that had escaped her braid. Enjoying the sleek feel of the strand between his fingers, he murmured, "Ye have nay reason to fear, Kate Campbell. 'Tis only a room, and I am only a man."

"Ha!" She snatched the hair from his hand and tucked it behind her ear. She then pulled on the latch with both hands. "There is naught *only* about you, MacKay."

"Hmmm, and here I was imagining that we were on better terms. Have ye forgotten I have rescued ye thrice? Once in the hall, once in the bailey and now just down below. Surely ye can bring yerself to call me Ian."

"Fine. Ian. Now move so I might open the door."

He sighed. "As ye lust, but be forewarned Campbell's men are likely lurking in yon hall."

Her hands fell away from the latch. "Might they be?"

He shrugged and straightened. "Mayhap aye, mayhap nay. I canna be sure since I am on this side of the door, but were I he and as obviously angry with ye as he appears to be . . ."

He left the rest unsaid, allowing her imagination to take flight as he was sure it would. No woman screeched as she had without just cause.

Hoping she'd eventually tell him why she had keened, he walked to the fire, gave the ashes a poke and threw in another handful of coal. He straightened and found Madame Campbell lifting the flagon with a shaky hand. "Halt!"

He took the amber vessel from her hand and pulled open the shutter. He then jumped up onto the eight-foot-deep sill and began pouring the flagon's contents out his room's cross-shaped aperture.

Kate, hands on her hips, a frown gracing her lovely face, muttered, "No wonder your Albany waters his mead, what with you all tossing it out without so much as a sip."

Ian shook the flagon to be sure all was gone and jumped down. "Katie, my dear, *visgebaugh,* the water of life, has naught to do with water. 'Tis whiskey."

"Whiskey?"

"Aye, lightning in an oak barrel, a distillation of barley. And a word to the wise whilst yer here: never drink anything that been sitting in yer room unattended."

She blanched, her hand at her throat. "B-b-b-ut I drank the mead below."

"Aye, but 'twas intended for all to consume and therefore safe enough." He held the flagon up to the candle. Nay residue. Good. But he would still rinse it out, just as he did every night before refilling it from one of the many casks in the distillery. No small wonder half the country thought him a sot.

He turned toward her then, thinking to ask if she would like something to eat and found her teary-eyed. Frowning, he closed the distance between them and lifted her chin with a finger. "Hey, what is this?"

She shook her head and walked to the fire.

He followed and took a gentle hold on her shoulders, shoulders not near as wide as his but damn close as high. A decidedly curious sensation. "Lass, talk to me."

Instead of turning into his arms and burying her face in his chest as most women would, she kept her back to him. "I never should have come."

He couldna argue with that. Alistair Campbell would nay doubt like to see her hide stretch above Ardkinglas's portcullis. "What did Campbell say?"

She took a shuddering breath. "'Twas naught he said. 'Twas his blade pressing into my breast that had me a wee bit upset."

His *blade?* Ian spun her so he could look into her lovely eyes. Frowning, he pictured the receiving room as he burst through the door. Aye, Campbell had had his hand on the hilt, but . . .

"Lass, are ye speaking the truth? For if ye are, then the bloody bastard—"

She placed a firm finger on his lips. "There is no need to curse." She heaved a sigh and lowered her hand. "God knows I have heard enough this night."

"I didna curse. Alistair is a bastard, the product of a handfasting that lasted but a year and a day. Yer dearly departed husband was Sir Gregory's only legitimate heir."

Her eyes grew wide. "No."

"Aye. Now, the truth, lass. Did he or did he not threaten ye with his blade?"

Kate swallowed, trying to remove the sudden thickness in her throat, wishing she could cut out her tongue while MacKay's amber gaze bore into hers.

If she reiterated the truth, what would he do? Kill Campbell? Sir Gregory had warned her about MacKay, had said he was more than an able swordsman. Aye, but then the old fox had lied to her by omission.

He had deliberately neglected to mention his son's deformities and the fact that Robbie had been his only legitimate heir. That she—as his supposed wife—would also be considered an heir. She took a deep breath. When next she laid eyes on Sir Gregory she'd definitely clout him. Then trounce on him for good measure.

"Kate, the truth."

MacKay was still staring at her. His gaze hard and assessing, demanding.

"Let the matter drop." What ramifications would come from that decision she had no idea, but better no action than Alistair's blood on her hands. Now if only MacKay would listen.

He shook his head, causing his golden mane to brush his shoulders. "Nay."

"Yes, you must, Ian, please, for—"

"*AWK*, please Ian, *AWK!*"

"Aaack!" Kate jumped a foot and plastered her body against MacKay's, her hands digging into his arms. Looking over her shoulder, her gaze raked the room for the intruder. "Who is that?"

MacKay patted the small of her back. "Dinna fash. 'Tis only Leo."

As if to confirm it, "*Awk!* Leo," came from behind the wooden screen Kate hadn't taken note of before.

"*Awk*, ah, Ian, *awk!*"

"Leo, shut up!"

Kate jerked and MacKay murmured, "Forgive me," then carefully extricated himself from her grip.

He walked toward the flat-paneled screen in the corner, leaving her shaking by the fire, her arms wrapped about her waist. "Dear God, I really do need to leave this place."

MacKay began folding back the screen. "Lady Campbell, may I introduce Leo."

Kate blinked, not believing her eyes. On a table sat a sturdy bronze cage and in it sat a large gray bird, its red-tufted head cocked to one side as he studied her in turn with a round, unblinking eye. "*Awk, beidheach eun!*"

It said *pretty bird.* "Oh, my. It's a parrot."

"Aye, and a noisier or messier beastie I have yet to encounter."

Kate took a hesitant step forward. "Wherever did you get it?" She'd heard tell of parrots, knew mariners were said to favor them, but she'd never actually seen one.

"He was a gift, from a grateful Turk."

She took another cautious step. "You were in Turkey?"

"Nay, in Venice, where I had the misfortune of pulling a drowning man from a canal. As a reward he insisted I take the bird. Come closer. He doesna bite. Well, he does, but only if you poke a finger at him."

"Leo," Kate murmured. "Is that short for Leonardo, then?"

MacKay grinned. "Nay. When he's in a snit he can do a very impressive lion's roar."

"Truly?" The bird must have spent time in Africa. Oh, my. "How do you know it's male?"

MacKay shrugged. "Truthfully, I dinna ken what it is, but it has yet to lay eggs."

"Mayhap it's not old enough."

MacKay opened the leather pouch sitting on the table, pulled out a handful of walnuts and dropped them into the cage. "I suspect it might be. Amir claimed to have had the bird for more than a decade before gifting him to me and I have had him for almost as long."

"Oh, my." The bird was nearly as old as she. Wanting a better look, Kate edged closer, and the bird, apparently wanting the same, used his remarkable beak and claws to grasp the front of the cage. Hanging sideways on the bars, he whistled at her.

She grinned. "He is certainly agile."

MacKay snorted. "He is tha—"

A hard rap sounded on the door.

Before Kate could catch her next breath, MacKay's powerful left arm wrapped about her like a steel belt. He hauled her behind him and pressed her to his back. In his right hand he held his dirk.

Chapter 7

Ian, his muscles tensing too much, flexed his fingers around the dirk's ornate hilt to keep blood flowing and shouted, "Enter."

The door swung wide and Shamus stepped in. "There you are. Albany wants ye."

Ian blew out a breath and relaxed his hold on Kate. Returning his dirk to its sheath, he growled, "Brother, knock the way ye have been instructed or one of these days ye'll find my blade betwixt yer ribs."

"Sorry." Shamus's gaze shifted to the left and he grinned. "Hello there. Who might ye be?"

Ian glanced right and found Madame Campbell grinning at his brother over his shoulder. "Humph." So much for protecting the lady's identity and therefore her reputation.

He stepped to the side. "Madame Campbell, may I present my brother, Sir Shamus MacKay of Siar Dochas. Shamus, Madame Katherine Campbell of France, widow of Robbie Campbell, formerly of Ardkinglas."

As Kate dipped into a curtsy, Shamus arched an eyebrow and silently mouthed, "Seriously?"

Ian nodded. "Now what does Albany want?"

Ignoring him, his brother stepped forward and took Kate's hand and brought it to his lips. "My pleasure, madame."

After Kate murmured in kind, Ian glared at his brother. "Albany?"

His brother let loose of Kate's hand. "He didna say, but looks fit to be tied."

Ian silently cursed and turned to Kate. "My lady, if ye will excuse us." The bird squawked, drawing their attention. Seeing Kate smile at Leo, he murmured, "Ye two get better acquainted while I tend to Albany."

Kate nodded, her gaze coming back to him. "As ye lust."

As he lusted. Humph. If wishes were horses, she'd be on her back, he riding above her.

He bowed and reached for his claymore. "Come, Shamus."

Striding down the hall shoulder to shoulder, Ian murmured, "What goes on?"

"Alistair Campbell has apparently petitioned for a court hearing. I dinna ken why, but he was sequestered with Albany for well over an hour before a messenger arrived, disrupting them. And now Albany wants ye."

Jogging down the well-worn steps, Ian murmured, "Campbell isna happy with the appearance of Robbie's widow."

Shamus chuckled at his back. "I still canna believe that wee shit was married to the lady in yer chamber. There must be some mistake."

Never one to waste words, Shamus had succinctly stated precisely what had been bothering Ian since first meeting the lady. Envisioning Robbie Campbell simply touching Kate, his stomach turned.

He stopped and looked up at his brother. "No one goes into my chamber whilst I am gone."

Shamus nodded. "Done."

"And that means ye as well."

His brother looked at him oddly, then laughed and clapped him on the shoulder. "Ye randy goat."

Irritated, Ian knocked his brother's hand away and waved him back up the stairs, then continued on.

Entering Albany's suite, he found his seventy-two-year-old regent scowling, gazing out an open window. "Yer grace, ye summoned me?"

Albany faced him. "Aye. A messenger just handed me this." He held out a crumpled missive.

Ian flattened it on the nearby desk and held it up to the oil lamp.

A McLellen captain reported that whilst reiving cattle across the border, a fire started, but not of their making. The English had retaliated by torching two of their outlying villages. Several men had been injured, and one woman and two bairns were dead.

"God's teeth." Fire had to be the worst of deaths. "Where is the McLellen?"

Albany collapsed into the heavy chair King Robert had used as a throne. The one James I should be sitting on. "On his way home, his contingent with him. I fear," Albany sputtered, "if this reiving continues, war with England will be inevitable."

"Aye." And the border lords had been warned time and again to keep their men on this side of the wall. Fearing there would be a McLellen reprisal for the deaths, which would nay doubt spawn a massive English counter-response, Ian asked, "Any chance we can call on the French to cause another distraction?"

Their allies across the channel were at best fair-weather friends but effective.

"Aye, but for how much this time?" Albany stood and began pacing, setting his once-red but now sepia beard to swinging in pendulum motion.

"We are caught in a chasm, my friend. We canna afford an all-out war with England nor can we afford to keep doing what we have." He slammed his fist on the desk. "Christ's blood, canna these fools see what their raids are doing? We dinna have the coins to reclaim Murdock, much less our king. And we will never have them if we have to keep paying the French to nip at the lion's paws! I swear I could hang them all for their friggin' avarice!"

Having no words of comfort, Ian said nothing and reached for the wine. Murdock, the duke's eldest son, had been captured by the English nine years ago. God only kenned what condition the man was in now.

"Here, my lord." After Albany took a drink, Ian asked, "Where do ye wish me?"

"Here for now. I am proposing a tax in the morn to increase our coffers so we might someday see our lads home. Some, I fear, willna take kindly to the proposal."

Albany collapsed on the chair again and turned to the window, the moonlight magnifying all the chasms lining his face, evidence of the man's years of angst and fashing. "Ye were but a gleam in yer da's eye the last time we ransomed a king. Bankrupted the country it did. Bairns and women starved by the thousands. And when the English came, they marched right up to these verra walls and took control. Took us, with barely a pockpud killed." He looked at Ian then, fire in his water-blue gaze. "I willna bankrupt this land again to ransom a bairn that canna lead, can do us naught but a world of harm."

Ian's heart stuttered despite kenning the man's logic. He'd heard the auld ones tell of those dark times past and shuddered to think of his clan going through them again. But to leave the lad languishing in an English tower was also unthinkable. Worse, should he die—and many a man had in prison—Scotland could find itself in civil war.

"Aye, my liege."

At the door he turned and asked, "What has Alistair Campbell concerned?"

"Verra little gets past ye I see." Albany grunted. "Campbell intends to sue Robbie's widow. He doesna want to pay her a bawbee, much less a penny, nor does he want her under his roof, where he claims she could interfere with the security of Loch Fyne and subsequently Ardkinglas and his sept. And as acting liege he does have the right to be heard before the council." Albany shrugged. "I tried to convince him otherwise but gave up. The court will convene in four days' time."

Chapter 8

When the door closed behind MacKay, Kate blew through her teeth and turned her attention to the brass cage sitting on the table.

Edging closer, she murmured, "Hello." The bird cocked his head as if listening intently and she grinned.

Oh, how I wish I could touch you.

She placed a finger on the bar, hoping the gray and white creature would come closer. "Hello, pretty bird."

Mayhap she should spend her coins on a parrot instead of a horse. Horses lived for only a score, and they certainly didn't speak. A parrot might live two score, and could prove grand company.

The bird bobbed in comical fashion, making her laugh.

"Aye, 'twould be fun having a pretty bird."

"*Awk!* Pretty bird! Pretty bird!"

Oh! He'd repeated her. *In English!*

"Oh, no. No, no. *Beidheach eun,* Leo, *Beidheach eun.*"

"*Awk,* pretty bird!"

She flapped her hands at him. "Shhhhh! Shhhhh!" Merciful mother in heaven. What to do, what to do? She could not have the bird screaming *pretty bird* when MacKay returned. He'd likely run her and the bird through and ask questions later.

Kate pressed her face to the bars. The bird trilled and bopped in response. Very good. He's paying attention. Mayhap if she changed her tone?

As quietly and calmly as she could manage with her heart beating itself black and blue against her ribs, Kate whispered, "*Beidheach eun,* Leo, *beidheach eun.*"

"*Awk.* Pretty Leo."

Augh! She wrung her hands and knelt before the cage. Mayhap if she could distract him . . .

"Ian, Leo, Ian." The bird *could* repeat that.

The bird ruffled its feathers and stretched its neck. In a high feminine voice it keened, "*Awk,* Ian, oow, ooow, ah, ah, sooo big, aye, oow, oow, oh, oh, oh, ooh, oooooooh, Iiiian!"

Mouth agape, Kate stared at the parrot. Having spent a goodly number of nights in a crowded Salisbury great hall she recognized only too well what the bird mimicked.

"*Awk,* ugh, ugh, ugh, ugh," the bird told her before making an impressive masculine growl, then heaving a huge sigh. He then ruffled his feathers and winked at her.

Kate burst out laughing. First she'd been kissed nearly senseless, then deserted, then threatened at blade point, and now a parrot was telling her the infamous Thief of Hearts's intimate secrets. She laughed even harder.

"*Awk, bhahahahawhaha.*"

Oh, lord. She covered her mouth in an effort to

muffle her peals. My, my, my. Did MacKay know about this? Picturing his ire, she laughed all the harder, making her middle burn.

"What, may I ask, do you find so funny?"

Kate tumbled backward. Seeing MacKay frowning in the doorway, his arms cradling enough food to feed Henry's army, she dashed her mirth-induced tears from her cheeks and scrambled to her feet. "Nothing."

"*Awk,* Ian, oh, oh, Ian."

"Silence, Leo!" Ian placed the food and wine on the table, then strode toward the cage. "I have heard quite enough for one night." MacKay dropped a cloth over the cage and pulled the screen back in place. "Miserable beast."

Kate had all she could do to keep her expression placid. "I find him quite entertaining, actually."

Scowling, MacKay moved about the room arranging the table and stools to his liking, and her gaze followed. Unlike most men who thumped about with splayed feet, MacKay's large feet headed quietly in the direction he intended to go. His calves were long and well muscled. His thighs——what she could see of them whenever he bent to pick something up——were as thick as many a tree in London. His hips were narrow as was his waist, then he flared long and muscular to incredibly wide shoulders that rolled as he walked. Yet as solid as he was, there was something fluid, dare she say predatory, about his every move. Hmmm. And how odd that she should notice such. By and large she noticed only the face and gait of a man.

He returned to her side and held out an amber keltie, a large glass goblet with a rounded bottom. "Splendid," Ian muttered, "he's yers."

She gave herself a shake. "Who is mine?"

"Leo."

"You can't be serious?" Who in their right mind would want to give away so unique a creature? The bird would fetch a small fortune in any market.

MacKay had positioned the stools on either side of the cross-legged table and motioned for her to take a seat. "I am verra serious. I have been trying to give him away for years, but none will take him."

She could well understand why, having heard the bird squawk, but then . . .

Kate reached for the slice of coarse dark bread he held out to her. "I should like to think on it."

"By all means."

She tasted the wine, found it surprisingly good, and then tried to set the goblet down, only to realize she could not without spilling its contents. Humph. She took another sip.

MacKay, his amber eyes hooded, raised his goblet. "To the loveliest lady in Stirling."

She arched an eyebrow. "And who might that be?"

Looking affronted, he murmured, "Why ye, of course."

Picturing herself alone in the dark bailey, again feeling the sting of betrayal, hearing the parrot mimic an unknown lady *oowing* and *ahing* at the top of her voice, Kate took her time raising her goblet. Looking him in the eyes, she murmured, "To the handsomest liar in Stirling."

He cocked his head much as the bird had. "Ye wound me, lass."

She snorted in decidedly unladylike fashion. "Better ye than me."

"Ack." He took a sip of his wine. As if reading her

mind he said, "My lady, Fraser finding me at yer side would have done ye irreparable harm."

She narrowed her eyes at him. "Yet here I am in your chamber and well your brother knows it."

He smiled at her. "Ah, but the difference lies in my brother kenning me well whilst others, not kenning, often think the worst of me."

"Oh." Well, mayhap she could give him the benefit of the doubt. Not that all this really mattered. She'd be long gone before she crossed his thoughts again.

MacKay drained his goblet, laid it down and pierced a piece of venison with his dirk. To her surprise, he pulled it from the blade and held the meat to her lips. Not something a near stranger would do.

She looked at the offering and then into his eyes. He said not a word. Didn't have to. Amber and gold sparked, challenging her. Heart thudding, she parted her lips. He eased the meat into her mouth. His index finger and thumb gently slid across the side of her tongue and then the inside of her lower lip before departing. The simple act of his feeding her caused an immediate quiver in her middle and heat to bloom much lower still.

His gaze shifted to her mouth. "Tell me of Robbie."

Her gaze settled on his beautifully shaped lips. "Robbie?"

Double dimples suddenly bracketed either side of his mouth. "How soon we forget. Yer husband?"

Oh!

She straightened, giving herself a good mental shake. What was it about this man that he could so easily distract her? "Umm . . . He was five and twenty."

MacKay arched a brow and speared another piece of meat. "That I kenned. Was he kind?"

Kind? Given what Laird MacDougall had said but a few hours ago, she suspected not. Preferring not to get caught in a lie, she shrugged and looked about. Hoping to distract MacKay from his disturbing line of questioning, she pointed toward the armory propped in the corner by his bed. "Lovely crossbow." In her experience men could go on for hours about their weapons.

He grinned. "Thank you."

Thank you? That is all? Ugh. Seeing a number of books on the wooden trunk at her side, she reached for the one on top. *Epitome,* Flavius Vegetius Renatus.

Out of habit born from having too few books of her own and the need to keep the reading fresh, she set the book on its spine and let the text fall open as it would. She closed her eyes and touched the page. Where her finger landed, she read, "It is much better to overcome the enemy by famine, surprise or terror than by general actions, for in the latter instance fortune has often a greater share than valor."

How dreadful.

She looked up and found MacKay, keltie in hand, studying her from beneath hooded lids once again. "It is the nature of war," he quoted, "that what is beneficial to you is detrimental to the enemy and what is of service to him always hurts you."

The wine which had tasted so sweet just moments ago suddenly turned to vinegar in Kate's middle. Closing the book, she murmured, "Words to live by." Or die by.

"Yet they disturb ye."

"I believe I shall go to the ladies' chamber

now." She started to rise, and he placed his hand over hers.

"Please stay, eat. Ye have had verra little, and I dinna want ye getting ill."

He released her hand and leaned forward, placing his elbows on the table and resting his chin on his clasped hands. "Ye read well."

Aye, Ian decided, verra well indeed, and it had been too many seasons since a lilting voice had read to him. Decades, actually. Too, Kate Campbell did much well, kissing not the least among them. And he was in sore need of distraction.

Since leaving Albany, his gut had been in turmoil. Did the man really plan to ransom Murdock before ransoming their king? Logical, aye, given Albany was already an auld man and Murdock had years of battle experience, but still the idea didna set well. Second, the lady before him would soon have to face twelve lieges, something he suspected wouldna set well with her.

He held another piece of venison out to her.

Hands clutched in her lap, she shook her head. "Nay. I must go now."

He popped the meat into his mouth. As he chewed he studied her, trying to fathom what about her specifically was holding his imagination captive. "Why are ye really here, Kate Campbell?"

She blanched and looked to the door. "Ah . . . the music."

He laughed. "Not an hour ago ye were complaining our pipes squawked." When she blushed to her hair roots he murmured, "Ah, Kate, be at yer ease, lass. None here would take offense. Pipes are an acquired taste, something ye will eventually feel in yer heart and bones should ye stay long enough."

"I cannot stay."

Humph. He held out another piece of meat, hoping she'd take it. She eyed him warily for a moment, then did, her full lips parting, her even white teeth closing over the pink flesh and his fingers. Ah, her mouth felt as slick as satin. Hmmm, the possibilities. After she chewed and swallowed he asked, "And when will ye leave?"

Instead of answering she drained her keltie. He grabbed the flagon and refilled it before she could put it down.

Her brow crinkled. "Now why did you do that? I told you I need leave."

"Aye, ye must, but not so soon." He held out another piece of meat to her and this time she snatched it with her fingers, her eyes narrow and assessing, like a hungry hound ready for a hunt.

She then tipped her head and studied him. "What do ye want, Ian MacKay?"

"Hmmm. Peace, a good crop, a mild winter."

She huffed. "You ask for the truth, yet you do not answer in kind. What do you *really* want?"

Clever lass. To garner confidences one often had to share confidences. So why was he hesitating to do so? Humph. "As ye lust. I want to see ye safe."

"Why? You know me not."

Why indeed. "The truth? I find ye unique to the point of being totally distracting." He leaned forward and took her hand in his, admiring the long, fine bones, the skin far softer than his own. He then looked into her eyes and pondered how they had captivated him from the verra first moment they looked upon him. "For I dare swear, without doubt, that as the summer's sun bright is fair, clear, and hath more light than any planet is in heaven"—he quoted Chaucer—"the moon or the stars seven, for all the world so had she surmounts then all of beauty, of manner and of comeliness, of stature,"—he grinned for that was most certainly true—"and well set gladness, of goodlier so well be she."

Kate, rather than swooning, gaped at him for a long moment, then burst out laughing. To his annoyance she continued to laugh until tears streamed down her cheeks.

Taking a gasping breath she managed, "Ian MacKay, how have you survived so long? You're such a poor liar."

He blinked. "I beg yer pardon?"

Taken aback, his jaw muscles now twitching, he sat silent as she drained her keltie, wiped the tears from her cheeks and strode to the door.

Ack! The blasted woman was rebuffing him. *Again!* He, the Thief of Hearts, the man who can set any woman's knees to quaking by simply smiling? *The hell she was!*

As she pulled open the door, he came up behind her and slapped a hand against the wood, slamming it shut. He then placed both hands on the door, effectively trapping her betwixt his arms. "My dear, we are yet through."

Her back to him, she tugged on the latch, "Oh, but we are."

He grinned. *Not so, my lady, not by a longbow's shot.*

He slipped an arm about her slender waist and hauled her to him, her skirt brushing the tops of his boots. Groin to lovely round hurdies, aye.

Eyes round, both her hands now on the door for balance, she tipped her head, trying to see what he was about and inadvertently gave him ample access to her long neck. He brushed his lips across the smooth white flesh just beneath her jaw and she gasped, her skin pebbling.

Inhaling the scent of rose and woman, he murmured, "'Tis petal soft, Kate, just as I imagined."

"Cease imagining!"

He chuckled and stroked her earlobe before taking it into his mouth. Feeling her breath hitch, he suckled and was rewarded by her soft keening, "Aaah."

His lips edged lower still and he felt her pulse pound. Suspecting her neck might prove her Achilles' heel, his tongue trailed lower, then licked. She shivered. Splendid.

Ian then did what he had been craving to do since holding her in the garden. He latched—his teeth gentle but his mouth firm—onto her neck where the soft flesh met the slope of her lovely shoulders. As he sucked his left hand slipped up her ribs and palmed the weight of one ripe breast.

"Ooh." Her moan, breathy and high, came as her legs buckled. To keep her upright, his right hand slipped from her waist to her stomach, the soft roundness coming as a delicious surprise. Immediately her palms flattened on the door and her back arched, bringing her heart-shaped hurdies into perfect contact with his swelling shaft. Feeling her soft yet firm flesh inadvertently cradling him, he nearly groaned aloud himself. Good God, she felt like a thick, overstuffed, downy mattress waiting to envelope him.

"Must go," she panted as his thumb gently stroked the underside of her now-heaving breast.

"Mmm," he agreed, pressing against her while sliding his right hand over her stomach, just a bit closer to the apex of her thighs. In response, her muscles quivered as a virgin's might. Unexpected yet delightful.

She craned her neck to look at him but was thwarted by his very closeness. Her pulse raced beneath his lips as she managed, "Must go . . . now."

Ack, she's still thinking too much. He nuzzled her ear, kenning his breath to be hot and moist. "In a moment."

He brushed a finger across her nipple and felt it grow taut, the breast swelling in his hand. He could barely wait to lay eyes on them, to discover if her nipples were pink, dusky rose or cinnamon. Ack, to suck—

Bham! Bham! A pause. *Bham! Bham!*

Kate, startled, turned to wood in his arms. Her body tense, ready for flight.

Shit!

"Shhhh, Katie, 'tis all right." Deep breath in, deep breath out. "Shamus, what do ye want?"

Too long a silence, then, "How did ye ken it was me?"

His brother would prove the death of him. Since toppling off his destrier last year, Shamus could be so astute one minute and then be so damn dense the next . . . and because of the dreadful inconsistency, Ian's cross to bear.

He rested his forehead against the door, his hold easy on Kate, who had thankfully started to relax. "Ye used our secret knock, Shamus."

"Oh. Right."

Deep breath in, deep breath out. "What do ye need, Shamus?"

"Albany said to tell ye and the lady that the tribunal has been moved up to Wednesday eve. And that the lairds will be drawn from a bowl so Campbell canna cry foul."

God's teeth. Could naught go right this day?

He grunted in resignation. "Thank ye, Shamus. Good night."

Shamus *humphed* on the other side of the door. When his footsteps faded away, Ian straightened, and Kate turned in his arms.

Eyes round with alarm, she asked, "What tribunal?"

He patted her back and placed a kiss on her forehead. "'Tis naught to fash about. Alistair has asked for a hearing to be sure ye willna gain overmuch from his brother's death."

"But I . . . I want naught!" She spun out of his arms and began pacing before the hearth. Wringing her hands, she muttered, "I do not understand this. I told that loathsome cur not but two hours past that all I wanted was the brooch he took from me." She stopped and looked at him, her face nearly as stark as the whitewashed wall at her back. "Will they interrogate me? Should they find in his favor, will they lock me away?"

"Oh, lass." He went to her and wrapped his arms about her. "Nay, they willna do any such thing. The very worst that can happen will be that Alistair is declared sole heir to Robbie's entitlements. 'Tis all." He brushed a lock from her cheek and grinned. "We are civilized people, Kate. We neither lock our women away nor lop off their heads like the vile pockpuds—English."

Chapter 9

I do believe I am going to be ill.

Pockpuds. Could MacKay have used a more derisive term? No. And it certainly left no doubt in her mind as to what he thought of her ilk. Merciful mother of God. The only man who had ever kissed her, the only one she had ever felt a liking for—in truth, felt lust for—loathed what she was.

And what of the inquisition they planned for her? How could she possibly answer questions about a man she knows naught of? From a brother, no less!

Should she find her way clear, should she ever again find herself in the bosom of her home, she would find Sir Gregory Campbell forthwith, and not only clout and stomp on him, but drive a stake through his miserable, conniving heart.

"Here."

She startled, finding MacKay at her side, a full keltie in hand. "Thank ye." When MacKay wasn't trying to seduce her he could be rather kind. She brought the goblet to her mouth and gulped. And then gulped some more.

MacKay placed a hand on her arm. "Whoa, lass.

There is nay need to drown yerself." He took the goblet from her hands and gently stroked her cheek. "And there isna cause to fash. Trust me, Albany has taken precautions to ensure that Alistair canna stack the court against ye. Too, I will be at yer side throughout the whole process."

Oh, grand. Both my accuser *and* my likely executioner will be at my side. Aaugh.

Proof or nay proof of who wants King James back on the throne, I have to leave this place before Wednesday next.

MacKay lifted her chin with a finger, forcing her to look into his eyes. Oh, such lovely gold eyes. Tears burned at the back of her throat, and she sniffed.

"Katie, no harm will befall ye, I promise."

She sniffed again. What little he knows. And he'd called her Katie twice now, the endearment her Nana always used . . . when she could remember Kate at all. "Aye, you're right, of course." She let out a shaky sigh. "I need go to my bed now." She would need the night to think.

"Ye can stay here." He grinned. "I will sleep on the floor."

Was that wistfulness in his voice? Nay, likely just kindness. "Thank ye, but I think it best that I go to the ladies' quarters."

He had an odd look in his eye as he stroked her cheek again. "As ye lust."

On the fourth floor, Ian stopped in the hall before the first of two doors, the one that opened to the ladies' quarters where the household's unmarried daughters and women slept. Across the hall stood the entrance to what he had come to think of as the Whelps' Den, where bairns too old to sleep with their parents yet too young to be shipped off for fostering—not yet seven years—slept.

He took Kate's hand in his. "Are ye sure, lass?"

When she nodded, he resigned himself to a lonely night in a cold bed and eased open the door, only to find there wasna a square inch of bed or floor to be had. Humph.

He backed up so she could see the situation for herself. As she looked about she nibbled on her lower lip. When she stepped back he eased the door closed and whispered, "Ye can have my room. I can settle in the great hall. Lord kens I have done it often enough."

She shook her head. "'Tis most gracious of you, but I cannot allow it. I will settle in the hall." Seeing he wasna the least happy about that, she laid a hand on his arm. "Given my current situation," she whispered, "it might prove wisest for me to be seen sleeping alone."

Stubborn woman. She was right, of course, but sitting upright in a corner, nay doubt fashing the night away, imagining all manner of dire things that could happen to her three days hence wasna what he'd choose for her. But what to do?

Ack, he'd think of something.

He held out a hand, "To the hall, then."

At the formal entrance to the hall, he pulled back the curtain and looked about the darkened interior. The answer to his dilemma—finding something for Kate to think about, to fash over, besides her upcoming inquisition—sat huddled by the far wall. He let the curtain fall and took her hand. In a whisper he said, "Come, we need enter from the other side."

She sighed in resigned fashion.

He led her through a dark passageway and turned

into the anteroom of Albany's chambers. In the far right corner he pushed on a panel. The wood swung open on silent hinges and he pulled her, owl-eyed, into a close space and closed the door.

When she started to protest the total blackness, he stepped behind her. "Shhh, dinna fash, we are here." He reached over her shoulder and pushed on the wall before them, allowing the secret panel to open only a matter of inches. Wrapping his arms about her as he had in his chamber, splaying his fingers across her belly, he whispered against her ear, "Look, all are asleep save the couple to yer right against the wall."

As he'd hoped she looked where he indicated and felt her breath catch. The couple before them were quietly copulating, the man sitting on a recessed bench, the lady, her modest breasts exposed and facing him, rocking on his lap.

Ian grinned. Nothing like a wee bit of voyeur to set a lady's fashing mind on an alternative path.

When the man leaned forward and took the woman's breast into his mouth, Ian murmured against Kate's ear, "Tsk, he's doing it all wrong."

He waited and as expected he felt her body heat rising under his hands.

Finally she whispered, "How so?"

Good lass. He exhaled against her neck. "There is a right way and a wrong to everything. See how he's pushing into her breast as if it were a pillow?"

She nodded, barely.

"'Tisna good. A man needs to lift the breast like so . . ." His left hand slid up her ribs and palmed her glorious right globe. His fingers gently kneaded. Rewarded by a quiet moan and her weight settling more fully against him, he ran a finger across her nipple. Feeling it grow rigid, Ian kissed her neck. "He should now suckle like so." He gently rolled her nipple betwixt thumb and finger, then gently tugged in rhythm with the couple rocking across the room.

She moaned and closed her eyes.

No cheating, my lady. "Look at them." Seeing her gaze return to the couple, he pressed his swollen manhood against her and rocked in matching rhythm, his free hand slowly easing toward the apex of her thighs. He gently latched onto her neck as he had earlier. She groaned and arched her back, her arse pressing into him. Oh, aye. Better, my lady, much better.

Needing to stroke flesh on flesh, he captured her lips with his. With the flick of a finger at the top of her gown, the fabric slid from her shoulder and the glorious weight of her naked breast slid into his hand. She gasped.

"Sshh, no one can see."

He gently tugged on her nipple—large and cinnamon, he was pleased to note—as his tongue delved into the delicious warmth of her mouth. Hearing her sigh, he slowly gathered up her skirt and slipped a hand beneath the hem. Her breath caught and her flesh quivered as his hand glided over her thigh.

Halfway to his goal her hand latched on to his wrist and stayed his hand. He looked into her eyes. "'Tis naught to fear, Katie, I willna harm ye."

Although heat radiated off of her like a fired kiln, although she panted and her cornflower eyes were dark cobalt and unfocused, she still appeared unconvinced. He caught her lower lip betwixt his teeth and stroked it with his tongue. When she licked back, he almost grinned. Aye, he had her full attention again.

His hand slid higher, brushing the curls at her apex in passing, and again settled, fingers splayed, over her belly, where he began to gently massage in slow, easy circles. He pulled his lips from her and whispered into her ear, "See how he strokes her with his hand between her thighs?"

"Ah . . ."

"Look at them, Katie. Can ye imagine what she's feeling as he strokes and slides within her?"

Kate, breathless, barely had time to nod before Ian's lips again captured hers. Oh. Oh. She felt afire, and God help her she did not want his touches and kisses to stop, but surely they must, he must, someone had to stop. This could not go on. Surely she'd combust like a pyre.

His kiss deepened, taking the last of her breath away. As his tongue swept across the confines of her mouth, her heart stuttered. His tongue then slid deep, toward the back of her throat, retreated, then plunged in again, much as the man did into the woman before her. Her knees gave out.

And apparently she was not alone with this feeling. Ian's breathing was every bit as ragged as hers. The heat coming off him in heady, musk-scented waves made her head spin. Who knew a man could smell so truly delectable or do such incredible things with his hands? His thighs, as hard and thick as the timbers above, felt delicious as they slid against hers. And his staff as it slid tauntingly against her buttocks in slow, steady strokes . . . ahh.

She wanted him over her, in her, all about her. But why was he doing this? She was not so lithe and svelte that she should induce such lust. Nor did he love her. So what was the point? Aye.

Despite her grasp on his wrist, Kate felt his fingers brush the curls where the worst heat sat. Once, twice, his fingers swept ever so lightly past, and then a third. His hand then stilled, and he lifted his mouth from hers. When he looked into her eyes, she groaned, could not help it, seeing the fire there. Of their own volition her hips flexed forward, giving him better access if he would but take it.

And God help her, she did want this extraordinary man to take it.

She released his wrist and reached for his nape, drawing his mouth to hers.

Ian growled deep in his throat as Kate's hand pressed on his neck and her lips parted. Aye, lass, now ye ken. Nay thought, just feel, flesh on flesh, heat and sweat.

He closed his mouth over hers and he slipped two fingers into the curls and found her path slick, ready, her sensitive nub swollen and taut, and not surprising, just a wee bit more prominent than those he had fondled before. God, he loved it. Sliding a finger to either side, he gently stroked. She, in turn, groaned into his mouth.

Aye, and now to send ye spiraling off the side of the earth.

He increased the pressure ever so slightly. Her fingers dug into his neck. In response he delved just a wee bit farther with each pass, slipping deeper into the moist cavern he craved to occupy. His shaft ached, throbbed, as she panted and ground her hurdies against him with increasing urgency.

Come on, lass, ye are nearly there. Come.

He felt her back start to arch then; her thighs and

buttocks tighten against him. Her panting was escalating. Ah, here we go.

Despite the painful need to push his kilt aside, lift the back of her skirt and thrust into her from behind, he continued to merely stroke, take what pleasure he could from the feel of her velvety vagina. His time would come, but later.

Kate went rigid in his arms then, the muscles of her satin sheath contracting in wee waves around his fingers, a high keen carrying his name, escaping through lovely, very puffed lips.

Gratified, he smiled.

He turned her in his arms, her face to his, and held her. While he waited for her breathing and pulse to slow he scanned the room. None stirred save the couple they had been watching, who were now panting and grinding for all they were worth. Humph. Lennox really did need to work on his touch.

After a while her hand slid over the plains of his chest. "Your heart still beats so hard."

He kissed the top of her head and reached for her wrist. He brushed his kilt aside and placed her hand on his swollen shaft.

"Oh!"

"Katie, 'tis what ye have done to me."

Her fingers wrapped around him in tentative fashion, then slid up. Groaning, he closed his fingers over her hand and squeezed.

God, if she so much as breathes I'll shoot the full quiver into her hand.

"Need I do—

"Shhh." He took a steadying breath and eased her hand away and back onto his chest. "Ye now ken what my hands can do. I want ye now to think on how I might feel within ye." He brought her hand to his lips and licked her palm. He then lifted her bodice and covered her delightful breasts. Seeing that the couple they'd been watching had collapsed into blissful slumber, seeing that Kate was put back together properly, that her legs were again steady, he turned her about and pushed wide the door. He whispered, "Sweet dreams," and patted her lovely arse, sending her into the hall.

He kept watch until she found a corner to herself and settled. He then closed the door.

With his balls aching to the point of nearly making him blind, Ian slowly climbed the stair back to his room. He hoped she would fall into the satiated sleep, but if not, that she'd at least think on what he had intimated rather than on what awaited her at the tribunal.

He sure as hell would.

Alistair collapsed against his mount's stall, the only place he had been able to find within Stirling Castle's crowded walls that would provide both warmth and privacy.

"God's teeth! This canna be happening. Not again."

Even in death that cretin half brother of his was trying to reach out for what should have been Alistair's by birth.

For thirty years he'd bided his time, accepting whatever boons his miserable father had deemed to hand down to him, whilst watching Robbie collect his due, hand over fist. And all because he—the first son—had been born on the wrong side of the damn blanket.

But he was laird now. With Robbie dead and his father imprisoned—and he had nay intention of ransoming the bastard prior to his dying—Alistair finally had all he had ever craved. Authority and Ardkinglas.

But could he commit cold-blooded murder? He'd killed in battle, but never with deliberate and callous forethought.

He blew through clenched teeth. He would have to or see all that he now held dear slip through his fingers. Would the court side with him? There was nay telling in the current political climate. He had made allegiances with the Donald. But would that be enough?

What if the tart produced proof of her marriage to Robbie? Custom dictated he offer her shelter, but he fully intended to claim that she, a coigreach, posed a real threat to Ardkinglas's security. If the court finds that she does own a third of Robbie's property, his back would be put to the wall. He hadna the coins for a protracted legal battle much less to buy her portion of the inheritance he and the witch shared. Had he the coins, he would have thrown them in her face and been done with her. Humph.

What would be the least bloody? The least likely to point toward him? Poison immediately came to mind.

Chapter 10

I will never, ever, drink mead again.

With her back to the cool paneling, her legs tucked beneath her, Kate tried to ignore her pounding head and the turmoil in her middle and focus on her most pressing problem: finding a subtle way of asking dozens of lords how they felt about ransoming James I. But the words wouldn't come.

Because of him.

And what on earth had she been thinking letting Ian touch her in such fashion? She hadn't been thinking at all, obviously, save for all the incredible sensations he had fired within her. Augh. And wily devil that he was, MacKay had made sure she would think and dream of naught else by taking her hand and placing it on that long, swollen shaft of his. Her middle quivered yet again recalling its throbbing heat and satin texture, the moist tip, imagining what it might feel like within.

Augh! She had definitely lost her mind.

She gave herself a shake. No way could she continue to just sit here and think on Ian MacKay. And to hell with being seen to be sleeping alone in the hall. She needed food and fresh air to set herself to rights.

She rose and headed toward the doors but found them barred by twelve-inch beams only two burly men could lift. She cursed under her breath, turned and tiptoed around dozens of slumbering bodies that reeked of stale ale and sweat and made her way to the heavy tapestry she knew covered the stairs to the kitchen. She lifted the corner and found the hall pitch black. No matter, as long as she was careful. She knew the curve of the stairs and where they would lead.

At the bottom of the stairs she pushed on the door. Soft light from a lone lamp, the scent of last night's roasted meat and snoring from the distillery greeted her.

Finding a bowl of dried apples soaking in water on the massive center table, she wrinkled her nose and looked about for something more palatable. Finding a wheel of hard cheese she cut off a slice. In a crock she found some oatcakes. Her prizes in hand she went to the door. It too had been barred by heavy beams but of a decidedly more manageable length. She pocketed her food and as quietly as possible lifted the beams and set them to rest in the corner. There was an advantage in being a "cow" on occasion.

The door creaked on opening, and she held her breath. Blessedly none within the distillery stirred.

She passed through the garden, hiked up her skirts and leapt over the low wall, only to be assaulted by thoughts of the incredible yet exasperating man who had once lifted her over it.

Finding the bailey quiet, Kate mindlessly nibbled

on her cheese, her thoughts going back to the last time she had stood in the bailey.

The vision she had experienced when MacKay had lifted her hadn't proved accurate. He'd not lain upon her and he certainly hadn't been bare-chested when he held her in that dark passageway, so mayhap the vision she had seen when James had wrapped his arms around her and the one involving Lady Beth wouldn't come to pass quite as she imagined them either. Could she dare hope for the best and leave?

Nay. Other visions had come true in horribly accurate fashion. She couldn't risk it.

Ugh, she really wished she'd never come.

And if you had not, a little voice in her heart whispered, you would have died a shriveled woman never having been kissed breathless, much less fondled.

Hmmm. There was that.

And you're falling under his spell, the voice mocked.

Nay, she was . . . Well, she didn't have a word for the feeling. One moment she simply felt wonderful, full of anticipation. The next she was terrified and the next her heart simply ached . . . painfully.

"Are ye all right, Madame Campbell?"

Kate jumped. Feeling an errant tear slip from the corner of her eye, she hastily brushed a hand across her cheek. "Oh, Lady MacDougall, you startled me."

The lady of Blackstone, her straight brown hair loose about her shoulders, her white night rail billowing about her long legs, drew closer. "I am sorry. I came down to the kitchen to get something to eat and noticed the door ajar. I wanted to be sure nothing was wrong."

Kate shrugged. "The hall was so hot and crowded."

Lady Beth bit into her oatcake. After a moment she said, "I heard there is to be a tribunal on Wednesday, a matter of yer husband's estate?"

Did the whole castle know? "Aye."

"Ye needna worry. Ian has apparently taken an interest in yer cause." She arched a brow, her curiosity evident.

Kate scowled. "How so?"

"He spoke to Duncan and then with Angus of Donaleigh. And John Campbell of Dunstaffnage as well, I think." Lady Beth tipped her head and studied Kate. "I think he's taken with you."

"Me?" Kate snorted. "Nay, he's simply bored."

More accurately, he was randy, and Kate had proved herself an easy toy. He would be chasing after some petite beauty within the week. And why that should cause a burning sensation around her heart she refused to think on.

Lady Beth laughed. "Nay, dear. I know the man, and I tell you he couldna take his gaze off ye in the hall. He's smitten, I tell ye." She broke off another piece of oatcake and popped it into her mouth. "And about time if ye ask me."

Kate's heart leapt. Could this woman see something she couldn't?

After a moment Kate sighed. Nay, Lady Beth was more likely one of those women obsessed with matchmaking. Some could make a living at it. To redirect Lady Beth's thoughts, Kate murmured, "'Tis lovely here, what with the castle being so high above the rest. So peaceful. Your King James must miss it dreadfully."

Lady Beth walked to the battlement. When Kate joined her, the lady pointed to the wide fields before her. "See that flat plain over there? Four years ago it was the site of the tournament Albany had held in honor of James's birthday. I was a new bride then and new to this country." Her gaze shifted over the hills and valleys for a moment. "In only four short years I have come to love this place, its glens, lochs, its mountains." She bit into her lower lip, then faced Kate. "As a mother I cannot imagine what that wee lad must be going through, being locked away so far from all of this, from all he knows."

Kate placed her hand over Lady Beth's. "I have thought the same." After a moment, she asked, "Is your husband of the same mind?"

Lady Beth nodded. "Aye, he's been hording what loins he can—'tis a pitiful amount, really—in the hopes that we will be given a ransom demand. Many others are saving as well."

Kate gaped, not believing her ears. "You've not been told how much the ransom is?"

Lady Beth shook her head. "Nay, that heartless bastard in London has yet to tell us."

The woman's words made no sense. Kate was sure a ransom demand had been made. Oh, dear God above, had Albany received it and not told his people? More importantly, what will James think when he hears of this? "Lady Beth, who else wants their king returned?"

She shrugged. "Nearly every clan in the Highlands, as far as I can tell." She named several and Kate committed them to memory. "As to the Lowlanders, I cannot say."

"Forgive me. Being French, I find that confusing."

Lady Beth nodded. "I know the feeling. Have ye noticed that we speak three languages?"

"Aye, but usually mine, French."

"The mountains are the cause. The Highlanders,

isolated in glens and valleys, speak Gael and their law is that of the clan. Think of it as 'our leader, right or wrong, do or die.' The Lowlanders, on the other hand, have the Norman system and speak Scots. Few can speak both. Thanks to marriage and political alliances, however, both speak French, so . . ."

Kate rolled a piece of gravel along the edge of the battlement. "But Ian speaks both Gael and Scots . . . and French."

Lady Beth grinned. "So it's Ian, is it? Nay, dinna bother denying it. Ye are smitten as well. And he speaks eight languages."

Kate blinked in surprise. "Truly?" She spoke four and thought herself well schooled.

"Aye. He also speaks Italian, Spanish, Latin, German and . . ." Frowning, she silently counted on her fingers, then brightened. "And English."

English? He speaks English! Augh. She could have gone a lifetime without knowing that.

"Did I say something to distress you, Madame Campbell?"

Kate forced a smile. "Nay. So why are the Scots not united in getting their king home?"

"In the south matters are complicated. The two most powerful families, the Donalds and the Douglases, can both lay claim to the throne of Scotland. Both have as much right to the crown as the Stewarts. You see, Donald, Douglas and James's father, Robert, were all grandchildren of a previous king. The sword put the Stewarts on the throne, and right now only patience is keeping them there. Should James not return, should Albany die, who knows. Either Douglas or Donald might become king."

"Are all in the south just biding their time, then?"

Lady Beth laughed. "I doubt it. Division runs

amok in Scotland. Too, James is a Lowlander, speaks Scots, so he's one of their own."

Noticing the sky turning violet, Kate murmured, "I've kept you overlong with my questions. Forgive me. You have made a great deal much clearer."

Lady Beth patted her hand. "I have been a stranger in a strange land. Ask me anything at anytime."

Thinking now was as good a time as any to confirm the accuracy of her vision, Kate asked, "How many children have you?"

"Three. A lad of four years, a lass of three and another lass of one year." She grinned. "We would like another son. Mayhap another lass."

"How blessed you are." Aye, Lady Beth had a husband who adored her and she would have another son, one that looked very much like Laird MacDougall, dark and burly.

Kate sighed. What would Ian MacKay's children look like? They'd be tall, of course, doubtless beautiful and highly intelligent. Would that she be the one to birth—

Lady Beth startled Kate, saying, "I enjoyed our time together. And, as I said, ask me anything."

Kate, embarrassed she'd been woolgathering, felt heat rise in her cheeks. "One more question, then, if you do not mind. Where do you come from?" The woman's French was understandable but just barely, thanks to an atrocious accent. More importantly she spoke English.

Lady Beth looked a bit wistful and murmured, "America."

Kate, well read, frowned. "I've not heard of this place."

The corners of Lady Beth's lips lifted ever so slightly. "No one will for many more years to come."

With that she kissed Kate's cheek and turned toward the castle.

Feeling a chilling breeze, Kate wrapped her arms about herself as she watched Lady Beth disappear into the kitchen.

What a lovely woman.

And if Kate did naught else, she would make sure James knew the MacDougalls were ready—sacrificing—to welcome him home.

But would James believe her? She had been prepared to take back to England whatever list or coins Lady Margaret was to provide. Now she would have nothing to prove that she'd spoken with these people, much less prove that she'd even been here.

Oh, she could readily describe Stirling and all that she'd seen, but would James believe her? He had grown so bitter and suspicious of late he'd likely accuse her of lying.

Kate paced the bailey. As the sun broke over the wall and bathed the castle in gold, she saw the solution to her dilemma. The flag. She couldn't take that, of course, but she could take something from the castle that had once belonged to James and bring it back to him. Something he perhaps cherished. But what? And where would that something be now?

Well, if anyone should know, it would be Ian MacKay. Yet the very thought of trying to get the information out of the man without making him suspicious—or ending up naked—made her mouth go dry.

She huffed. There had to be another solution.

"God's teeth, where could she possibly be now?"

Ian's gaze raked the crowded hall for the third

time, looking for the tall widow in black he'd been obsessing about all night.

And why had he been obsessing instead of tupping her mindless? Because she thought it best that those in the hall saw that she slept alone. Being a gentleman he had concurred and to what end? All were stirring from slumber and Kate was nowhere to be seen.

"Ack."

He wanted to take her on a ride before another crisis arose, before the midmorning General Council convened. She'd not seen the countryside and likely needed the distraction from the upcoming tribunal, and should they find themselves in a secluded glen, well . . .

If he could find her.

Having already checked the entire keep, he had nowhere to look but outside.

He took the stairs two at a time and nearly ran over Lady Beth. "Good morn, my lady. Have ye happened to have seen Madame Campbell?"

Beth, still dressed in her night garb and with her hair flowing, as was a lady's custom while in private quarters, smiled in enigmatic fashion. "Why, aye, I have."

"And?"

"And you look very handsome this morn."

Ian frowned, wondering why his donning a new jerkin should cause comment. Aye, he had taken care with his ablutions this morn, but then he did so every morn. "Thank ye. And where might ye have seen Madame Campbell?" Deep breath in, deep breath out.

"Oh. In the south bailey."

How appropriate. Kate was in the Killing Field. "Thank ye, my lady."

Waving distractedly at the scullery lasses who hooted at him as he passed, Ian strode out the kitchen and hopped the garden wall. As he scanned the south bailey—the scene of their first kiss—he grinned, picturing Kate with her hands on her hips, her eyes spitting fire, and telling him "Bullocks." Lord, the woman was a challenge but then, being attractive and lusty, she was worth the effort. She would make a man a fine ladywife. Not him but some lucky man.

Why that thought should make his skin crawl he couldna imagine. "Humph!" He gave himself a shake and scoured the bailey again for a sign of her.

Finding naught, he cursed. Thinking she might have wandered down to the nether bailey for a look at the village, he strode around the magazine storerooms and entered the broad lower bailey, the least defensible part of Stirling, and found only three guards, their bows and quivers on their backs. A slight unease bloomed in his chest as he walked up to the closest guard.

"Have ye seen Madame Campbell?"

The man blinked. "I saw two ladies not a moment ago, but canna say if one was Madame Campbell or nay."

"Tall, in widow's garb." He cupped his hands and held them before his own chest, the universal language for grand breasts.

The man grinned. "Aye, that one . . . She went there." He pointed toward the north end of the castle grounds.

"Thank ye." If Kate wasna there, he would muster the damn guard.

* * *

Kate, her face to the wind buffeting the rampart, her loose hair and gown being whipped behind her, wished with all her might that she could take flight. Soar like a hawk over the village below and continue south. Aye, all the way to Salisbury.

Lost in the image of flying free above the untamed landscape she yelped, feeling a strong pair of hands gripping her waist. She spun and found herself chest to breast with the very man she wished to escape.

Dressed in an elaborately tooled, shrunk-leather sleeveless jerkin, white shirt, yards of dark blue plaid pleated about his narrow hips, then draped over his shoulder and secured by a solid brass brooch, and what appeared to be doeskin boots, Ian MacKay was a sight to behold. Sun bounced off the golden waves blowing about his incredibly broad shoulders as he purred, "Good morn."

Handsome as sin or not, Kate slapped his iron-hard chest with a flat hand. "You frightened me near to death."

Apparently not the least contrite, he chuckled and kissed her forehead. "Should be a glorious day. Come ride with me."

She glanced over his shoulder. "The guards."

He nodded as he followed her gaze. "Ah, that is what they are all right."

"But they'll see."

"So? Last night I could understand, but now? 'Tis broad daylight."

Unable to do anything else, given his hold, she glared at him. "My point precisely, and you really can be annoying."

"Me? I think not." He wrapped an arm about her waist and started toward the rampart's stairs. "Come, hinnie, we need fill our bellies before we're off."

Kate tried to pry his fingers loose. "Off to where?"

"Ye will see."

"Will you please stop!"

Apparently surprised by her tone, he did. "What?"

"I have yet to . . . to do my ablutions."

His features softened and those delightful dimples came forth yet again. He stroked her cheek with a gentle finger, sending chills down her spine.

"How thoughtless of me. Take the time ye need. The Council willna meet until midmorn. We'll have ample time for a ride. I am most anxious for ye to see the area. Quite lovely in places, truly."

Kate nibbled on her lower lip and looked down at the long fingers threaded through hers. She wanted to go with him. The thought of riding with Ian had sent her pulse racing and every part of her heart shouting, "Do it," but what good was a heart if she had not a life? "I think it would be wrong for me to go."

His beautiful broad brow furrowed and he let go of her hand. "Do ye fear the gossip?"

Tears began to burn at the back of her eyes and throat. "I just think it wiser that we not . . . be together."

He did look contrite now. "Ah, lass. Did I frighten ye last night? For if I did, I apologize most profusely, for 'twas never my intent—"

Heat scorched her cheeks as she placed a firm finger on his lips. "Nay, do not apologize. I knew that had I but asked, you would have . . . not proceeded. 'Twas my fault entirely that matters got so out of hand."

Goose! Could she have chosen poorer words? She blew out a breath, the hurtful band encircling her heart growing tighter. "We simply need to keep a distance betwixt us so we have no reoccurrence of . . . you know."

He lifted her chin with a finger, forcing her to look into his eyes. Beautiful amber eyes with tiny flecks of gold.

"Lass, ye canna deny ye enjoy my touch. So what do ye fear?"

Why was he being so impossibly persistent? Could he not tell she was dying inside? "I . . . I am still in mourning, and you should be pursuing a marriage-able lady of quality."

He grunted. "And who might ye suggest?"

She threw up her hands. "How should I know?" She turned her back to him and wrapped her arms about her waist. "Surely you know dozens who would gladly accept a proposal of marriage." Hundreds, more likely.

He edged closer and leaned on the battlement, sheltering her from the wind. "Aye, but I have nay desire for them." After a moment he asked, "What did the beast ye were married to do to ye, lass?"

Surprised by the question, having nothing to say since she had never laid eyes on Robbie Campbell, she swallowed convulsively.

She needed to leave. Now. The man only wanted a convenient plaything who'd pose no obligations, make no demands on his heart. Fine. Hers would not become a trophy for the Thief of Hearts. Hers would stay squarely in her chest.

"Ian!"

They turned to see Shamus, his blond hair flying

in the wind, his broadsword bouncing on his back, jogging up the steps.

At the top, he bowed to Kate. "Good morn." He then turned to Ian. "Albany summons ye."

His gaze on her, Ian muttered, "In a minute."

"Nay," his brother said, "now. The Lennox has apparently left to join McLellen."

Ian cursed under his breath, then took her shaking hand in his and brought it to his lips. "My lady, I must leave but think on this while I am away. We are not finished."

Chapter 11

Waiting for Albany to complete whatever he was reading, Ian rubbed at the fire burning at his breastbone. First the damn tribunal, then the damn border chieftains and now Madame Katie was doing her utmost to avoid being with him. Jesu, next they'll will be telling him Henry's army was setting up tents and laying siege to Edinburgh.

And he didna care what Kate said, something in her past still haunted her. And he'd find out what it was if it meant driving them both wode.

"MacKay!"

He looked up to find Albany glaring at him. "Aye?"

"What on earth is wrong with ye, man? Have ye heard a word I've said?"

Ian straightened. "My apologies. What is it ye need me do?"

Albany, looking none too pleased, handed him a shaft of papers. "These are the proposals I am putting forth in less than an hour. Read them over and tell me if ye ken any who will have a serious problem." He then stormed out the door.

Ian gave himself a good shake and focused on the task at hand.

An hour later, the bile in his stomach was trying to burn its way through to his backbone. Not only was Albany proposing a crippling tax on all imports but he had written "our subjects" instead of "the king's subjects," in suspiciously regal fashion. *Twice.*

More unsettling was the wax seal Albany had placed on the last page of the document. It wasna the king's as it always had been. The new seal read *Sigillium Roberti duce Albani gubernatoris Scocie,* the seal of Robert, duke of Albany, governor of Scotland.

Highlanders would be angry and likely ignore the edicts, as they tended to do when displeased, but the Donald was going to go through the friggin' rafters.

Albany had already made an enemy of Donald by refusing to settle the issue of the earldom of Ross. Aye, both the Douglas and the Donald wanted it, but the Donald had the most solid claim through his wife, and well Albany kenned it. Add the insult of this verbiage and the seal . . .

Ian shuddered.

For years, he had held tight to the belief that Albany, an intelligent and able administrator, was a man whose heart and interests lay solely with Scotland. That Albany believed himself simply a throne holder, that he held no personal ambition for the crown, but this . . .

Albany was courting war.

Ian tossed the document onto Albany's desk and raked his hands through his hair. Mayhap he was overreacting. Mayhap the man simply wanted an accurate historical . . .

"Ack!"

* * *

Kate wrung her hands as she paced the upper hallway before Frazer's room. Given the council's lengthy session, the man's affection for mead and his age, she prayed he would not be holed up in his garderobe for hours.

Poor Sir Charles. If someone was to take advantage of her Nana the way she was about to take advantage of Fraser, she'd cut their bloody heart out. But there simply was no one else she could ask questions about James's possessions who would forget her questions as soon as she posed them.

Finally hearing shuffling footsteps behind the closed door, she blew out a breath and smoothed the front of her pleated gown. Yanking down on the annoying cowl encircling her chin, she knocked.

The door creaked opened and Sir Charles grinned up at her. "My dear, is something wrong? You look like ye have seen a ghost."

"My pardon, Sir Fraser, but I need to ask you something."

He motioned for her to enter. "Please make yerself comfortable." He wiggled a wooly eyebrow at her. "'Tisna often I have a lovely lass come into my room."

The old fox. She couldn't help but grin. "You need to let the ladies know you are available, my lord. I will wager you'll have more than you can handle in a fortnight."

He laughed in rusty fashion, then, growing serious, asked, "Lass, is something amiss? Do ye want me to fetch MacKay?"

Oh, good graces no! "Thank you, my lord, but no. I just need a moment of your time."

Fraser shrugged and took the chair opposite her. "As ye lust."

She looked about the small, monastic room, so different from Ian's. There were no crossbows, no broadswords, no mountains of books. No massive trunks filled with who knew what sitting beneath the shuttered window. Just a bed, two stools, and a small table with a bundle of candles, a flint box and a candlestick. "You have little of yourself here, my lord." She blushed. "I mean no disrespect; it's just so little for so long a stay."

Fraser looked about as if seeing the room for the first time and sighed. "At my age one travels with the clothes on his back and little else. All those trunks you saw belonged to my son's family and the men. They are of an age to fash about the weaponry and finery."

"I see." Only too well. No one had bothered to be sure he had brought extra clothing should it rain or grow colder still.

Before she lost courage or her conscience got the better of her, she asked, "My lord, did you know King James?"

The old man smiled. "Aye, lass, that I did. Looks like his da, redheaded and all. A bit of a Devil's buckie he was, wild but clever, too. I remember the time he had come with his da to Muchalis Castle, fell over the banister he did——ye ken the one, 'tis by the dais——and broke a tooth; a milk tooth it was, so 'twasna a bother but still bled like a bugger." He chuckled, his watery gaze not on her but on some distant place only he could see. "Two days later, the scamp nearly drowned falling into the burn. Scared us all out of a year's growth. Sad to say the next— and last—I saw the lad was at his mother's funeral.

The poor laddie looked so forlorn, draggin' that floppy cloth pony of his about by one leg, tears streaming down his wee round cheeks. Near broke my heart, it did."

A cherished cloth pony. Perfect. "Does he have it still, do you suppose? The floppy pony?" She knew for a fact that he'd not had it on arriving in the Tower.

"Heard tell he finally put it away when his da, auld King Robert, bought him a real pony."

Hating her duplicity, Kate pushed harder. "I do not suppose his infant toys were put on the ship when he sailed for France."

Sir Fraser shrugged. "I dinna imagine they shipped more than what he was interested in at the time. Mayhap his chess set, his kites, that sort of thing."

Meaning the rest had been stored away or . . .

"I hope Albany hasn't destroyed what remained. James might want his keepsakes when he returns."

Fraser grinned. "'Tisna our way, lass. All that was his, that was left behind, is in storage somewhere around here, awaiting his return. Dinna fear on that account."

Bless ye, Charles Fraser. She had only to find the right storeroom. A maid, a gillie, mayhap even a guard, was about to become her new best friend.

She rose. "You've been dear. Thank you. Will you join me at board?" Given all his help, she could keep him company for awhile, tend to his needs.

Blushing, Fraser came to his feet. "Ah, 'tis sweet of ye to ask, but I need to rest for a bit before the Council reconvenes. Too damn much shoutin' and arguin' for these old bones."

"As you lust." At the door she kissed his brow. "Sweet dreams, dear friend."

Looking a bit bemused, he waved and closed the door after her.

Kate stared at Fraser's door. How difficult it must be being old and alone after years of a good marriage. Particularly if one suspected one's grip on matters is not what it once was. How frightening that must be.

As she turned away she sighed. At least Fraser had had someone who had loved him, could hold dear to those memories. She would spend her declining years with a cat on her lap, recalling what might have been whilst listening to a parrot squawk.

Footsteps on the stair caught her attention.

Please do not let it be Ian. I feel maudlin enough as it is.

Her heart tripped seeing Alistair Campbell round the corner and come to a huffing stop, just feet from her. Her gaze flew to his sheathed dirk.

He noticed and, grinning, stepped toward her. "Why if it isna"—he huffed for breath—"Robbie's whore."

Why you miserable—

Kate's right hand lashed out and caught Campbell across his cheek.

As he gaped and took a step backward, she gasped. Never having struck anyone in such fashion before, Kate's hands flew to her mouth.

Oh, my word, what have I done?

Did she have a death wish? It was one thing to verbally challenge the man who had proved capable of sticking a blade in her breastbone, but totally another to strike him.

Campbell, in turn, turned florid and suddenly barreled toward her, his girth taking up most of the hall's width as he came. Instinctively, Kate scrambled backward, tripping on her hem, her hands out before her. "Do not come near me!"

She hit a wall, and he came to within an arm's length of her. Teeth bared, spittle oozing from the corners of his fleshy lips, he growled, "Henceforth, mistress . . . Beware of every drop ye drink and every bite ye take."

Chapter 12

God's teeth, where the hell is she now?

The bloody woman was driving him wode. Normally, if Ian showed even the slightest interest in a woman, he was all but tripping over the lass. But not Kate. Nay, he'd come to consider himself lucky if he even caught a glimpse of her in passing. Which he had done just a bit ago when she bolted out of the hall and toward the main staircase.

Thinking she'd gone toward the baileys again, he had gone down and out, only to learn he'd misjudged. By the time he'd charged up the stairs she'd disappeared without a trace. Ack!

She was deliberately avoiding him. He was sure of it.

Giving serious thought to tethering her should he ever find her again, he was knocked sideways by Kate as she came racing around the corner of the staircase at breakneck speed. He reached out a hand to steady her. "Whoa, my lady!"

Seeing Kate's normally bright, honey-colored countenance ashen, her eyes as glossy as wet sapphires, he cursed under his breath and pulled her to him. "What is wrong?"

She shook her head and tried to jerk free.

"Katie, my lass, I have had quite enough of this."

Since he'd been old enough to sprout hair on his balls, women had been seeking him out to share their woes. He need only hold their hand and murmur a few sympathetic "mmms," and he'd ken all from their first breath to their last tup. But nay Kate. She had to be the exception that proved the rule. And he was bloody sick and tired of it.

He wanted to ken what made her so feisty one moment and so shy the next. He wanted to ken why she sighed when he kissed her yet kept saying nay whenever he tried to get her alone. He wanted to ken what she adored, what she disliked and most importantly what she feared.

And *why* he wanted to ken all these things didna bear contemplation, for it might mean he could be falling in love for the first time in his life, which was simply unthinkable. 'Twas the wrong place and the wrong time.

He threaded his fingers through her right hand and headed down the stairs. "Come, we need talk."

She moaned and pulled back. "Please, Ian, not now."

"Aye, now." Without bothering to look back, he kept walking, pulling her behind him.

Suddenly he was jerked to a halt. He looked back and was astounded to find Kate lying on the stairs, her heels dug into the wall's mortar and her free hand holding onto the safety rope for dear life.

"Ack!" He leaned over her and pried her fingers off the rope, and then grabbed her by the waist. Muttering a string of Gael curses, he tossed her over his shoulder. Her head and shoulders behind him, her lovely round hurdies in the air, her long legs flailing before him, he started down the stairs. When she nearly kicked him in the head, he clasped her ankles in an iron grip.

Her fists pounded his back. "Let me go you, you . . . *brute!*"

"Nay! Ye be mine until such time as I say otherwise."

In response Kate swatted at his arms. "I hate you, Ian MacKay!"

"Nay, ye dinna. Ye adore me, but ye are frightened, and I mean to find out why."

"Aaugh!"

Just as he passed the entrance to the great hall, Lady Beth stepped into his path, her hands on her hips, a scowl distorting her plain countenance. "Ian MacKay, put that woman down right this minute!"

"Lady Beth, this isna any concern of—"

"I mean it, Ian, or I screech bloody murder. Right here. Right now."

Warily, he eyed Duncan's cantankerous ladywife. He had heard tell she'd brought Angus the Blood to his knees on one occasion. Lips in a tight line, she waited, tapping her foot.

Damnedable woman.

His jaw muscles clenching, he set Kate down but kept a tight hold on her hand.

Kate, throwing a scathing glance his way, tried to straighten her eschewed headdress with her free hand. "Thank ye, my lady."

Lady Beth shook her head at both of them. "Behave like bairns, ye get treated as such. Now come. We are to dine together."

Scarlet-faced just a moment ago, Kate now blanched. "No, no . . . I'm not hungry. And . . . And I do not have my blade."

Lady Beth took Kate's free hand. "Ye can use Ian's. I am sure he willna mind."

* * *

At a long table before the raised dais where Albany and several other lords and ladies sat, Lady Beth waved toward the open seating next to Laird MacDougall. Through clenched teeth she hissed, "Sit, the pair of ye."

Kate, her middle roiling, her palms sweating, sat. Ian, fuming at her side, heat shimmering off him in waves, sat. He was apparently as upset as she but for entirely different reasons.

Hoping to find an excuse to leave, she looked about and found Alistair Campbell staring at her from across the room. He raised his goblet and grinned. Oh, no. Had he already poisoned the food? No, he had not had time. But then . . .

Ready to plead illness, Kate turned toward Lady Beth and found a girl weighted down with a square leather budget nearly as tall as she. From its depths her quick hands pulled trencher after bread trencher out and placed them before each of the men. Right behind her came two lads of about thirteen. The first lad took each goblet from the table and filled it from the bulging budget that the second lad carried. Behind them came the squires carrying huge pewter trays laden with all manner of meat and fruit.

Kate held her breath as the boy filled the MacDougall's goblet with wine. Before he could pick up the one before Ian, Kate snatched it up and began wiping out the goblet with the edge of the tablecloth.

Ian leaned toward her and whispered, "What are ye doing?"

Praying she had removed any poison that might have been in or on the goblet, Kate muttered, "'Tis dirty." She managed to smile when she held the goblet out to the boy.

Ian filled their trencher, then whispered in her ear, "Kate, I truly wish for ye to trust me."

A pleading note in his tone caught her attention and she faced him. His eyebrows were contracted over the bridge of his slightly crooked nose, his gaze searching hers for a clue as to what she might be thinking. So beautiful.

Kate licked her dry bottom lip and his gaze followed. Her middle trembled. Wishing he wouldn't do that, she looked away. How was it possible that even a look could tear at her heart? Life was so unfair.

"Here." Ian held a piece of egg out to her. She stared at it. Logic dictated Campbell could not have known which platter she would be served from but her hand still shook as she took it from Ian's fingers. Before she could bring it to her mouth, shouting erupted at the far end of the hall. All around her men stood, their hands reaching for their dirks. A woman keened, benches toppled and pandemonium ensued.

Ian, his gaze locked on the combatants, put a hand on her arm. "I will be right back." He then strode away, the MacDougall and several others following.

Kate glanced at Lady MacDougall and found her—along with every other woman in the hall—staring or pointing toward the shouting men.

Her pulse bounding, Kate looked about again. 'Tis now or never.

She backed away and hurried from the hall.

* * *

In the ladies' chamber, Kate frantically searched through the bed coverings and pallets piled haphazardly in the right-hand corner. She'd placed her satchel right here, in this corner of the room. She was certain of it. She straightened and huffed, her gaze raking the cluttered room. Where could they have put—

"Thank God." Her battered leather bag sat on a trunk beneath the window. She snatched it up and heard something fall. She looked down and saw a small velvet pouch at her feet. Frowning, she stooped and picked up the little blue bundle. A tag was attached by a narrow ribbon.

Sweets for the sweet.

—Ian

Her heart tripped. He'd given her a present?

Tears stung the back of her throat as she brought the pouch to her lips and caught the unmistakable scent of cinnamon, which called to mind a stolen apple tart and their first kiss.

She took a deep breath, inhaling the fragrance through the velvet, recalling the feel of his lips on hers, the scent of him. Delicious and warm.

Dear God, she would miss him so.

A loud shout and the clang of metal on metal jerked Kate out of her reverie.

Now what?

Heart thudding, she strained on tiptoes to peer out the window and found a large crowd circling the inner close. The fight that had started in the hall had apparently moved outside.

The fates were being kind. Those in the hall were

still fully occupied. She needed to go while she still could.

Kate brushed the tears from her cheeks and carefully placed Ian's gift next to her satchel. Later she'd have time to open the pouch and think on the man who had given her the gift. One thing was certain. She would never eat whatever the pouch contained. They were the only tangible proof she would have in the years to come that the incredible Ian MacKay wasn't an illusion, a product of her lonely yet fertile mind.

Praying her meager belongings hadn't been pilfered, she opened her satchel and was relieved to find her two hooded capes, her two other gowns, her stained slippers, a sliver of rose soap and her hairbrush. What jewelry she had she already wore: a jet belt and a plain gold band that had once belonged to her mother. Her blade, a gift from her Nana, was tucked in her pocket.

She donned her black cape and placed Ian's gift in the satchel, being careful to pad it well. She then took a deep breath and peeked into the hall. Finding it empty, she raced down the stairs that would lead to the windowless lower level.

Jogging along the cool, deserted hallways that ran around Stirling's great foundation, she opened each door she passed, looking for the one that held James's possessions. Her every rattle and step echoed, making her cringe, but she continued to make haste. After turning left yet again, her breath caught. Before her at the very end of the hall stood a door with a gold and scarlet crest on it. As she drew closer, her heart began to race. Twin lions adorned the seal. She'd found it!

Heart hammering, she ran the length of hall, only

to find the door secured by a rusty wrought iron lock. Augh!

Kate dropped her satchel and pulled out her blade. She then routed under her headdress and pulled out two sturdy pins. There was something to be said for having heavy hair.

She then knelt before the lock and examined the keyhole. Someone had taken the time to oil the lock. Very good. When she'd seen the rust, she had feared the inner workings would be frozen in place.

She had picked only one lock in her life and that had been the one on her grandmother's wedding chest after she had lost the key, but surely the works were similar. A lock, after all, was just a lock.

Catching her lower lip between her teeth, she carefully fitted the point of the blade into the hole to hold the lock stable and then slipped in a hair pin.

Hearing a familiar feminine huff, Ian grinned. He'd finally found her. Verra considerate of her to hide in such a dark, secluded place.

Mayhap now he could find out what truly ailed her without being interrupted. Once he kenned all her secrets and put her fears to rest, he would then kiss her senseless and give her the gift he'd been carrying in his sporran for the last four hours.

Grinning, he peeked around the corner.

What the bloody hell?

Kate knelt before the royal storage room, her hands frantically working at the lock.

Nay. This canna be. She's a thief?

His earlier joy in finding her evaporated as he eased forward, staying close to the exterior wall and out of her line of sight should she turn.

Just feet from her, he pressed his back to the wall and looked heavenward.

Please dinna let her be doing what I ken she is doing. Please.

As if in answer, he heard the lock's inner workings click. He then heard Kate heave a sigh and the lock drop to the stone floor. A heartbeat later she muttered, "About bloody time."

English.

Pain bloomed in the pit of his stomach. She'd spoken in English just as a Londoner might. Son of a bloody bitch!

Deep breath in, deep breath out.

Think! What the hell does she seek? 'Twas naught within the chamber but auld clothes, toys and a few pieces of furniture. Mayhap a painting or two.

Naught made sense, and because it didna he would wait. Wait for her to lay hands on whatever it was she had risked her verra life to get. For she had done that.

Chapter 13

"Augh!" Kate shuddered, reaching through a cobweb to push another cradle, the third she had found, aside to reach a small chest tucked in the back. Praying this chest was the one she sought, she lifted the lid and found a collection of motheaten garments, dusty perfume bottles, brittle hairbrushes and a dozen tarnished combs. "Damn."

She straightened, placing one hand on her moist forehead, one on her hip. She had opened ten chests and still no floppy pony. No toys of any kind, for that matter. But they *had* to be here somewhere.

She shoved aside a tall metal shield decorated with the king's coat of arms and found another chest, this one depicting horses.

Oh, please let this be the one.

She held her breath and lifted the lid. Blankets. She lifted those and found a stout chamber pot with more horses decorating it, another blanket and beneath that an irregular piece of gray slate, a few chunks of chalk and a set of lead soldiers. This is it! She dug deeper still, carefully placing the treasures she had no interest in on the tall chest at her side. Near the bottom, she found a tattered cloth pony.

"Thank God." She crushed the floppy brown toy to her chest. Now James would have to believe her.

"I canna put into words how disappointed I am in you at this moment."

Kate's heart stopped, and then restarted with a painful kick. Still the room tipped.

Oh, no. No.

She staggered to her feet. Tucking the pony into the folds of her skirt, she swallowed the thickness in her throat and turned.

Ian MacKay, his arms crossed over his massive chest, his expression lethal, filled the doorway. "Who are ye?"

Kate caught her lower lip between her teeth, "You know me."

"Answer me!"

Kate jumped as *meeeee* echoed down the corridor. *Oh, God, I am in so much trouble.*

Ian took a deep breath, then another. In a somewhat calmer growl he reiterated, "Who are ye?"

Hoping to excuse her presence in what should have been a locked chamber she sputtered, "I was . . . I was simply curious to see—"

He closed the short distance between them and grabbed her arm. "I want yer name!"

She cringed as pain shot to her shoulder. "You know it's Kate."

His face expressionless, Ian increased the pressure on her arm, his fingers closing with the force of a steel trap.

She cried, "Kate!"

He jerked her closer so that her chest pressed his. "Kate what?"

English! He had just spoken to her in English.
Oh, merciful Virgin Mary, he knows. Oh, no. No,
no, no. She would never see her Nana, or Mister
Boots or her father ever again. She was dead. Oh,
oh, oh. A squeaky voice in her heart screeched, *Pla-
cate him. Tell him the truth until you can think of a means
of escape.*

She gasped as the pressure on her arm grew.
"Kate . . . Kate Templeton." Seeing fire spark in his
eyes, she blubbered, "Katherine Margarita Templeton."

His left hand grabbed her jaw, forcing her head
back, craning her neck. His gaze searched her face.
Something—what might have been regret—flickered
deep within the golden depths of his eyes for a too-
brief moment before they turned a cold, flat brown.
"Well, Katherine Margarita Templeton, ye are about
to die, but before ye go, ye will suffer, for I will ken yer
every thought and deed."

"No!" The pony forgotten, she flailed behind her,
searching for a weapon, anything to defend herself
with, and came in contact with something cold and
hard.

Her breath hitching, her heart careening about
in her chest, she took hold of the object and swung
with all her might. Not until it crashed against Ian's
head just above his left ear, sending blood everywhere, and he fell in a heap at her feet—all six feet
and four gorgeous inches of him—did she realize
she'd hit him with the royal chamber pot.

Mouth agape, hand to her throat, Kate stared at
the blood pooling beneath Ian's head.

"Dear God, what have I done?"

Her stomach heaved as she dropped to her knees
and placed a shaking hand on his chest. The solid
leather jerkin made it impossible to feel if he

breathed. Frantic, she tore at the leather straps holding the leather secure.

Please, please, please don't let him be dead. Please, I didn't mean to kill him even though he was going to kill me. Oh, please, I know he didn't mean it. Well, maybe he did, but I'm sure he would have thought better of it eventually. Please, please, please, oh please, don't let him be dead. He's too beautiful to die. Oh please, please.

The straps gave way and Kate, holding her breath, slipped her hand under the leather shield and waited for Ian's chest to rise. The moment it did, the tears building behind her lashes spilled and splashed onto his chest.

Thank you, oh, thank you.

She ran a gentle hand down his cheek. "I am so sorry." She then noticed the pool of blood on the floor had grown. "Oh, dear God!" He was bleeding to death.

Sheeting. She needed sheeting to stem the flow and she had seen some somewhere. She tossed the contents of several chests in all directions until she found the sheeting, but her shaking hands made tearing it impossible so she used her teeth.

After carefully swathing his head she pulled a blanket from James's chest and made a pillow. She used the remaining blanket to cover him up to the chin. Studying the beautiful planes of his face she managed to whisper, "I will never forget you."

A band of pain squeezed her chest as she picked up the slate and a piece of chalk. After scratching out a short missive of parting, she leaned over him and kissed his warm but too-still lips.

Kate picked up the pony and rose on shaking legs. When next she saw Sir Gregory she would not only clout, stomp and stab him in the heart but she would then rip it out.

She made her way to the outer door and peered into the outer close. The sounds of men battling and the cries of an appreciative audience rang around the inner bailey. Keeping to the wall, she made her way to the outlying barn. Dozens of sad-dled destriers and palfreys were tied before their stalls, but there was no groom to be seen. They were doubtless at the fight.

She hurried down the line of horses, discounting this one or that due to its small size or the look in its eye. Finding a glossy black destrier that was defi-nitely stout enough to carry her she stopped and placed a hand on its rump. The animal immediately shied and let fly a hoof, barely missing her leg by inches. Yelping in alarm, she jumped back, causing several other horses to shy.

At the end she spied a massive white destrier who remained calm while all the others shied right and left as she drew closer.

She placed a tentative hand on his heavily mus-cled white rump. The warm flesh quivered and the horse's head turned toward her, its beautiful black eyes calmly assessing her. Taken by the shape of its head and long white eyelashes, she murmured, "My, you are a pretty thing."

He nodded as if agreeing. She ran her hand over the well-defined muscles making up his shoulder. His huge feathered feet, on the other hand, gave her pause. A crushed foot was the last thing she needed.

As if reading her mind, the destrier snorted in quiet fashion and gently bumped her chest with his head. Kate scratched his cheek, then reached for his lead. "Aye, you'll do nicely."

"For God's sake, wake up."

Ian felt a firm hand on his shoulder, opened one eye and found his brother hovering over him, his expression worried. Wondering why his head ached—he hadna been in his cups, had he?—he growled, "What?"

"What? What the bloody hell are ye doing lying here in a pool of blood and covered in bairn blankets?"

What the hell was Shamus—

Kate! Ian bolted upright. "Ack!" Blinding pain seared through his brain. Fearing it might fall out of his skull, he reached up with both hands and felt a massive wad of fabric, and yanked it off. It was soaked with blood. He threaded tentative fingers through his clotted hair and winced, touching a two-inch gash.

I am going to kill her.

He reached for his brother's arm. "Help me up."

Shamus, still looking bemused, hauled him to his feet. As Ian wavered, trying to get his balance, his brother handed him a slate. "I found this on yer chest."

Ian had to blink several times before the feminine swirls on the slate would settle into a logical pattern.

I am so very sorry.

                    With love,
                    Kate

Ha! She was sorry all right and would be sorrier still once he got his hands on her. "Have ye seen her?"

"Aye, heading to the outer close, but didna think anything of it."

The stable. She was gone. He could feel it in his bones.

Shamus picked up a piece of broken crockery. "I'll wager this is what she conked ye with."

Recognizing what Shamus held, kenning many a royal ass had sat upon it, Ian decided outright killing would be too kind a punishment for Madame Kate.

Shamus dropped the bloodied shard and headed toward the door. "I'll summon the guards."

"Nay! One word of this, and I will gut ye." Bad enough that he'd been felled by a woman—a damn pockpud at that—he wouldna be made a laughing stock. He would never live it down. "I'll go after her. Alone. Just make my excuses should anyone ask where I am. I'll be back by nightfall."

She couldna have gotten far.

Picturing Kate hanging in the donjon by shackled wrists and ankles, he brushed past Shamus and headed for the stable.

A moment later he stood cursing before Thor's empty stall.

"God's teeth! She stole my friggin' horse!"

And where were the bloody grooms and squires?

Blood seething, Ian reached for the lead on Albany's destrier, his mind conjuring all manner of macabre tortures for the lady in black. The horse shied, he cursed again and gathered the reins, forcing the horse to tuck his head, and then vaulted into the elaborate saddle Albany favored. To Ian's consternation the horse wheeled, then reared. Leaning

forward, he kicked the gelding's belly and the horse
dropped back onto all fours.

"Do not screw with me, horse. I am not in the
mood."

He turned the horse toward the north gate and
kicked again. Albany's mount frog-hopped a few
feet before snorting and taking off at a fancy collected trot. Ian ducked as they entered the curved
passageway that made assault by an enemy difficult.
Clearing the outer portcullis and coming into the
sunshine, he straightened and kicked. The horse responded by breaking into a rocking canter and Ian
groaned, finally recalling why his aging liege favored
the animal. The beast's gait was as smooth as ice and
as slow as cold honey. Ian blew through clenched
teeth. He hadna time for damn prancing! He
kicked again. The horse, frightened and confused,
broke into an all-out run down the high street leading into the village and beyond that to England and
nay doubt Lady Katherine Margarita Templeton.

Kate, the wind chafing at her damp cheeks, kept
a death grip on the thick pommel before her. She
was making good time, the horse's powerful legs
were eating up ground at tremendous speed, but
she desperately wanted to pull the horse to a halt.
Her knees burned unmercifully from being turned
out for so many hours by the heavy stirrups and her
shoulders and neck ached from constantly checking
behind her. But she could not stop, not yet.

As best she could tell they had been traveling only
for four or five hours, and she had no idea how soon
or how many would be after her.

She glanced at the setting sun again, saw that it

had drifted too far behind her and tried to correct the horse's direction by tipping his head more to the left; a difficult task, given her hands were fully occupied with keeping herself upright. Augh.

Initially, she had kept to the roadway but realized from the position of the sun that the road had made a slow turn. She had been heading west, going deeper into Scotland. She then decided to go as the crow flies, straight through pastures and fields—through no matter what—so long as she was heading south, home. The horse appeared to enjoy the change, particularly when chest-deep in fodder. He continually wrenched on the reins to lower his head and grab mouthfuls of hay or oats as he went. Oh, that she were so fortunate.

Her correction finally made, the sinking sun now directly to her right, she tried to focus on relaxing her legs instead of thinking about her growling belly. Why had she not thought to grab some food? She knew why. Her thoughts had been consumed by Ian: the pain he might be in, when someone might find him and his ire when he found her gone.

She would miss him. Miss the way he smelled, looked at her, teased her, kissed her. She'd even miss his obstinate nature and anger. The undivided attention he had lavished on her, though undesired and certainly unwarranted, had made her feel special for the first time in her life. As if she was truly a woman worth taking note of, someone a man might even love.

Yes, she would likely spend the next fifty years—should she live that long—missing him. And what of him? Would he even give her a thought? Most likely not after a day or two, after his wound healed and his anger waned.

The thought of his forgetting her caused a burning at the back of her throat and her eyes to glaze with tears. She sniffed and gave herself a mental shake. "I can't be thinking of him, or what might have been." She had a mission to complete and mayhap even a future, and she could not be calling this animal *horse* whenever she tried to gain his attention. He needed a name. Better she thought on that.

"How does Pearl strike you?" she asked him. No, that sounded like something one might name a fat white cat. "Ivory? No. Dove?" Augh. As mile after mile flashed past she thought on things that were white: marble, quartz, diamonds, the moon, geese, swans, chalk and teeth. None would do. As the wind kicked up she shivered and sniffed the air. Good, no hint of rain or snow—

That is it! Snow! But Snow what? Snow Flake? No, too fragile sounding. Ball? He certainly had those. The largest she had ever seen beneath a stud. Hmmm, Snowball. She leaned over the pommel and patted his neck. "What do you think? Snowball?" He snorted and she took that as a *yes*. "Good, Snowball it is, then."

The horse suddenly startled and she nearly fell off. Grabbing the pommel with both hands, Kate frowned, seeing Snowball arch his massive neck. His ears, once relaxed and flopping, were now upright, the tips nearly touching as he focused left. She peered in the same direction, thinking he might have spotted a deer. When next his back suddenly hunched under her and his steps hesitated, Kate's curiosity turned to alarm. Her gaze raked the wooded copse again but she found naught to be alarmed about. Yet the horse continued to prance, sensing a threat deep in the dense shadows.

She shuddered and turned his head to the right. He obeyed but reluctantly, his steps short, his powerful hooves flashing high before him, his attention still on the woods. Oh, not good. She clucked. "We need hurry away, Snowball."

He paid her no heed. Augh! Gritting her teeth, Kate kicked as hard as she could. Her knees— already in agony—revolted, shooting hot pain up her thighs. When Snowball finally sprang into a lope Kate had all she could do to keep from screaming.

She could not have said how long they ran, being in too much pain to think, but finally the wood was far behind and the horse felt more relaxed beneath her. Unable to bear any more jostling, she pulled back on the reins and Snowball, huffing and blowing, settled into a sedate walk.

She reached down, patted his hot neck and her hand came away covered in foamy sweat. "You poor thing."

She needed to find water for him, and they both needed to rest.

As the three-quarter moon started to rise, they came abreast of a small loch surrounded by tall, long-needled pine. She edged the horse closer to the boulder-strewn shoreline for a closer look. Seeing that all appeared safe, she pulled up beside a boulder in a grassy patch. "We will rest here for a bit." She leaned forward and patted his neck again. "You're such a good boy, Snowball. Such a good boy." His owner would no doubt miss him very much.

When she pulled her right leg out of the stirrup, it felt like someone had stabbed her. She groaned. The ground suddenly looked a mile away.

* * *

I'll strap her to a rack.

Aye, he would have to build the torturing device since Stirling didna have one, but no matter, the end would be well worth the effort. He'd take great pleasure in turning the screw, hearing her scream. He blew through his teeth. Nay, hearing Kate scream wouldna be tolerable. He'd have to come up with something else, but definitely worthy of her deceit and the pain now burning in his chest.

Unaccustomed to a woman's rejection, much less from one he had begun to fancy himself really caring for, he couldna fathom what he was to do with the bile and fury building within. And how could he have not seen through her? Why had he not grown suspicious when she—a striking woman—had claimed to be married to that cretin Robbie? When he learned that she spoke Gael—a language nearly impossible if ye werena born into it? When she deflected his questions about her marriage and reacted with more fear than was warranted upon learning Alistair was taking her before the tribunal? Why had he not kenned then?

Had he become so enamored by her luscious breasts and hurdies that he'd become coddle-brained? Aye. That's precisely what had happened. And with a bloody pockpud at that! God, how stupid could a man be?

Focused on Kate, he almost missed the trampled path heading due south through a field of ripening hay to his left. Frowning, he reined in and dismounted. He walked into the field some ten feet, then knelt to examine the ground. He grinned, recognizing Thor's shoe prints. None came larger or had the toe cleats intended to tear another horse's rear end to shreds. Humph! Clever lass. She had apparently realized she'd been heading west and changed course.

Jaw muscles twitching he remounted. Soon. He would have her in his clutches verra soon, and she'd wish she never been born.

Two hours later Ian spurred Albany's reluctant destrier in the sides for the hundredth time and entered the outskirts of Airdrie.

Finding the village in total darkness, save for a lone lamp that burned in the publican's window, he dismounted. Suspecting Kate might have taken refuge within, Ian secured Albany's cantankerous mount next to the water trough and made his way to the wattle-and-thatched stable. His mood grew darker as he went from stall to stall. At the end, he cursed.

Where the hell could she be if not here? Surely she wouldna risk her life or Thor's by racing over unfamiliar ground in the dark. His destrier could see well enough at night—better than he—but there was always the risk when traveling fast of falling into an unseen *glack* or over a cliff.

Ian collected the black and led him out onto the main road. He could do naught but ride on and pray the moonlight would be enough to keep the pair ahead of him safe.

Just before dawn, having crossed several burns and climbed numerous hills and as many crags, he heard a woman's bloodcurdling scream. One he would recognize anywhere.

Chapter 14

Kate, jolted out of a sound sleep, screamed as someone grabbed a fistful of her hair and jerked her head backward. He tried to slap a hand over her mouth while another, a man with fetid breath and broken teeth, grabbed and twisted one arm behind her, then tried to grasp her other. Pain suddenly burst to life behind her eyes. Blood . . . She saw only blood. Dear God!

She fell backward, praying that at least one of the men behind her would topple with her and crack his head on a rock. Hearing a grunt and feeling her arm come free she tried to scramble to her feet, only to be yanked backward again by the hair. She screamed and lashed out behind her, her fingers curled like claws.

The man holding her hair shouted, "Damn it, Kieth, leave the destrier be and give me a hand with this friggin' bitch!"

Kate's gaze flew to the right where she had left Snowball tied to a low-hanging pine bough. Totally consumed with her own terror, fighting the men who had awoken her, Kate hadn't given a moment's thought to the horse until the man had spoken.

She heard panicked whinnies and jerked to the right in hopes of seeing him. Her hair was pulled again and she screeched in pain, sure she had just lost a fistful. She toppled sideways and caught sight of Snowball just before a vicious blow landed on her cheek and she saw stars.

Snowball, spinning on his hind legs and pawing the air, was also fighting for his life. A rangy man in rags held on to his reins while another tried to grab on to a stirrup.

Oh, please, please do not let them hurt him!

Suddenly a tremendous weight pinned her legs and painful fingers dug into her thighs. Searing cold shot up her spine as her hips were pressed into the unyielding stones beneath her. The stout man— the one who had been trying to catch Snowball's stirrup—was now straddling her and pushing at her skirts. Having no success he hauled out a knife and started slashing at the bodice of her gown.

"No!" She clawed at the stones with her free hand. Clutching one, she swung. Blood spattered onto her face and the man collapsed onto her chest, knocking the wind out of her.

I can't breathe. Oh, Merciful Virgin, I cannot breath.

As suddenly as the weight had landed, it lifted, the pain at the back of her head subsided, and her arms were free.

Not daring to look, heartbroken that she should come to so inauspicious an end so far from home at the hands of ruffians, to never be able to write to Ian and tell him how sorry she truly was, she curled into a ball and sobbed in earnest.

Hearing a deep, bone-rattling scream, then cries

of pure anguish, grunts and more screams, Kate covered her ears and squeezed her eyes shut. She couldn't bear to see what other horrors awaited her.

And what would become of poor Snowball? It didn't bear contemplation and she sobbed all the harder.

Suddenly she was being lifted. *Oh, God, now what?* She could do naught but scream.

"Shhhhh, Katie, shhhhh, 'tis I."

Strong, warm arms wrapped around her and began rocking her.

"Ian? *Ian!*" Her arms flew above his shoulders and she buried her face against his neck. She continued to sob, this time from pure joy. Oh, he was alive and well, and he smelled so good despite the sweat. He was as strong and beautiful as ever, and she was alive. She could apologize for coshing him on the head, and tell him—

His pulse vibrated at a horrendous rate against her lips as he asked, "Did he . . . Did the bastard rape ye, lass?"

Kate shook her head, her face still buried against his neck. "No, you came . . . in time."

And she would love him forever if only for that. Yes. Had he not come when he had, she and Snowball would have—

"Snowball!" She bolted upright. Not seeing him by the tree, she struggled to stand. "Where is he?"

Ian lifted the hair from her face with a gentle hand and brushed away her tears. "They are all dead."

Kate looked behind her then. Blood. Severed limbs. Bodies lay everywhere. Seeing the carnage Ian MacKay had wrought in rescuing her, she suddenly grew light-headed.

Bile rising, gagging, she covered her mouth and took hold of his arm to keep from falling. The scene—far worse than she had envisioned—was not, she reminded herself, Ian's fault. Had she never come he never would have done this. Would never have even contemplated doing this. It's not his fault, but my God, he had proved himself dangerously lethal all the same.

She took a deep breath. "Snowball. We have to find Snowball."

He frowned at her. "Who?"

Kate flapped her hands and frantically scoured the shoreline for even a splash of white. "The beautiful destrier I stole—borrowed from Stirling."

Ian gripped her arms and held her out at arm's length. "Snowball." He made a disgusting sound at the back of his throat, then let loose an ear-piercing whistle that nearly startled her out of her skin.

Oh oh. His face was now ruddy and something in his eyes told her not to utter another word if she wanted to see sunrise.

Within a heartbeat bushes began thrashing, wood was snapping, and the ground began vibrating beneath her feet.

On the next beat Snowball, snorting, peered over Ian's shoulder at her.

"Oh."

Ian's gaze shifted to her rent bodice and exposed breasts. "Katherine Margarita Templeton, meet *Thor*."

I am in soooo much trouble.

She clutched at the fabric, trying to cover herself. "Had I know he was yours, I never—"

"Silence!"

Without saying another word, he picked up her

cape, gave it a shake and threw it at her. He then picked up his bloodied broadsword and hauled her by the arm to the water's edge where he rinsed the sword off. She flinched when—with the flip of one powerful hand—the claymore sang as it swung through the air and slid into the sheath at his back. He then hauled her, tripping and stumbling, through the woods. A moment later she was tossed onto a black horse—the one that had tried to kick her, if she wasn't mistaken—and tied, wrists together, to its saddle.

She twisted her wrists. "Is this *really* necessary?"

Ian growled deep in his throat to keep from shouting himself hoarse. The wench wouldna get away from him again. Teeth clenched, he untied Albany's mount and led it toward Thor, who patiently awaited him.

He had never been as frightened as he had when he stole up to the loch's edge with claymore in hand and found Kate flat on her back, keening for all she was worth with that fat pig lying on top of her. Blind rage had sent blood pounding into already-tense muscles, and he saw naught but red. What happened after that he couldna say. All he kenned when the fury ebbed—when Kate was finally in his arms—was that which his eyes saw. Four dismembered men lay at his feet.

He shook, dispelling the image and reached inside his saddle bag for Thor's lead rope. He growled seeing Kate's frippery. He pushed the garments aside, found the rope and tied it to the black gelding's bridle.

Without a backward glance at Kate, he vaulted into his saddle and turned Thor due north.

He had missed yesterday's General Council meeting but he'd be damned if he'd miss today's.

Snowball. He shuddered, dropped his reins and nudged his heels into Thor's sides. When the destrier immediately responded, moved into a collected trot, he relaxed a wee bit. Had Kate ruined his mount, he'd have skinned her on the spot. His verra life depended on Thor responding without direction from the bit should his hands be occupied in battle.

Hearing Kate groan Ian glanced over his shoulder and found Albany's mount frog-hopping like a fool and throwing his head. Examining Kate's bruised face, picturing her bruised thighs, his gut inexplicably twisted, and he picked up the reins. Thor immediately slowed to a sedate walk.

As angry as he had been when he heard her speak English—had kenned she'd been playing him for a fool—as furious as he'd been when he found Thor gone, none of that could compare to his blind fury finding her fighting for her life beneath that animal.

And why that should have driven him wode, caused him to blindly slaughter, didna bear pondering since he had yet to come up with the perfect torture for Katherine Margarita Templeton, spy extraordinaire.

Ack!

A mile up the road while slogging through bog, Kate murmured, "How is your head?"

He gritted his teeth and hunched his shoulders. She had dropped all pretenses and spoken in English. And his head still ached and would bear a scar, its first, thanks to her.

A mile later while climbing through dense forest Kate murmured, "I am sorry for causing you such trouble. I truly am." He again ignored her. She didna ken the meaning of sorry but soon would.

Two miles farther, deep in a field of grain, she

murmured, "I am thankful naught untoward befell Snow—Thor because of me."

That he could believe. She had appeared most distressed thinking Thor injured or gone. Too bad she hadna the same concern for him when she smashed that bloody chamber pot over his head.

After a mile more she asked, "I don't mean to bother ye, but do ye have any food?"

He turned in the saddle and glared at her.

Blanching, she tucked in her chin and mumbled, "Forget I asked."

Now how the hell could he do that? He hadna eaten either in almost a day thanks to her. Ack.

In another three hours they would make Airdrie. While he dined on whatever the publican had to offer, he'd see to it that she had bread and water. Enough to keep her alive until he could come up with a truly *fiendish* torture for her.

At a bubbling burn an hour later, while the horses drank, he studied the way water splashed and rolled over the moss and lichen-covered boulders. Humph. He'd heard tell they dunked witches on a long pole. Nay, she'd scream, then likely drown, and then he'd be no wiser as to why she had come to Scotland than he was now.

But water did have appeal. 'Twasna sharp nor hard. Surely he could use it in some fashion to drive her wode without causing her pain. Have her begging for mercy, willing to answer any question. Hmmm.

Riding along a shale cliff, Kate shouted, "I need stop."

Humph. "Nay." They had to make Airdrie within the next hour if he was to make the afternoon session. Albany was an effective administrator but not a warrior and tempers were likely at a boiling point in Stirling.

"But I need . . . privacy."

He rolled his shoulders. "I said nay."

Kate huffed, "Fine," and after a moment added, "I will simply . . . piss in yer saddle, then."

"Ack!" He pulled up short and spun to face her. Teeth bared, he growled, "Dinna ye dare." Albany would have his hide.

She glared back. "If you will not stop, then what choice have I?" She turned away, muttering under her breath.

"*Grrrrrr.*" Aggravated that she had a point, he looked about. A narrow, isolated glen lay beyond the deep, rock-strewn *glack* to their immediate right, but there was also scrubby pine and cedar near the cliff edge that could offer her bit of privacy. Better—there was nowhere for her to run. Perfect.

He dismounted and stomped back to her. "If ye want down ye need answer a question first. Were ye ever married to Robbie Campbell?"

Her gaze downcast, Kate shook her head.

Thank God for that. He reached for the rope and his fingers brushed hers. Feeling cold metal on the middle finger of her left hand he examined her ring for the first time. Dented and scratched, the thin gold band appeared older than she. "Then whose ring do ye wear?"

Blushing, she looked away and shook her head.

"*Humph.* Mayhap sitting in chains in a dark, rat-infested donjon for days on end might make ye a bit more talkative."

She looked at him then, her magnificent sky blue eyes huge in a now stark-white countenance. Good. There were nay rats at Stirling, hadna been since they'd introduced the wee wiry terriers after they discovered the rats were eating all the cats they'd brought in. But she needna ken that.

He started untying the ropes. "If ye so much as breathe wrong, ye will wish ye had died at the hands of those pigs back there."

She nodded, her lower lip caught between her teeth.

"As long as we ken each other." When the rope fell away, he grabbed her by the waist. She placed her hands on his shoulders and slid toward him. Catching her, her breasts pressing against him, looking her in the eyes, something tightened in his chest.

Damn you for making me feel this, this . . . Ack!

He let go, and she dropped the four wee inches that separated them in height and staggered back. It took all his willpower not to reach out and steady her.

Jaws clenched, he pointed to the dense clump of brush and trees that hung perilously close to the fifty-foot drop to his right. "There, and be quick about it."

Muttering, "Thank ye," she slowly hobbled away.

The moment Kate squatted behind the dense brush, she burst into tears. The donjon. Rats! Good God, she had to get away and quickly. But how? A cliff sat at her back and he stood between her and the horses. Oh, she never should have come, visions or nay. Good intentions or nay. Rats.

A sob escaped her, and she slapped a hand over her mouth. She couldn't let him know how frightened he'd made her.

A high-pitched call caused her to look up. The kite soaring above her cried out again as a gust blew open her cape and slapped at her exposed chest, making her skin prickle. Oh, that I too could fly from here. Sitting hip deep in brittle grass, she looked over the ravine's edge. Mayhap she should just throw herself over the edge and be done—

I *could* without actually doing it! Why not? Hope bloomed in Kate's chest as she tore off her cape and pulled her gown over her head. Shivering, she stuffed her gown with the weeds at hand and then pulled off her hose and stuffed them with grass. Using the lace from her hair she hurriedly attached her stockings to the bottom of her gown. Cursing the loss of her headdress, which would have added a bit more reality, she kicked off her slippers and shoved them onto her supposed legs.

She nearly jumped out of her skin when Ian yelled, "Make haste, woman! We havena all day."

Her heart thumping near to breaking her ribs, Kate managed to squeak, "Aye, just a moment!"

After tying her cloak over her gown, she sat and, using her feet, shoved her headless self over the edge. If it all fell apart before landing, then so be it. At least she tried. Not able to stand the suspense any longer she peered over the edge. Ha!

The dummy had landed chest-down between two boulders, appearing at a distance as if her head had dropped down between them.

Thank you, thank you, thank you.

She then picked up the largest rock she could reach without showing herself and scrambled backward into a prickly thicket. Murmuring a quick prayer, she heaved the rock over the edge and screeched, letting her voice fade as if falling away.

Ducking down, she heard Ian shout, "Oh shit!" and then his running footsteps. He barely came to a stop at the edge of the ravine before dropping onto his belly and scrambling down, cursing himself and every living thing on the earth as he went.

Hearing the way he called her name, hearing him keen, "Please God, dinna let her be dead," Kate's eyes filled with tears. Oh, he did care for her . . . in some fashion. Not so much or in the manner she cared for him, but at least now she knew.

But still she had to go.

Muttering, "Forgive me," she rose and raced around the copse to where Ian had left the horses unattended. She reached for the black's reins, only to have him shy and prance away.

"Frig it." Tears streaming down her face she reached for Thor's reins. God, she sounded like one of the Tower guards.

Her possessions, the cloth pony and Ian's gift were all still in his saddle bags anyway, and she had no time to transfer them, much less dress or chase down the black and coax him into standing still. She had no idea how quickly Ian would climb back out of the ravine, and she certainly *did not* want to be around when he did.

Finally mounted, she glanced at the ridge and whispered, "I will return Thor to you, I promise."

She then turned Thor's head south and kicked for all she was worth.

Chapter 15

"KATIE!"

Eyes locked on the still body below, heart in his throat, Ian slid feet first down the steep embankment without making an effort to slow his descent. Christ's blood! How could he have been so stupid as to stop in such a place as this? "Katie!"

Please let the lass be alive, please.

He wouldna be able to live with himself if she broke her back, much less died. Such a pretty thing . . . Ack! Or if she were now brain-coddled. Oh God, please, nay.

Landing hard on the rocks, his heart beating at a frantic pace, he scrambled across the uneven boulders. "Katie, answer me!"

He dropped to his knees at her side and gently took hold of her shoulders. Something—

"What the hell?"

A scarecrow? She'd made a friggin' *scarecrow* and let him think she'd fallen to her death? Light-headed, he rocked back on his heels and gulped in some much-needed air.

Nay. She couldna have done this to him. Frightened him near to death. But the evidence lay before him.

He stood on still-shaking legs, his gaze scouring the ridge line looking for her.

"Ye walk on the sod of truth, Katie! Do ye hear me? Ye are a dead woman! D-E-A-dead!"

He raced to the wall and, grabbing a protruding root, kicked the toe of his boot into a crevice.

I am definitely going to kill her!

Aye, and using a rack would be a kindness. Better that he draw and quarter her and then impale her parts on the four corners of Stirling's keep. And when he finally left Stirling, he would bring her remains to Seabhagnead where he'd place them on four tall spikes at the four points of the compass so he might take great pleasure in viewing them each and every day when he awoke. Where he could stand on his rampart sipping mead, and gloat.

"'Twasna bad enough that she had lied, that she stole me horse, but to—"

His horse!

She wouldna. She simply wouldna dare a second time.

He scaled the rock like a crazed spider, his arms and legs burning with the doubled effort. Huffing at the top, he scrambled to his feet and raced around the scrubby copse.

Seeing only Albany's destrier, his ears pinned back and legs splayed, Ian let loose an ear-shattering whistle. He held his breath, hoping Thor was within hearing as the black took off at a dead run.

Ian threw back his head. *"Aaaaaack!"*

Cursing his stupidity for relying on a woman's means of killing, Alistair Campbell paced outside

Albany's receiving room where the tribunal was about to commence.

Yesterday whilst all were in the inner bailey watching the enraged Babcock and MacFarlane try to kill each other, he'd visited the ladies' chamber and discovered that the velvet pouch with its deadly treats and the satchel he had set it upon were missing. But his joy had been short-lived, discovering a few hours later that MacKay had also disappeared.

Was he looking for her?

If they had gone off to tryst and now MacKay lay dead . . .

Alistair shuddered.

None would fash about the whore's death. She was naught but a coigreach intent on upsetting their lives, but if MacKay was found dead with her—and with the sweets that had been liberally dusted with dogbane at his side—then suspicion, in particular Albany's, would fall squarely where it should: on his shoulders.

And he'd been a bloody fool making his distrust of the woman clear to any and all who would listen.

His stomach turned, realizing he might also have inadvertently garnered the wrath of MacKay's lunatic liege, Black Angus. The man would go to war over a stolen pullet. The killing of his brother-by-marriage would send him into a friggin' bloodlust.

Should the worst occur—should MacKay be found dead with the whore—could he depend on Donald to come to his aid? He had signed that secret pact with the Donald to support the man should he decide to make a bid for the crown, but would the Donald reciprocate in kind should he be the one in peril?

Alistair seriously doubted it.

His sire, the rightful liege of Ardkinglas, was still verra much alive, making him, the bastard son, a redundancy in some minds. Should he hang for murder, a Stewart cousin, or mayhap even the Donald himself, would likely take control of Ardkinglas.

Ack!

Seeing Shamus MacKay round the corner Alistair's pulse quickened. Mayhap the brother now gleaned more.

"MacKay, have ye news of yer brother or Madame Campbell?" He waved an agitated hand toward the open door where the twelve liege lords waited. "They willna wait forever."

Shamus came to a stop and glared at him. "If I kenned where either of them were I'd tell ye, but since I dinna, cease asking."

Without another word Shamus shouldered past and headed down the hall.

Grinding his teeth, Alistair began to pray. He had nay liking for Ian MacKay, but he had sore need for the man to walk through the doors of Stirling.

Chilled to the bone, Kate pulled back on Thor's reins and brushed at the tears on her wind-chafed cheeks. She was so lost.

Dressed in naught but her rent cotton shift, she'd been most grateful for the heat pouring off Thor's sweat-caked body, but now he needed to rest and she needed to dress and think.

She steered Thor toward a nearby stand of pine and dropped the reins. As Thor routed around in the pine needles for something to nibble, she routed around in the saddle bags for clothes.

Her breath hitching, Kate hauled out her spare

gown, slippers and cloak. As she struggled into them, Thor occasionally glanced at her as if wondering why she would not stop crying. God knows she had tried, but the more miles that passed, the more hours she rode, the more guilt consumed her.

She would never forgive herself for causing the terror she'd heard in Ian's voice. And he'd likely never forgive her either. And he should not.

She sniffed as her near-frozen fingers fumbled with the bone catch of her cloak.

'Twas time to go again. She needed food. She'd not eaten in . . . days, maybe. She wasn't sure.

She picked up the reins and urged Thor around the boulder she had taken shelter behind and back onto the trail she had been following. She looked up. Clouds for as far as the eye could see; wet-wool gray, slung low from horizon to horizon. What to do? Without the sun she had no idea in which direction she faced, much less in which direction she should go.

Having seen the paths she had made through the grain fields as they had headed north, understanding how Ian had tracked her so easily, she now kept to the winding goat paths the Scots called roadways. Whenever she came to one heading south she took it. If it ended and she had a choice of heading either right or left, more often than not she turned left, reasoning that London lay to the southeast. And still she was thoroughly lost.

"Well, Thor, shall we go?" If she didn't find food soon she'd perish.

Topping a rise a short time later, Kate's heart sank to the pit of her stomach. Before her sat a valley where two rivers met, the closest running to the right and the other to the left and on the headland betwixt the two sat a massive castle. A village sat below. Oh dear. The village meant food but the castle likely meant soldiers and then there was the matter of the rivers, which blocked her path as far the eye could see. Mayhap if she skirted the edge of the river?

A few miles into the valley she met an old woman and her dog herding a small flock of sheep in the direction from which she'd come. Not sure how Thor would react to the bleating beasts and the clanging bells on them, she eased him to the side of the path and brought him to a stop.

The apple-cheeked woman, dressed in a coarse green kirtle and shawl, looked up at her in surprise, then smiled. Kate waited until the woman was beside her before saying in Scots, "What is that place by the river?"

The woman's eyes grew round. "'Tis Roxburgh, my lady."

Kate had never heard of it, but was pleased she had correctly guessed that the woman was a Lowlander. She was close to her goal: England.

"Is there a publican there?"

The woman shook her head, her gaze now raking Kate and from her expression not really liking what she saw. Conscious of her missing headdress, Kate ran a hand over her wind-whipped hair. "I have been traveling a long way."

The woman craned her neck to look past Thor, no doubt looking for some sort of escort. "May I ask yer name, my lady?"

"My apologies. 'Tis Lady Campbell, widow of Robbie Campbell of Ardkinglas."

The woman's hands flew to her cheeks. "Then what on earth are ye doing here without guards?"

Very unusual to be sure. "My mother, you see, word came she was dying, all very sudden." After a moment she asked, "Is there a problem?"

"Aye!" The woman made a tsking sound, then pointed over her shoulder. "'Tis Roxburgh Castle yon, once a Douglas stronghold but now in the hands of the Pockpuds. Has been for some years now. If ye dinna want to come to harm, my lady, may I suggest ye get ye bonnie self elsewhere."

Augh. If questioned, there would be no earthly way Kate could explain her presence here. Worse, she had already been abused enough by many a disgusting soldier that she'd had the misfortune of knowing at the Tower.

The woman huffed and looked at Kate as if she was a daft child. "May I ask where ye are headed?"

A reasonable question that Kate had no reasonable answer to, so she made up a name. "Shepkirk."

The woman's brow furrowed. "Hmmm, I dinna ken it."

Kate forced a smile. "'Tis a wee place near the auld Hadrian . . . Roman Wall."

"Ah. Well, ye are heading in the right direction, but 'tis still a fair piece, my lady, and many a pack of ruffians stands betwixt ye and it."

Kate didn't doubt it and reached down and patted Thor's neck. "With God's blessing, Thor shall get me there safe and sound."

The woman reached out a tentative hand and patted the destrier's shoulder. "I shall pray that he does, but he looks a tempting prize. He isna exactly what ye'd call porridge."

"Aye." Kate shuddered, the images of the four men who assaulted her still fresh in her mind. "So where might I safely cross the river?"

"'Tis a ferry by yon castle, but ye dinna want to be goin' there." After a bit of nibbling on her fingernail she said, "Ye had best head west, along the Tweed." She pointed to her right and the closest river. "Ye may find a shallow ford further down. To the east, 'tis the Teviot and its water runs deep."

Kate agreed going west might prove wisest. She thanked the woman for her help, and reached into her pocket, feeling for her coin pouch.

Augh! She'd neglected to empty her pocket before kicking her gown into the ravine! How stupid and careless. Now how was she to feed herself or Thor? And what if she couldn't find a ford, but had to pay a ferryman? Augh!

"My lady? Are ye all right?"

Kate, tears burning at the back of her throat, looked down at the woman who was frowning at her. "I wanted to reward ye for yer kindness but I seem to have lost my coin pouch."

"'Tis nay reason to reward me. I have done naught, but do thank ye for the thought."

"Still." Kate swallowed the growing thickness in her throat and picked up Thor's reins. "I had best be going now."

Wishing her Godspeed, the woman stepped away and Kate pressed her heels into Thor's sides.

Hours later and without yet finding a place to cross the river, she stood in a hamlet before a lone stall, bartering her last gown for a pork pie and two shriveled apples.

Walking away, leading Thor by the reins, she swore next she saw Sir Gregory Campbell, she would not only clout, stomp and cut out his heart, but she'd cut out his lying tongue as well.

Once past the last cottage and away from curious

eyes, she held an apple out on an open palm and Thor gobbled it up in one bite. Humph. So much for saving the other for her breakfast. She held out the second apple and it disappeared as quickly as the first. Better she starve than the horse, she supposed. She was dependent on him getting her home.

She settled the reins on his neck, and reached for the stirrup. With a groan she heaved herself up and into the saddle. "Let's find a ford, shall we?"

If one didn't come into sight soon, she and Thor were going for a swim.

"MacKay!" Robbie the Mole Graham thumped Ian's shoulder, then looked about to see if any had observed his arrival. Waving Ian into his modest, one-room cottage Robbie muttered, "Thought ye'd be in Stirling."

"I was." And would be still but for Katherine Margarita Templeton. "Can I impose on ye for a wee drink?"

Brow furrowed, Graham murmured, "Of course."

When they settled onto their three-legged cuttie stools before a peat fire with mugs of warm ale in hand, Graham said, "Ye look a bit tuckered. What is amiss?"

"There is trouble on the border." Seeing Graham's mouth grow thin and hard, Ian hastened to assure him, "'Tis naught to fash on just yet, but be aware. What is happening at Roxburgh?"

Graham shrugged. "They have a good six hundred within at any given time, and twenty or so patrols out from sunrise to gloaming. Usually in groups of ten. Rumor has it they've requested coins and manpower to repair and refortify."

Humph. Ian studied Graham's dirt-encrusted fingernails. "I see ye are still mining."

Graham chuckled and rubbed a calloused hand across the top of his sandy hair. "Heard about that, have ye?"

Ian laughed for the first time in days. Graham had to be the best under-the-curtain-wall tunnel borer in all Scotland. "Let me just say I couldna picture ye sitting on yer hands while the pockpuds walked yon ramparts thumbing their noses at ye."

Graham shrugged his thick shoulders. "A man's got to do what the good Lord set him to do. If 'twasna Roxburgh, then I'd be digging under something else, to be sure." After a bit, he asked, "Why are ye really here?"

Ian drained his ale, then cleared his throat. "I am looking for a woman who might have passed through. Verra tall, hair the color of a raven's wing, big blue eyes, and riding a white destrier."

Graham stared at him for a moment, then broke into laughter, nearly toppling off his stool. Grabbing the mantel and righting himself, he hooted, "She stole yer horse!"

Feeling heat rise up his neck, Ian grumbled deep in his throat. "There isna a damn thing funny about this, Robbie."

"Oh, but there is, as I'd been wondering why ye were riding that gelding." He took Ian's mug and walked to the leather budget hanging by the door. Muttering to himself, "The Thief of Hearts gets nipped himself," Graham erupted into another peal of laughter.

Ian could do naught but seethe. He had lost Kate's trail and time was fleeing.

Finally gaining control of himself, Graham wiped

the back of his hand across his eyes and handed Ian his full mug. "My, oh my." He cleared his throat, then asked, "What can I do for ye?"

"I need ye to go into the village and ask about. I canna do it, not with the roving patrols about."

"No problem. Make yerself at home. I will be back in a wee bit." His friend rose and left. Ian could still hear Graham chuckling as he disappeared behind the smithy's.

I am going to kill her. I swear it.

Annoyed he had lost track of Thor's hoofprints in the hard gravel miles back, fearing Kate had gotten herself into some sort of trouble, Ian paced, peeked out the door for sight of Graham and paced some more.

The sun had set long before Graham ambled back up the hill. Throwing the door wide Ian muttered, "Well?"

Graham grinned. "Aye, she has been and gone. The lad who had bartered with her said yer mighty steed was following behind her like a besot pup."

Ian blew through clenched teeth. He'd kill the horse, too. "How long ago and in which direction did they go?"

"Not more than four hours ago, and west along the Tweed. She asked the lad if there might be a crossing further along."

Kate was still trying to find her way south. Good. But why hadna she simply crossed at Roxburgh? More importantly, why hadna she sought refuge there? "And is there a crossing?"

"Aye, some ten miles further to the west."

Ian slapped a hand on Robbie's shoulder. "Thank ye. I am in yer debt." He reached into his sporran for a coin and his fingers came in contact with the gift he had hoped to give Kate. Pain bloomed again beneath his breastbone, forcing him to take a deep breath. He pushed the cross aside, pulled out a gold pound and, taking Robbie's hand in his, placed the coin in his palm.

Realizing what he held, Robbie blushed scarlet and tried to hand it back. "Nay, I canna—"

"Aye, ye can, if for naught else than to shore up yer damn tunnels."

And the coin might buy Graham's silence, although Ian wouldna bet on it. The retelling of the tale might prove too tempting an entertainment.

Robbie followed Ian behind the sheep pen where he had hidden Albany's mount. As he swung into the saddle, Robbie said, "Ye take care. Ye should be safe until dawn, then keep an eye out."

Ian could only pray Kate would be as cautious. Soldiers who had nay women tended to take advantage whenever the opportunity presented itself.

Hiding in a small copse as dawn broke, Kate nearly drooled staring at the dozens of speckled chickens pecking around the garden soil next to a stout wattle-and-thatched cottage. Had someone told her a week ago she'd be stealing, much less salivating, over the thought of raw eggs, she would have laughed herself silly, but she wasn't laughing now. She fully intended to get herself a handful of eggs or die trying.

A shift in the wind carried the scent of burning peat. Oh, nay. She parted the bushes to her right for a better look at the cottage and found a lamp had been lit within, sending a bright splash of citrine through a partially open door.

Cow pies! Those within were awake.

So be it. She had to get her hands on those eggs before someone came out to collect them.

She checked Thor's reins a final time, collected her skirts up between her legs and, back hunched, crept out of the copse. Keeping to the far left, she scrambled into a rock-strewn gully that ran along the side of the garden. Keeping low, she followed the depression until she thought she was directly across from the hen house.

Lying on her stomach, she peeked over the rise. No one had come out, and the chickens were still pecking away. Too, she could now see that what she thought might be a square hen house was in truth just a lean-to shelter built into a small hill. The door faced the rear of the cottage. Praying the cottage did not have a rear window, she eased out on the gully on her hands and knees. Two forward creeps and she fell onto her face. Augh!

There was no way she could cover the distance crawling in a gown. She huffed, righted herself and, gathering her skirts up again, scrambled to her feet.

In for a penny, in for a pound. She ran.

Cackling chickens scattered as she raced past, her gaze locked on the hen house. At the door she knelt and frantically pawed through the nests. Five eggs! More than enough, but then . . .

She should take a few more. She certainly didn't want to be going through this again tomorrow.

Her eggs collected, four in her pocket, four in her hand, she gathered up her skirts. She hadn't taken ten steps when a horrendous, deep-throated honking erupted behind her, nearly stopping her heart. She spun and found the largest goose she had ever laid eyes on rushing toward her, its chest thrust high and its huge wings frantically beating the air.

"Ah!" Kate ran and the goose came after her. Not a moment later the cottage door flew open and a woman half Kate's height and twice her width, and armed with the largest broom Kate had ever seen, screeched, "Halt! *Thief!*"

Kate felt a sharp crack on the back of her head and wings suddenly slapped her ears. She spun, and the goose dropped to the ground but then flew at her chest, trying to beat her to death with its wings.

"Eeeeeek!" The eggs in her hand broke as she batted at the goose. Dear God, how could feathers hurt so?

She dodged left, only to get cracked on the head by a broom. *"Oooow!"*

She tried running the other way and the goose charged her legs. "Cease!"

Kate got slammed in the middle of her back. *"Ooow! Ooch!"*

Her head jerked back. "Ouch! Ouch! *Eeeyyy!*"

To her horror, the goose had latched on to her hair with its beak. Hanging down her back like some bizarre veil, he tried to gain purchase on her back with his clawed feet while trying to beat the stuffing out of her with his enormous wings.

"Ouch! *Ayyyy! Oooh!*" Kate spun in the hopes of dislodging the beast. The woman, not to be outdone and still screaming, hit her front and back.

Chapter 16

There is a God.

Ian leaned against the thatched cottage's wall and crossed his arms over his chest to watch Kate battle her outraged assailants.

The goose, an adult gander by the looks of him, would have done anyone's Michalmas banquet proud. The rotund owner looked to be the kind of woman who grabbed hold of life with both hands, as evidenced by her girth and the way she was swinging her willow broom.

Ian had been trotting past the cottage when the screams and horrendous honking started, had ridden into the copse to investigate and been reward with finding Thor. Peering through the bushes with claymore in hand, he then spied Kate and her attackers. Thinking she deserved a good thrashing for scaring him near to death—and more than pleased he wasna the one having to do it—he decided to let her fend for herself for a wee bit while he tended the horses. After tying the gelding behind Thor, he took his time leading them to the cottage.

Ack. A thin red slash appeared on Kate's cheek. The sight made something in his chest contract and he straightened. *"Enough!"*

The old woman spun at the sound of his voice, her nearly ruined broom waving over her shoulder. Her eyes grew wide when they found him, and the broom slipped from her hands. "My lord!"

"Mistress."

The goose, on the other hand, paid him nay heed.

Striding past the gaping woman, Ian grabbed Kate by the waist and knocked the goose in the head with his elbow. It immediately fell at his feet, floundered a bit before it gave itself a good shake, and apparently deciding it had done its duty for the day, quietly waddled away.

Kate, her chest heaving, tears streaming down her face, collapsed against him. "Ian! I just . . . I was so hungry . . . and then the goose. Oh God." She buried her face against his shoulder.

Ian rolled his eyes. "Mistress, ye will have to pardon my ladywife." He made a swirling motion next to his ear with his free hand, silently indicating Kate was seriously wode. When the auld woman's eyes grew wide, Ian nodded and murmured, "As a belfry bat. She escaped and, well, I thank ye for catching her and will pay for any damage she has caused."

Kate, apparently calm enough to listen, suddenly pushed off his chest. Looking absolutely appalled, she asked, "Did you just tell this woman that I'm mad?" She slapped his arm. "How could you? Augh!"

Taking a shuddering breath, she pushed the hair out of her eyes and faced the woman who had nearly been her undoing. Pointing an accusing finger back at him Kate shouted, "This . . . This *man* intends to torture me. Aye. He plans to put me in a donjon where rats will eat my toes and all because I coshed him on the head with a chamber pot and then stole his precious destrier and . . . and . . ."

Ian grinned as Kate stuttered to a stop, apparently realizing she was making matters worse for herself. What he didna expect was for her to calmly straighten her bodice with both hands, lift her chin to a haughty angle and then take off like a deer on the run . . . for the horses.

"Ack!"

Damn those long legs of hers!

He thundered after her, his claymore slapping his back. Only feet from Thor, he snatched her up by the waist, swung her about and threw her over his shoulder. "Ha!"

Kate kicked and bucked, her fists pounding on his back. "Let me go!"

Not in this lifetime. "Nay, now hush or I will gag ye."

"You wouldna dare!"

He laughed. Oh, he most certainly would. "Thor, down."

When the horse dropped to his knees, putting a strain on the lead rope attached to Albany's gelding, Ian grabbed the length of leather attached to a ring on his saddle that he carried for repairs. None too gently he pulled Kate off his shoulder and tied her wrists together. He then tossed her onto the saddle and squeezed in behind her, his hips pressing her into the high pommel. Pulling his sporran out of the way he muttered, "Up, Thor."

Grunting, his dependable mount rocked back onto his haunches, and rose, first onto his front legs, then lifting his rear. He then shook like a wet dog, making Kate gasp and grab for his mane. Good. She hasna grown overconfident.

Ian guided Thor toward the auld woman, who stood gaping in the garden. "For yer trouble, mistress. I do apologize." He tossed three coins at her feet and turned toward home.

How he was going to get past the roving pockpud patrols in broad daylight whilst on a white horse with one of their countrywomen tied to his saddle he had yet to fathom.

Two hours later, Kate muttered, "My hands are going numb."

Ian reached forward, his left hand brushing her breast, and placed it over hers. "Dinna fash, they are still warm."

"You really are insufferable." Her left breast tingled where his hand had slowly grazed, and she would bet her next meal that he had done it deliberately.

Ian snorted. "So ye say."

"I do say." Truly insufferable. He'd not only caught her and was taking her back to Stirling where rats and God only knew what else awaited her, but his hands were not the only things driving her to distraction. His hot thighs and groin were causing her an inordinate amount of discomfort, calling to mind their intimacy in the passageway, which she had absolutely no desire to recall. Which, of course, she now had.

He startled her out of her reverie by asking, "Why did ye not seek protection in Roxburgh? Ye kenned I couldna have reached ye there."

True. But she had had no choice but to bypass

to the right, and immediately they were racing along the rocky riverbed, icy water flying, soaking them to their knees. How the horse tolerated such cold was beyond her.

Moments later, Ian turned Thor into a nearly vertical, heavily forested incline. Merciful Mary! How were they to get through such? A heartbeat later she found out.

What Thor's chest could not break through, they went around. Sort of. She wasn't really sure. Fearing her eyes might be plucked out before she scant realized they were in danger, she folded over Thor's neck as best she could and used her arms to protect her head.

Thor finally leveled beneath her, his hooves clopping on what sounded like stone. She was no longer being whipped by branches, no longer awash in the scent of pine sap but being buffeted by a crisp wind. Not trusting that they weren't simply in a tiny glen and that she would soon be assaulted again, Kate murmured, "Is it safe to open my eyes?"

Ian whispered, "Depends on what ye call safe."

More aware of the wind, she opened her eyes and her breath caught.

There was naught to her left but a straight, hundred-foot drop dotted by a few precarious scrub cedar and below that hectares of vertical forest.

"Aaah . . ."

Ian tightened his hold on her waist and whispered, "Shhhh. Yer voice will carry."

Kate swallowed convulsively and licked her lips. Loose shale slid beneath Thor's hooves. In a tight whisper she managed, "Surely none would be so foolish as to follow us up here?"

"A few might."

As if to confirm his words she heard a sharp cry at some distance and then something tumbling down, snapping branches as it went. Her back went rigid. Oh, dear God preserve us.

He pressed his lips against her jaw. "Dinna fash. Their cattle havena been bred for our terrain."

Don't worry? She could do naught else and she desperately wanted to close her eyes but could not.

What seemed like a lifetime later they rounded a huge stone outcrop and there before her were dark green bands of forest between patchwork valleys, black lakes, silver rivers and hundreds of pale purple mountains at a much farther distance. "Oh my."

Out of the corner of her eye she saw him grin. "Aye, and we are almost there."

"There?"

"Our hidey-hole."

Of course. A hidey-hole. On top of a mountain. Well, not a mountain exactly but certainly higher than Stirling had been.

True to his word, at a short stand of cedar, Ian brought Thor to a halt and murmured, "Duck." A moment later they were through the cedar and entering a cave.

Ian slid out of the saddle and reached for her waist. Her legs wobbled as she tried to stand, and he slipped his arm about her shoulders. "Ye did well for a sassenach."

Augh. At least he hadn't called her a pockpud.

"We'll stay here until the sun sets."

Kate, her hands still tied before her, looked about. At the front, the cave was tall, wide and well lit, but farther in, where it grew dark, the floor appeared to rise up to meet the downward-sloping ceiling. In total it looked like a gaping clam. "You've got to be out of your mind."

Ian grinned and threw Thor's reins over the pommel. "About staying in a cave?"

She stomped her foot, kicking up a cloud of fine dust. "No! About going down this mountain at night."

He shrugged. "'Tisna a mountain but a hillock, and Thor can see well enough at night."

"But . . . But I can't."

"Nor can I. Well, not as well as I'd like."

"Augh!" The man was impossible.

He pulled out his short blade and motioned her to him. "Come."

"Oh, nay." She backed up, fear making the hair on her arms stand, her throat constrict. Alone, atop this bloody *hillock*, he could torture her in any manner of ways and none would be any the wiser.

She backed up farther, her gaze raking the shadowy cavern for something to hide behind and found naught large enough. Ian cleared his throat and her attention snapped back to him. He followed, his eyes narrow, his gaze never leaving hers as he stalked, muscles rolling in the confident way of a skilled predator. Caught by a narrow band of sunshine, his eyes began to glimmer like polished brass. Oh no. Her knees hit stone. Caught off balance, she yelped and plopped onto her bottom.

Ian grabbed Kate's wrists. To his annoyance, she keened and pressed her face against her arms.

He dug the tip of the blade into the knotted leather holding her hands. Given the way Kate's legs were shaking and the uneven cave floor, he thought it wiser to free her hands so she might keep her balance. The last thing he needed was for her to fall and knock herself out. She had yet to tell him all he needed to ken. Besides, he had nay intention of holding her skirts should she need *privacy*, which this time she'd find only at the back of the cave.

The leather fell away and she looked up, surprise written all over her lovely countenance.

He cocked an eyebrow. "Did ye expect that I'd slit yer throat?"

Her gaze darted away as she caught her full lower lip betwixt her white, even teeth.

"Humph. Ye did." He slipped his sgian duhb into the sheath strapped beneath his arm. At Thor's side, he ran a hand down his legs, then patted his sweating neck. "Good lad." Thor had foraged and drunk whilst they had waited in Roxburgh, so he'd be good for the rest of the day.

From his saddle Ian lifted the ale bag Graham had kindly provided and pulled out the stopper. "So what brings ye to Scotland, Katie?"

As he expected Kate's gaze locked on the bag. "I told you already."

"Nay, ye admitted that what ye had told me earlier was a lie." He put the bag to his mouth and took a much-needed drink. His thirst appeased, he wiped his mouth with the back of his hand, "Ah, lovely. I needed that."

Seeing that Kate looked about to cry, he held out the bag. "Oh, did ye want some?"

Nodding, she rose, her tongue licking her parched lips.

He grinned. "So, it appears I have something ye want, and ye have something I want." He plugged the bag. "But ye go first. What are ye doing in Scotland?"

Kate, her gaze still locked on the bag, rubbed at

the grooves encircling her wrists. "I told you, I wanted to return the brooch to Lady Margaret."

"And how did ye happen to come into possession of it? Ye admitted to never having been married to Campbell." No small blessing that.

"All right . . . I was given it. Now may I have a drink?"

Humph. To what end was she given the brooch? Who in their right mind expected a lone woman to accomplish anything? He pulled the stopper and held out the bag. Kate reached for the bag but he pulled it away. "Nay, I will hold it."

He allowed her to bring the bag to her lips and take a wee mouthful, before lifting it out of her reach.

Kate stomped her foot. "You said I could have a drink. You call that a drink?"

He brushed past her, the bag held out of her reach. "Who gave ye the brooch, Kate? The man whose ring ye wear?"

She nibbled on her lower lip and nervously spun the gold band. "It's my mother's."

Ah, that explained the wear. "So were ye ever married at all?"

"No, if you must know."

Humph. For some reason the tightness in his chest eased just a bit. Never married. A virgin, all of whom he steadfastly avoided. Yet this one he had nearly deflowered. Ack.

"Here." He allowed her a longer sip before pulling the bag away, kenning she was still parched but nay longer ready to expire.

A virgin. But then . . . He might make some use of that. "So who sent ye here?" The man was an idiot, whoever he was.

Kate folded her arms across her chest and turned her back to him.

Seeing she was determined to be needlessly stubborn, he grumbled, "Ye dinna want to answer? Fine. Die of thirst."

She glared over her shoulder at him, slaying obviously on her mind.

He'd let her stew for awhile. He needed to check the trail to see if any had had the balls or the horseflesh to follow. He tossed the ale bag over his shoulder. "I will be back in a minute." At the entrance, he looked back, scowling. "Stay quiet and dinna touch so much as a hair on that horse. Ye do, and I swear I will bind ye hand and foot, stick a gag in yer mouth, and leave ye for the wolves."

Kate swallowed convulsively. "Wolves?"

"Aye. Did ye nay notice those bones in yon corner?"

"Oh." Paling as far as her honeyed skin would allow she collapsed onto a boulder.

Humph! That should keep her fashing for a bit while he was gone.

As he eased around the outcrop to peer over the edge to the forest below, he could hear Kate sputtering in outrage above him. So much for his order to remain quiet.

Well, let her rant. She wouldna be making a run for it, at any rate. Even if he hadna put the fear of God into her, she couldna ride out of the cave without warning, and a whistle this close to Thor would bring him to a bone-jarring halt, likely tipping her out of the saddle. Too, there was something amiss about her not seeking shelter at Roxburgh and her not shouting for help when she spied the pockpud patrol.

Seeing naught stirring below, he returned to the

cave and found Kate, tears streaming down her cheek, sitting on her boulder, opening a small velvet pouch.

Looping the ale bag on to the saddle he asked, "What have ye there?"

"The gift you left for me in the ladies' chamber. I was going to save the sweets but, since you refuse—"

Kate yelped when Ian lunged, knocking the pouch from her hands and sending the bag and its contents flying. He then grabbed her by the arms, brought her face close to his and started sniffing her mouth like a hound on the scent.

Heart thudding, Kate reared back. "What on earth is wrong with you!"

The muscles in his jaws jerked and his fingers dug deep into her arms. "Did ye eat any?"

"No! Not yet." Mercy, what had she done wrong now?

To her shock he shook her. "Did I not tell you to never eat or drink anything left unattended?"

"Yes, but, but . . . The gift came from you." The man was absolutely daft! And frightening.

"Nay. I never gave ye a gift."

"But, but . . . you did. See . . . the note." She pointed as best she could to the bit of paper poking out from beneath the dark blue velvet at her feet.

Ian looked down and to her monumental relief let go of her. She stumbled backward, rubbing her arms as he dropped onto his haunches.

A moment later he raked his hands through his hair and then looked up at her. "I didna send this to ye, Katie."

"No?"

He shook his head.

Oh, my God. The sweets were poisoned. Feeling bile

rise in her throat, unable to breathe, she collapsed onto a stone outcrop. Someone had tried to kill her.

"But who? I don't—" She knew. Had no doubt as she whispered, "Alistair Campbell."

Ian rose. "'Twould be my guess unless ye made another enemy whilst I was out cold."

Finding naught the least humorous in the situation, feeling tears smarting at the back of her eyes, Kate crossed her arms at her waist and turned her face away.

She heard Ian squat before her. His voice, normally deep and velvet smooth, sounded a bit raw as he murmured, "My apologies, lass, but seeing ye . . ."

He huffed and left the rest unsaid.

Confused that he should be threatening her with rats and wolves one minute, then panicking, thinking she had ingested poison the next, she sat mute as Ian collected the pouch and its scattered contents, then walked to the cave opening and disappeared.

And he called *her* an enigma?

Kate looked down at the dirt embedded under her nails and the stains marring her lone gown. Why had naught gone as she'd planned?

She'd been careful. Had followed Sir Gregory's every order to the letter, yet here she was hungry and parched, a prisoner at death's door, and worse, half in love with her aggravating captor.

Groaning, having no answers, Kate buried her face in her hands. "I so want to go home."

Home to Mister Boots and hot pork pies, to her cramped apartment and feather pillow, to a hard day boiling her father's white shirts and at the end a welcoming hot bath and her rose soap. Was that so much to ask? She thought not.

At this point she would even welcome her father's mindless interrogations.

And should she, by some miracle, see her way clear of this . . . this nightmare her life had become, she would never, *ever* respond to another vision ever again so long as she lived.

"Are ye thirsty, lass?"

Kate dashed the tears from her cheeks and straightened to find Ian standing before her with ale bag in hand, his handsome features looking like a perfect chiseled mask, his eyes a worrisome, flat light brown.

Augh. "What have I done now?"

He pulled the stopper and held the bag out to her. "Drink, and 'tis naught ye have done, but those below."

From Ian's expression she could only assume that they'd set the mountain on fire, intent on burning her and Ian out. She grabbed the bag and drank deeply. Her thirst quenched and her courage bolstered, she finally asked, "What has you so concerned?"

"They have set up camps below for the night. We canna leave."

Kate glanced at the opening, realizing for the first time that it was almost dark. Having had little desire to race down a mountain in the middle of the night anyway, she dared to ask, "And you find this upsetting because . . . ?"

He threw up his arms. "Because I have nay bloody idea what is going on in Stirling—they could be waging war for all I ken. Because the pock—Sassenach are down there filling their bellies whilst we are up here starving. Because the night will grow colder still and we canna start a fire for fear the smoke will draw them to us."

She frowned. His worrying about those meeting in Stirling might hold merit, but . . .

"Forgive me, Ian, but if you had been living as I have for the last few days, sleeping under pine boughs and eating when you could—and I assume you have since you caught me so quickly—why angst so over the lack of food and heat now?"

He humphed, shaking his golden mane. "Never ye mind."

"Fine!" Don't tell me. *Grrrr.*

An hour after gloaming the wind changed direction and the night grew decidedly colder. As hour after hour passed, the air grew colder still. The only saving grace: they could see fairly well by the light of the stars and the waning moon.

Behind him, Thor slept, three knees locked, one leg cocked. Kate, huddled in her thin silk cloak, sat opposite him at the opening of the cave, her chin resting on her knees, her arms wrapped about her legs, her lovely blue eyes now black as she stared at the broad expanse before them with her lower lip caught in her teeth. With each breath she took she shivered, causing the moonlight to play across her high cheek bones and shimmer off her waist-length hair. And she hadna spoken a word since growling her last *"Fine!"*

Feeling his blood heat, his groin swell just looking at her, he shifted his gaze to a safer target: the Sassenach's fires below.

God kenned he hadna meant to frighten her so, but when she'd told him that the open pouch on her lap had been from him, his heart had nearly stopped. What if he'd been delayed? He would have found her cold as a bloody stone, her mouth full of foam. He shuddered, and not for the first time.

And what was he to do with her? There was nay way he could torture her into answering his questions, not with something twisting in his chest every time he looked at her, and he certainly couldna let her go. She might ken something vital. Mayhap to Scotland's verra security.

Nay. 'Twas far more likely she was a pawn in someone else's game. At this juncture he could only hope that she would break down as they got closer to Stirling and tell him.

Ack! Never in his life had he faced such a dilemma and all because a jet-haired beauty had had the audacity to say "Bullocks."

He glanced at her again and found shiny droplets shimmering their way down her smooth cheeks.

Why me, Lord?

He strode over to her and she bolted upright, stiff as day-old bread.

Without looking at him, she murmured, "Have you ever noticed that your country at sunset resembles a mourning dove?"

Ian frowned. "Canna say that I have."

"It does. When the sun fades those hills nearest us appear to be that charcoal gray found on a dove's spots and wings. The middle distance turns to the bluish pewter of a dove's head and back, and the distant mountains appear to be that pale purple found on a dove's belly. They do. And now all appears black yet it's still green."

He pictured a mourning dove, pictured the land

he kenned as well as his brother's face and con-
cluded Kate desperately needed sleep.

He brushed the hair from the side of her face and
whispered, "Lass, ye canna spend the night sitting
here staring at naught. We need sleep or neither of
us will be worth a bodle by morning. Come."

She looked up at him, her eyes as glossy as one of
the wee locks below. "But the wolves."

Humph. There hadna been a wolf reported in
these parts for decades. "The fires below will keep
them away."

Her brow crinkled. "Are you sure?"

"Verra."

That seemed to satisfy her for she rose and let
him lead her into the back of the cave.

More by feel than sight he found the sandy spot
he had noticed earlier and asked for her cape.

"Why?"

He suspected she was scowling suspiciously and
grinned. "Trust me, will ye?"

She grumbled, but the silk came into his hands.
He laid it down, pulled his claymore over his head,
and unhooked his belt and the clasp holding his
breachen feile.

He took her hand and guided her down onto
their makeshift pallet, then settled beside her. Realizing his intent, she grumbled and tried to rise.

"Shhh, dinna fash. Two are warmer than one." He
grabbed her by the waist and hauled her onto her
side so that her back was to him, then draped his
plaid across her, tucking a good portion of it under
her arms and knees. "See, nice and cozy." Kenning
he'd get nay sleep lying so close, he murmured,
"G'night."

Lauds. Kate shuddered—as much from Ian's

closeness as from being near frozen—when his heavy arm draped over her waist. After a bit her teeth stopped chattering, and she was forced to admit that he had been right about one thing: two were definitely warmer than one. But it had naught to do with her. Ian threw off heat like London's royal bread ovens, and truth to tell he definitely smelled better than bread to her. Laud, why had they not met under different circumstances? Where there were no secrets.

Foolish girl. Even under the best of circumstances, he'd not have given you a glance. Better she ruminate on escape since she'd get no sleep this night.

As she discarded a plan for jumping off the ledge and pretending that she'd fallen to her death as being a touch too possible, she became aware of his long, even purrs. My stars, the man was already sound asleep. How was that possible? Not knowing how but grateful for it, Kate yawned and relaxed into his now much-safer warmth. As her back relaxed and a sense of security enveloped her, her thoughts turned to her mother.

Black, dreamless sleep slowly gave way to a golden hue.

Katie, never happier in her six years, skipped in circles. "Mama! Papa's getting me a puppet!"

Her mother chuckled as she scraped crumbs from the table. "Is he now?"

"Yes, he just told me. A lady puppet, Mama, with a green and purple skirt and a floppy hat with a bell."

"Katie, what have I told you about fibs? I was here when he said good-bye and he said naught about buying you a puppet."

"But he did, Mama—just not with words."

Suddenly her mother was kneeling before her, her beautiful face close to Katie's. "Child, how exactly did he tell you?"

"I don't know. He just did . . . when he picked me up."

Looking very worried Mama whispered, "Katie, does this happen often? This knowing?"

Sensing she was in some kind of trouble, Kate could only nod.

Her mother started crying. "Oh, sweet Lord, you have Nana's gift. Whatever shall we do now?"

Katie began crying, too.

"Shh, my love, shh. We just have to make this our little secret."

"A secret, Mama?"

"That you see things that have yet to come to pass."

Kate's head was beginning to hurt. "But doesn't everyone?"

"No, and that is why you can never, ever tell anyone. Particularly Papa. He must think that you're normal."

Frightened, Katie sputtered, "But I am normal."

"No, my love, you are fey."

"But I don't want to be fey, Mama!"

Her mother, tears streaking her face, grasped Katie's arms, hurting her. "Listen very carefully, child. You will never . . . ever . . . tell anyone about this, do you understand?"

Suddenly feeling very alone, Katie nodded. "Do you know things, too, Mama?" Oh, please, please say yes.

Still crying, Mama wrapped her arms around her and pulled Katie against her small breast. "Yes, love, but not such as you."

The pain and fear eased with her words and the world faded away to blissful black. She rolled over and became vaguely aware of something delicious near her. Hmmm. She snuggled deeper into the warmth. Blissful blackness returned.

"The truth!"

Kate's skin prickled hearing the man's nasal voice. It was familiar but she couldn't place it. The room where she stood reeked of acrid sweat, urine and burning oil. The huge stone blocks making up the room, however, did look familiar.

Where am I?

"Aaaugh!"

The agonizing cry caused Kate to spin about. She could see a man's hand wrapped about a pike, then part of a table and on it a pole wrapped in rope. Attached to the end of the pole was a wheel.

In the far corner, behind the legs of a table, she saw a pile of clothing and a pair of well-worn boots. Rope creaked and another scream tore from a man's throat. She screamed, realizing she was in the Tower, and the man on the rack . . .

Father!

Chapter 17

"Kate, shhh, 'tis only a dream, lass. Shhhh."

Covered in a cold sweat, Kate continued to lash out, and Ian tightened his hold. "Shhh, dautie, ye are all right."

After Kate had finally fallen asleep he'd dropped the pretense of sleep and tried to drift off but she'd started, and murmuring, flopped over. After nuzzling into his neck, she'd pressed a full breast against his chest, draped a graceful arm over his waist and then cocked a long, luscious leg across his thigh where it settled between his legs. That might have proved tolerable had she kept still, but did she? Oh, nay. She had to keep moving, rubbing her leg against him. Ack! 'Twas a miracle that his shaft hadna exploded.

"Got to go!"

He pulled her closer. "Nay, sweet, shhh. 'Tis only a dream."

Panting, definitely awake now, she hissed, "I need go! You don't understand."

He grunted, "Then tell me."

"I can't."

Feeling her breast press into his chest with every pant, Ian cursed. Mayhap if she could see she was safe, she would settle. "I will start a fire."

When he rose, she whispered, "Is that safe?"

"Aye." He could only hope. And again wondered why she appeared to be more afraid of her countrymen than she was of him.

A few bits of wood and dry grass gathered and set deep in the cave, Ian reached into his sporran for his flint. The moment the wee fire caught and flared, he heard Kate gasp.

"What?"

She was sitting up, his *breachen feile* clutched to her opulent breasts, pointing at him. Eyes as large as twin moons, face scarlet, she sputtered, "You're na-na-na—

Still squatting, he looked down. His shaft, thankfully, wasna pointing to the ceiling and only a bit engorged. "Naked," he pointed out helpfully.

"Yes! Naked! But why?"

Humph. He stood, hands on hips, his legs braced apart as was his way. "Because ye have my plaid, woman."

"Oh!" She frantically worked to extricate herself from his *breachen feile,* and he caught a lovely glimpse of her golden thighs as she struggled.

He blew through clenched teeth as she tossed it to him.

"Humph." Why he should don it now that she and he were both awake and had naught to do for the next two or three hours was beyond kenning.

Resigned to torturous celibacy, he wrapped the plaid about him, donned his belt and settled next to Kate. To his consternation she scooted off the pallet and huddled against the cave wall.

Ack! "Woman, did I bite ye? Did I rape ye? Nay. So will ye please be at yer ease and lie down so we might get some rest?"

Wrapping her arms about her knees, she shook her head. "I'm no longer sleepy."

He mentally cursed. "As ye lust."

Sure that she'd eventually get tired of staring at the night and settle down next to him, he curled on his side and closed his eyes.

He awoke with a start to the sound of Thor shying, Kate keening and then a heavy thump. One hand on his claymore, he opened his eyes.

Thor, his ears pinned back, was standing a few feet from where Ian had last seen him with his saddle slung under his belly and Kate, sniffling and batting at a cloud of dust, was on her back, her skirt up above her knees.

I really should put both of us out of our misery.

Rising slowly, he asked, "What the hell do ye think ye are doing?"

She yelped and scrambled to her feet. Tears were streaming down her cheeks as she faced him. "I need go!"

"Nay. Not until ye tell me what ye are doing feigning to be Madame Campbell." He desperately wanted to take her over his knee and thrash the bloody breath out of her.

He went to Thor to straighten the saddle before his destrier decided to kick it to pieces.

Keeping one eye on Kate, he jerked it upright, a saddle bag popped open, and the contents spilled at his feet. Among a spare set of spurs, his comb and a pair of spare breeches lay a bairn's cloth pony. Frowning, he bent to pick it up.

"No!" Kate lunged for the pony, but he was quicker.

She flew at him. "Give it to me!"

Trying to hold her at arm's length without hurting her, he turned the toy this way and that. "I remember this. 'Tis James's." Scowling at her, the pony still held out of her reach, he asked, "Now why would ye risk yer life for such as this?"

Kate, her teeth bared, slapped at his arms, trying to get the wee horse. "Give it to me!"

Ignoring her, he turned the toy over. Spotting a wee bit of paper in a rented belly seam, his gut twisted. 'Twasna the pony she wanted but what was hidden *inside*.

Cursing under his breath, he dug into the hole and pulled out the paper. Using both hands he pulled the horse to shreds in search of anything else, sending cream-colored down flying. Finally satisfied nothing remained inside, he dropped the fabric and unfolded the paper.

A band constricted around his chest as he read the list. Duncan MacDougall of Drasmoor, Angus MacDougall of Donaleigh, Brion Grant of Uruhart, Robert Mackintosh of Dalcross, and on and on the list went. Half the friggin' lairds. Notably missing were Douglas and Donald, and it was all written in Kate's unmistakable hand.

Kate keened and rocked on her knees, the remnants of the pony clutched to her chest.

In his heart of hearts he had been praying that she was simply a pawn in someone's scheme to defraud Alistair in some fashion. The evidence in his hand proved otherwise and something inside him died.

"What the hell is this?"

Not daring to look up, Kate began frantically gathering lighter-than-air down and stuffing it into what remained of the pony's head. "I can't believe you've done this."

"*I?*"

"*Yes, you!*" She had risked her life in the hopes of changing destiny and to what end? All was now lost because of *him*. Worse, thanks to her, her father was now in mortal danger and the only proof she had for James was unrecognizable.

Kate yelped when Ian grabbed her by the hair and pulled her head back so she was forced to look at him. Waving the paper before her face, he hissed, "Answer me, woman! What is the meaning of this?"

Caught in the first rays of the day's sun, the sharp planes of Ian's face glistened, appeared to be made of pure gold. Beautiful and deadly.

What did it matter now?

He was Albany's man and held the evidence against her in his hands. She was headed for someone's donjon or a noose.

But what if she told the truth and threw herself on Ian's mercy . . . Might he not let her go? He hadn't been cruel until this moment, had in truth been kind in a fashion.

With her hair still locked in his fist, Ian hauled her to her feet. "Damn it, woman, answer me!"

Looking into his scowling countenance she decided she had no choice. It was her only hope of getting home to her father, to apologize for putting his life at risk, to warn him to run if it wasn't already too late.

Stomach churning, her neck arched back near to breaking, Kate keened, "'Tis a list of those who want your king back! Who have been saving coins for his ransom."

He leaned over her, his nose nearly touching hers. "And who would ye be giving this list to?"

"To James."

He pulled back on her hair, making her cry out. *"James who?"*

Dear merciful mother of God, help me. "James Stewart, James I, king of Scotia!"

He hauled in a deep breath. "Woman, ye had best start speaking clear as well water or I will snap yer neck. Ye havena been out of my sight these last four days, so who supplied these names?"

Fighting her way through the pain, Kate stammered, "I was to . . . to go to Lady Margaret and get the list but she died and then I didn't know what to do so I asked Lady Beth. But please, *please* don't hurt her. She didn't know. But I couldn't allow her to die and her children with her because of James." Kate took a gasping breath. "He's so, so angry, and Sir Gregory understood, could see it himself, but . . . But now the pony's de-destroyed and he won't believe me. He thinks you've all forsaken him, yet I think you've not been told of the ransom and now I'm going to die and so is Father . . ."

Kate had all she could do to breathe, much less speak, so tight was the pain in her chest and at her head. If only she could give in to the pain. Better to die at Ian's hand and in this cave than be sheared and then hung before a wild-eyed and cursing mob.

Suddenly Ian's grip released and she fell, wheezing, to her knees.

After a moment she dared to look up and found him staring at her, the blood vessels at his temples pounding and his jaw muscles twitching. "What," he began, "do you ken of a ransom?"

Please, please let this mean he believes me.

"We were told Henry has demanded tens of thousands in sterling for James's release."

Ian took a deep breath, then another before asking, "Who is *we?*"

"Sir Gregory, James and Father. And me. There were others—three guards and an old woman—when James arrived in the Tower, but they were taken away. I have no idea where they might be now." She wasn't even sure if they were still alive.

"Describe Gregory."

Her first instinct was to describe Gregory as he had looked when he arrived in prison five years before, since that was how Ian would remember him, but then she thought better of it. Ian had no doubt seen men who'd spent time incarcerated. "Shorter than I by more than a hand, once proud in bearing, he's now stooped. His fair hair has gone gray. He's still bearded." Recalling his tales she hastily added, "And he has several front teeth missing that he claims were lost in battle."

And he would lose a good few more should she ever lay eyes upon him again.

Ian was quiet too long for comfort before asking, "Do ye ken to whom the ransom demand was sent?"

"Nay, but I learned of it several years ago."

"Several years . . ." Ian fisted his massive hands, then straightened and rolled his shoulders. "And ye ken all this how?"

Praying her answer would be enough—Ian didn't strike her as a man who believed in the fey—Kate mumbled, "My father, Hugh Dupree Templeton, is

James's tutor in English law and his subservience to the crown . . . and I . . . I am but a friend."

"A friend." Cursing, he walked to his destrier and grabbed the ale bag. After taking a long draw he surprised Kate by tossing it into her lap. "Drink. Ye have much more yet to say."

Covered in a bone-chilling sweat front and back, Kate did as he bid, thinking it might well be her last. Ian's color was ruddier than she had ever noted before and if possible, he appeared more furious now than he had been upon finding her list.

"How are ye his friend?"

Kate wiped her mouth with a shaking hand and held the ale out to him. "When James was younger I helped him with English by reading to him and he taught me Scots. We made a game of it. As Sir Gregory taught him Gael, I listened, although I need confess that James was the more apt pupil. But now"—Kate looked at her hands—"James insists that I address him as Your Majesty."

Ian stared at her for a few minutes, then walked to where her cape lay. He donned his sporran and scabbard, then picked up his claymore and returned to her. Broadsword in hand, his powerful legs braced apart, he stood before her. Kate held her breath, terrified that it might be her last, yet again taken with how impressive and fearsome Ian MacKay truly was.

He raised his claymore and lifted a strand of her hair off her shoulder with its gleaming tip. "I need check on those below."

She nodded, struck mute by the closeness of the blade.

At the edge of the cave opening Ian pointed the claymore at Thor. "Touch and die."

He spoke without heat, barely above a whisper, and she knew to her bones that he would slay her.

His blood boiling with pent-up rage, Ian quietly made his way toward the English encampment at the foot of the rushing burn some hundred feet below.

He hadna thought it possible that he could feel more fury than he had in discovering Kate's duplicity. Yet upon hearing that a ransom demand had been made yet none of the chieftains had been informed, his fury had reached new heights.

He didna want to believe Albany had been playing him false. He had invested too many years in serving the man. Moreover he had nay desire to believe Kate. She'd done all in her power to thwart him at every turn. His brain and heart fought it, but his gut said aye, do.

Ack!

He desperately wanted to strike out, hit someone or something, and had he remained in the cave he greatly feared that that someone would have been Kate.

His heart ached. Common sense told him she spoke some truth. How else could she have described Gregory Campbell so well? Or ken how many had been captured with his king? Possibly the most telling had been her repeatedly calling the lad James before her eyes grew glassy, admitting that James now demanded that she use his title. Kenning the mule-headed lad, he could easily imagine him— irate and confused that he'd remained so long in captivity—doing so.

But then there was a distinct possibility that she'd

been schooled and then sent to cause a greater rift between the house of Stewart and the rest. But if that was the case, why hadna she simply played the courtesan, gained his confidence—which she'd quite diligently and successfully avoided—and then planted the seeds of distrust?

Worse, he suspected she was still holding something back.

Ack!

He couldna confront Albany without proof and that proof could come only from his king. Ian heaved a resigned sigh.

Am fear a bhios a bharra-mhanadh a-mach, suidhidh e air fail chorraich. Aye. He whose destiny is cast does sit on a sharp cope.

So be it.

Hearing a rustle down and to his right, Ian dropped to his belly. He crawled forward to peer over the granite ridge and felt relief seeing the encampment below had yet to stir. None of their cattle had been saddled and nay fires relit. If he made haste, he and Kate could ride out without being seen.

But first he had to eliminate the lone guard standing some thirty feet ahead. Standing between him and the truth.

"This isna happening."

Shamus looked in Douglas's direction and found the man pale, sitting in stunned silence after Albany had announced the new earl of Ross. He then glanced at Donald and found the man, flushed scarlet, slowly rising. It was apparent to all within the great hall that Donald was beyond speech. Without uttering a word, he waved a hand and his party rose and followed him out. Alistair Campbell had blanched as well.

Bile rising from his gut, Shamus eased out the door and raced out down the spiraling stairs to the bailey where he found Donald and his party already mounted.

Raising his arm Shamus yelled, "A word, Donald."

The Lord of the Isles turned in his saddle. "MacKay, all that needs to be said has been. Albany will rue this day. Of that you can be sure."

"Donald, he stabbed ye in the back. I, too, believe Ross is yours by virtue of yer wife, but please, I urge ye, dinna do anything rash in the heat of anger. Lives, mayhap thousands, ride on us all staying calm at this juncture. If enough of us protest, rattle our swords, I am sure we can force Albany to relent."

Donald snarled, "Too late, MacKay. The die is cast." He then wheeled his destrier about and rode toward the gates of Stirling.

Ack! Shamus reentered the keep and was nearly trampled by three more enraged chieftains and their parties heading for their horses. Hearing a continuous roar coming from the great hall, he took the stairs up to Stirling's parapet where he could find some peace and think.

High above the plains surrounding Stirling Shamus looked west and caught sight of Donald's party riding hard. Had Ian been here he might have forestalled Albany's announcement, but Shamus seriously doubted that even his able brother could have prevented it. Albany was hell-bent on strengthening the Stewart's hold on Scotland and that is all there was to it.

A red flare suddenly arced high in the night sky

from where Donald had disappeared into the distant foliage. Only moments later, and some twenty miles ahead, another flaming arrow shot into the air. Then another farther west.

"Shit!" War signals. Donald had prepared for the worst, and had Shamus not been standing where he was, none at Stirling would be any the wiser.

He watched as one arrow after another shot into the sky until the flames were so distant and wee that they were almost negligible. Word was traveling west among the Donalds faster than their liege could travel. Prepare, he was telling them. Be ready to ride when I arrive. But to where? And with what force? Who besides the Donald's clansmen had been waiting, watching?

Shamus took the stairs two and three at a time. His first allegiance was to the clan MacKay and his liege, Black Angus, and then he would warn the MacDougall warlords. Shit!

After that he would tell Albany. Let the bastard be the one to break the news to those in the hall that war was imminent.

Chapter 18

Ian ran into the cave and Kate jumped to her feet. Hand to her throat, she asked, "What's wrong?"

Pleased she hadna moved since he'd left, he grumbled, "Naught. We leave now." He motioned to his left. "Grab as much ash as ye can. We need to mask Thor."

She hurried to the pile of spent embers. "But, but . . . go where?"

Ian strode to Thor and tightened his girth straps. "To London."

Kate stumbled and nearly fell. "London? I don't understand. Why would you risk your life to take me home?"

Because I have gone totally wode.

"Ye'll understand soon enough. Now do as I ask and start rubbing ash on Thor's hindquarters. He stands out against the forest like a boil on the proud man's nose."

"Proud man's . . . Ye have gone mad, MacKay."

Astute, he would give her that.

Kate, smiling from ear to ear, suddenly threw her arms about his neck. "Thank ye, thank ye!" She gave him a smacking kiss on the lips before burying her face against his neck.

Not kenning what to say, for bringing her home wasna his primary intent—he'd go without her had he the choice—he placed his hands at her waist, readying to push her away and heard her whisper as if to herself, "I do so love you, Ian MacKay."

His heart tripped. Nay. He couldna have heard her correctly. More, if she had said what he thought she'd said, surely it was only relief speaking, her joy in learning she'd live to see another day.

Feeling undone, as much by the feel of her breasts pressed against his chest as by her words, he eased her from him. "Enough. Go fetch the ash."

Kate, looking positively giddy, murmured, "As ye lust, my lord."

"Humph."

Together they slathered Thor with ashes from nares to tail. Within minutes, his mighty destrier looked a proper bloody ruin.

Ian clapped the dust from his hands. "Perfect. Now don yer cape, woman. We need go."

As Kate grabbed her cape, Ian threw Thor's reins over his head and led him to the entrance, where he caught the scent of smoke on the wind. Damn. The pockpuds would discover the dead guard at any moment.

He turned to hurry Kate along and found her, still grinning, running toward him. "Humph."

He tossed her into the saddle and vaulted up behind her. "Hold tight. The going will be steep."

Frowning, Kate looked left and then right over the rolling landscape dotted with the occasional copse and scattered black-faced sheep. Above them a warming sun was trying to burn through a dense buff haze.

Umm . . . If they were heading south, then the rising sun should be at her left shoulder, not dead ahead. She looked over her shoulder at Ian and caught him grinning. Why, she could not imagine. "You're heading in the wrong direction."

"We're fine."

"No." She pointed right. "The sun rises in the east, therefore south is that way." Since her father could take direction no better than the man at her back, she grumbled, "Is it your sex that makes taking direction so difficult?"

"My shaft is just fine, but thanks for asking."

She twisted to find his gaze on the horizon but his dimples struggling to make an appearance. "Augh." She poked him in the ribs, making him grin. "You know well what I mean."

"True, and we are heading east."

She gaped at him. "Whatever for?"

"Ye will see soon enough."

"I will see—?" She huffed in exasperation. Ian had said little since they'd left the cave. No doubt ruminating over her confession, but still, she would have greatly appreciated knowing why they were going east and what he intended.

She still couldn't believe he was taking her home. And the more she thought on his doing so, the more perplexing she found it. Oh, she was most grateful, no question there, but what had he to gain? Why would he—

Ian pulled back on the reins. "Look, supper."

"Huh?" She saw naught but acres of green oats on either side of her.

"Piss-a—beds. There."

Scowling, she looked down in the direction he pointed and found a patch of dandelions. "Oh!" They were edible. Hallelujah. Now, if they just had a pot to boil them in and some salted pork, they'd be all set.

Her mouth watering after the impossible, she asked, "Now why on earth would you call them piss-a-beds?"

Ian dropped Thor's reins. "Think on it."

She did. "Oh."

He stood in his left stirrup and started to dismount, then humphed and settled back behind her. Grabbing her by the waist, he muttered, "Best I stay in the saddle and ye gather, else I find myself a beggar again."

Kate rolled her eyes. No way would she even consider stealing Thor now that he was taking her home—albeit the long way, but then she had stolen his destrier on more than one occasion so supposed she couldn't fault him overmuch.

The dandelion greens gathered in a fold of her skirts, she stood and found Ian staring at her exposed legs. She cleared her throat and his gaze immediately lifted to her face. "Would you take these or give me a hand up?"

He grumbled, kicked out of his stirrup and leaned over. "Just put ye left foot there." She did as bid and his arm came about her ribs, his fingers brushing her breasts. As heat flashed in her middle, he hefted her with one bulging arm and she was in the saddle, squashed firmly betwixt his hips and thighs. A most distracting place if ever there was one.

Whilst he appeared comfortable enough with their riding arrangement and any gait, she found trotting the least distressing and wished he would do more of it. Whilst she bounced and struggled to keep her balance, she wasn't as aware of his heat, the feel of his powerful thighs rubbing against her thinner ones, as she was when they simply walked. And cantering . . . She shivered just thinking about how often he'd managed to stay deeply seated whilst she went up and down like a puppet, landing on or against his groin. In the last three hours it had become more than a bit too apparent that Ian had something besides London on his mind. Lauds!

She handed him a healthy share of the dandelions as they took off again. Chewing her first bite her lips and cheeks puckered. Good graces, she'd forgotten how bitter some raw greens could be. But bitter or not, they would ease the hunger pangs.

After a bit she said, "Tell me about yer life."

"Not much to tell. I'm an emissary and travel on court business, more often than not negotiating bride prices and treaties. Occasionally I travel to the continent."

Kate rolled her eyes. The man at her back was a good bit more but exactly what she was not sure. "And your family?"

"Ye have met Shamus. I also have a younger sister, Mary Kelsea, who is now married and has three bairns. My nephew, the youngest, will be two on Michalmas."

When he grew silent she frowned. "Parents?"

She felt him shrug. "Nay. They have been gone a verra long time."

"My condolences." Although she and her father were constantly at odds, even the thought of losing him she found appalling.

"Thank ye, and what is yer life like in London?"

She cocked her head to look at him. "Not so fast. What of your home?"

"Ye saw it. I live at Stirling."

That one room? How depressing. She and Father had three they could call their own. "What of a lady-wife?" Handsome as Ian was, he had to be a widower.

"I have never wed."

Surprised, Kate murmured, "Why ever not?"

He slipped an arm about her waist. "Enough of me. Yer turn."

Not satisfied but realizing she would get no more out of him, Kate sighed. And what was there to say about her life? It was porridge compared to his. "I get up each morn, make breakfast, clean, go to market, do laundry and if there is time before Father returns, I paint."

"Paint?"

"Yes. Anything I think interesting. I use pigments of my own making and apply them to whatever wood I can find."

"I'd like to see them someday."

She grinned. "No, you wouldn't." Her skills were so far beneath those artists decorating the chapels and cathedrals of London—her measuring rod of greatness—that he would likely fall down laughing.

Ian leaned forward and murmured in her ear. "Tell me . . . Is there really a Monsieur Bottes?"

His warm breath caused chills to race down her neck and spine. Worse, pride got the better of her. "Yes."

He gave her middle a tight squeeze. "Explain."

Umm. "Mister Boots was alive and well when last I saw him, but Father really dislikes him." Particularly when he would brush up against Father's best cloak and leave hair all over it.

"Humph. I think I like yer fa—*shit!*"

Having grown relaxed in the saddle, Kate fell back against Ian when Thor lunged forward and into an all-out run. Holding on to the pommel she yelled, "What is wrong?"

"Behind and to yer right. A large party."

Kate craned her neck to look past Ian's shoulder and saw several black dots and a large cloud of dust.

Looking forward, searching the area for a hiding spot, she shouted, "English?"

"I dinna ken and have nay desire to find out." After a moment Ian yelled, "Lass, can ye swim?"

"I don't know. I never tried!"

Kate thought she heard Ian curse.

A moment later she cursed, realizing they were taking a northern heading. Augh. She would never get to her father at this rate.

It wasn't until they crested a hill and she saw a wide, fast-flowing river to her right that she understood why he had asked if she could swim. Grateful he had changed course she now wondered how they would get through the thick band of forest before them.

Ian brought Thor to a halt, bounded out of the saddle and reached for Kate. "Hie, lass."

The minute her feet hit the ground he threw Thor's reins over his head and handed them to Kate. Pointing to a small break in the foliage, he said, "Lead him as straight east as ye can and try not to break any branches as ye go. I will be right behind ye."

After Kate pulled Thor forward Ian found a sturdy broken pine bough. Backing up, he started sweeping leaves and pine needles over Thor's distinctive tracks.

An hour later he was looking at a very familiar boulder, one he was verra sure he had passed not ten minutes earlier.

Ack. Kate was walking in circles.

Cursing, praying the men behind them had slowed, he followed the fresh tracks.

A moment later he squeezed past Thor and patted his rump. Coming up behind Kate he tapped her shoulder. "Kate."

She jerked around, her free hand flying to her heart. Looking annoyed she hissed, "You nearly startled me to death."

"What the hell are ye doing going in circles?"

Her mouth gaped open before she placed a hand on her hip and started thumping a foot. "And how am I supposed to know that? You said not to break branches, and I am not."

Deep breath in, deep breath out. "Kate, just look at the sun and go east."

She thrust a finger skyward. "And where might that sun be? Huh?"

Ian looked up at the dense canopy. "Humph."

He, and every man he kenned, instinctively discerned direction if not by the sun, then by taking note of everything from shadows to river flows, to moss growth and the direction of felled trees. But apparently, not so women.

No, Kate hadna seen anything the least odd in repeatedly passing the same friggin' *cottage-sized boulder!*

"Kate, can ye sweep?"

She straightened, her eyes narrowing and lips thinning. "Do *not* even think to mock me, sir, or you will rue this day."

God's teeth, may the saints preserve him. They didna have time for this. The enemy was, nay doubt, already sniffing along the tree line.

He placed a hand over his heart. "Kate, dearest, love, lambikins, I meant no insult. 'Tis just that we need move on with all due haste. The enemy, after all, follows. If ye would be so kind as to sweep over our tracks as I have been doing for the last hour, I would be most pleased to lead the horse east."

Appearing somewhat mollified, she huffed and snatched the branch from his hand. "Fine. By all means lead on."

In short order they emerged from the wood and Ian lifted Kate into the saddle. Pointing to the distant cottages before them, he murmured, "'Tis Cove. We will find food there."

Keeping to the gravel track, Ian pushed Thor until the destrier's sides were slathered in sweat.

Entering the wee village, he brought Thor down to a trot else he run over one of the scattering sheep or bairns. Before a wee barn, he reined in and jumped from the saddle. As he reached for Kate, the barn door squeaked open.

"MacKay."

Ian grinned at Bret Home, a wiry, dark-headed man of thirty or so, who made his living pirating. "How are ye, friend?"

Bret, his gaze locked on Kate, grumbled, "As fair as can be, given the times. Who is this?"

Ian made the introductions and led Thor into the barn.

Bret closed the doors behind him. "Bury yer tack and saddle beneath the hay. Mistress, a pleasure to make yer acquaintance. Now, fetch that bucket yon."

Muttering, "Lovely friends, MacKay," Kate headed

for the bucket as he reached under his saddle for Thor's girth strap.

Bret, his gaze on Kate's hips, grumbled, "How many follow?"

"Six, mayhap eight. About an hour behind."

Bret spit onto the straw-strew barn floor while Ian lifted the saddle from Thor. Answering Bret's unasked question, he murmured, "Greenwich."

Bret arched an eyebrow. Leaving Bret to think on it, Ian carried his saddle up to the loft.

Finally Bret called up, "I will fetch the manure, then get the Sea Witch ready. I need to make a wine run anyway."

His saddle and tack buried, Ian climbed down and found Kate, her sleeves rolled up to the elbows, washing Thor down with dung-colored water and his horse looking none too thrilled about it. He reached for the rag hanging over the bucket edge and started doing the same. "Where is Bret?"

Kate peered under Thor and frowned. "He's fetching meat and drink, bless him." She wiped between Thor's front legs. "This really is not a bad color. Ochre, I think."

"Humph." Looked like shit to him.

As she wiped down his destrier's face and he washed the poor beast's rump, Kate asked, "Will we spend the night here?"

He caught her hopeful note and reached for more foul water. "Nay, as soon as Bret returns and Thor's made safe, we go to the boat."

Kate froze midwipe. "Boat?"

"Do ye have a problem with boats?" Better he learn of it now than later.

She resumed rubbing down Thor. "No, no, you just surprised me."

A side door creaked open, and Ian's hand flew to the hilt of his broadsword. Seeing Home's wife, he relaxed and grinned. "Hey, Iona, good to see ye."

Iona—a stout, flame-haired Highlander who had never tolerated fools easily and had thus remained a maid well past her twenties—cast a wary glance at him. "If ye brought trouble down on our heads, Ian, ye will be sorry ye ever laid eyes on me."

Ha! She hadna changed a bit in five years. Grinning, he dropped the cloth and took the food and ale bag from her hands. "Lovely and as acerbic as ever, Iona. Ye are a dautie dear." He planted a smacking kiss on her cheek, causing her to blush.

Liking her and liking Bret, a Lowlander who, in Ian's opinion, had been in sore need of a wife, he had arranged their introduction and thus took full credit for their marriage.

Grinning, he leaned toward her and wiggled an eyebrow. "How goes yer love life?"

She laughed and slapped his arm. "None of yer bloody business."

The door creaked again and Bret entered. "Word's gone out to the crew. Best ye finish with that horse and eat, for the sooner we are off the better."

Thinking it wisest, Ian said, "We will eat on the way to the ship."

"*Ship*? But you just said *boat*!"

All eyes turned toward Kate. Ian closed the distance between them. "Aye, we'll take a boat to the ship, which lurks in the next cove. If there is a problem, Katie, speak now, lass, whilst we still have a chance to change course."

Kate smiled. "No, 'tis fine. Fine."

Despite her reassurances, the hairs on Ian's arms

stood at attention. Why was it that whenever Kate muttered *fine* in that tone it never boded well?

Thor was finally the color of dung from tip to tail.

Suspecting it would take a good year before he was white again, Ian patted Thor's nose and turned him out into the paddock. "I will be back, lad, dinna ye fash."

Thor blew derisively before grabbing a mouthful of sea grass.

Ian returned to the barn to find Kate and Iona whispering like conspirators in the corner. "Humph."

Bret handed him a familiar leather pouch. In it he found the forged documents he had left years ago and L100 in coin. A fortune to the man before him. "Thanks, friend."

Bret wiggled a finger at Katie. "We had best be off."

Ian took Iona's hands in his and pressed several coins into her palm, kenning better than to offer them to Bret. "Take care, dautie. I wish ye well."

Brow furrowed, she patted his cheek. "Godspeed, Ian." Almost as an afterthought she added, "Be sure to bring the lass back when next ye pass. I like her."

High praise.

He nodded, regretting how easily he could lie to a friend.

I do believe I am going to be seriously ill.

Standing knee deep in sea oats, Kate stared over the Cove's headland. The steeply pitched path before her led down to a black rock beach a good hundred feet below and on that beach sat the dinky little boat Ian fully intended to put her in. She had barely survived her first sea voyage with her mind intact and now this.

Her middle rumbled as wave after foamy wave crashed into the rear of the little boat, causing it to rise and thrust forward, only to fall back and scrape back across the rocks as each wave receded.

Look up. Don't think about what is happening below.

Her gaze settled on the ominous thunderheads lining the horizon. Not good. Find something else.

In the middle ground, she found only the roiling sea which hid every manner of beast laying in wait beneath its slimy, slate-gray surface. Sharks and killer whales with teeth as large as her fist. Squid that could suck a man's face off. Treacherous eels and slimy Man-of-War that would sting her to death.

Oh, God, when next I see Sir Gregory I am going to geld him and shove his balls down his throat.

"Kate?"

She opened her eyes to find Ian holding out his hand. "Come, lass, we need hurry before we lose the tide."

She swallowed, trying to loosen her tongue from the roof of her mouth. Reluctantly she took his hand, barely mindful of its warmth and strength.

Halfway down the treacherous slope, she garnered what little courage she had left to her and asked, "If put to the test, do you think you could slay a whale with that broadsword of yours?"

If he could, then surely he could handle a shark or a squid, although she did hear tell that there were squid as large as Spanish galleons. Augh!

She looked up and found Ian staring at her. "What?"

His brow was deeply furrowed. "A *whale?*"

She nodded most vigorously. "Yes."

"Of course, Kate, I am a knight. We do it all the time."

"Oh." She hadn't realized whale slaying was part of knight training. It did explain why she had never heard tell of a knight being swallowed by a whale despite them forever sailing to the continent and going off on crusades whilst multiple sailors—who everyone knew received no initial training since most were conscripted—frequently had been.

Feeling ever so much better she mustered a smile. "Thank you."

"My pleasure."

Why he shook his head when he started down the path again, she couldn't imagine. It wasn't as if knights spent their days talking to her. Ian was the first who ever had.

And she still didn't think much of getting into a dinghy that had spent its day scraping across rocks. If one really thought on it . . . How sturdy could the bottom possibly be after all that abuse?

Chapter 19

"MacKay, if that woman of yers doesna cease rapping on the friggin' hull, I am binding her hand and foot and strapping her to the damn beakhead. She is scaring my men half to death. *Do something!*"

Ack. Ian put down his book—which he hadna really been reading, as his mind had been fully occupied with reliving every moment he'd spent with Kate—and rolled out of his hammock. "Aye, Bret. I will tend to it immediately."

"Damn straight ye will. She is in the bow." His friend grunted and, shoulders hunched, headed for the companionway ladder leading up to the *Sea Witch*'s aftercastle deck.

Katie, ye are going to be the death of me.

Thinking it might relieve her fashing, he hadna said a word when she started going from bow to stern testing every board, beam and timber for soundness, for the ship was indeed sound. So confident was he in Bret's abilities that he had let her be and began to read, never giving a thought to the impeding storm, that its winds would set the *Sea Witch*'s quadruple masts to screeching in their holes—a natural and proper occurrence—and her hull to moaning.

Apparently, Kate had.

After a moment's search he found her hunched in the four-foot-high forecastle, slippers in hand, skirts gathered between her legs, sloshing through bilge and rapping on planks.

Bent in half, he touched her elbow and yelled over the gale and ship's moaning, "Katie! Come."

She swatted at him. "Can you not hear it? The planks are straining. Oh, this is definitely not good."

God's teeth. "Katie, for a woman of uncommon sense ye are behaving like a dolt!"

That caught her attention. She snapped upright and nearly knocked herself out on a deck beam. "Ouch!"

He grabbed her by the elbow and pulled her to him. "Enough. Ye are coming with me."

He hauled her through the tween deck, past the gun carriages and hammocks suspended from the *Witch*'s upper deck. The sailors off watch clapped and cheered, which thankfully caused Kate to cease her struggling.

In Bret's wee bulkhead cabin, Ian kicked the door closed and tossed Kate into his hammock. Unlike Bret's bed, which was built into the cabin and ran bow to stern, his hammock—because of its length— was suspended before the galley portals on great hooks and ran port to starboard.

As she grappled for balance, he caught the edge of the hammock, slid in and stretched out beside her. Wrapping his arms about her, he pulled her to his side.

"Katie, lay still or ye will get ill."

"But, but——

He placed a finger to her lips. Lord, he had never met a woman who thought so much. "Nay buts. Ye are here, ye are in my arms and ye are safe. 'To him who is in fear everything rustles.'"

Kate huffed. "Sophocles, and 'Dead men tell no tales.'"

Good Lord, he loved the odd way her mind worked. "I dinna think that is what the man meant."

"Well, *I do.*" She craned her neck and looked out the nearest portal. She immediately blanched. "Augh!"

Peering over her shoulder and seeing only a roiling slate sky and formidable, foaming swells, he decided he had best give her something else to fash over.

He loosened his hold and rolled onto his side. Kate immediately tumbled, pressing him breast to chest, groin to groin, thigh to thigh and toe to toe.

Mmm. Lovely how he and she seemed to align so verra well.

He tightened his hold on her waist before she could think to roll away and ran a finger along her pouting lower lip. "I have dreamt," he whispered, "of getting you into this verra position for days."

The tip of her tongue darted out and traced the path his finger had just taken. "Oh?"

"Ah huh. And ye?"

She blushed, her gaze scooting from his eyes to his throat. "No, I hadn't given it a moment's thought."

Ah, so she had. Verra good. He kissed that soft place next to her ear as he slipped a hand beneath her hair. Hearing her breath catch, feeling her skin pebble, he used his thumb to tip back her head so they were again eye to eye. "Ye have lovely lips, Kate. Made for savoring."

"Oh?"

"Hmmm." And he did, taking only the slightest nibble, but 'twas enough to cause her eyes to flutter shut and to make her sigh. He deepened his kiss.

As his tongue slid into her warm, moist interior, he gently thrust. Groaning, her mouth opened farther. That's the lass.

He delved deeper still; savoring her taste, mimicking with his tongue what his now decidedly hard shaft yearned to do farther below but never would.

He was rewarded with the press of her hips and breasts. A hand fluttered across his shoulders. Yearning to feel her caress, he jerked on his already-loosened shirt and guided her hand beneath the fabric. He nearly sighed when her fingers glided through the hair of his chest. When her fingers brushed his nipple, he did groan into her mouth, hoping to encourage her into further exploration. To his delight her hand slipped to his waist and he felt her fumble with his brass belt.

Ack, if she wanted to touch, who was he to deny her?

Keeping his mouth locked on hers, he slipped the belt cleat. One click, a lift of his hips, and the belt hit the floor. While he was at it he unfastened his brooch and tossed that as well. There. He was all hers to touch and stroke as she pleased.

She, thankfully, wore no such impediments. Just a wide-necked, deeply cut gown that easily slipped from her shoulder with the flick of a finger. He opened his eyes to examine his prize.

Her breasts truly were beautiful. So lush and taut.

More than a handful to be sure and just how he liked them.

Needing to taste, anxious to suckle, he traced the edge of her jaw with his lips, then slid along the long column of her neck. At her pulse he licked and she quietly keened.

He slid lower and grazed across the delicious swell of one breast. She arched and her fingers threaded into his hair. *Ah, I'd wager she had been thinking about that night, about what she saw and what he told her.*

He cradled a breast in his hand, relishing the weight and feel. As his fingers gently kneaded from below, he ran his thumb over its large cinnamon sphere. To his delight, she groaned and her nipple puckered to a perfect peak. The ship pitched into a trough as he latched on and gently suckled. When the ship rose on the next wave, he slathered the tip, then lapped the side of her breast. He repeated the process with the next several rises and pitches of the ship so she would hopefully anticipate.

Before long, Kate, panting, placed her hands on either side of his head and tugged. Ah, she wanted his mouth again, wanted to press fully against him. Not the least opposed, he did as she bid, while slipping a hand under her skirts.

As his hand rode up her thigh, her skin quivered in anticipation of where it might come to rest. Ah, his delightful Kate remembered well.

Had they been in a bed he would have preferred to kiss and lick her there. To suckle on her delightfully plump bud, then thrust his tongue into her until such time as she arched off the mattress and screamed. But given they were in a hammock he could do naught but fondle and stroke her, and so he did. First, by taunting, brushing ever so slowly by, and then waiting for her to lift her pelvis, which she graciously did with a good bit of moaning.

He pulled his mouth from hers and licked her earlobe. "Tell me what ye want, love."

Kate responded with a breathy "You."

For Kate did. Most heartily did she want Ian MacKay.

She had never wanted anything more in her life nor did she ever expect to have this opportunity again. To be with him in this most intimate of ways, to feel a fulfillment she craved to the very depths of her soul. They would part, mayhap never to see each other again, and she wanted his essence deep within her to cherish. To keep forever and sacred the knowledge that only he, the man she loved, could teach her.

He did drive her mad with his lips and his hands but that was no longer enough. She desperately wanted more. But how did she tell him?

The question evaporated as his fingers slid through the curls at the apex of her thighs and began stroking the greatest need. Oh, yes, please, do.

Oh, he could drive her mad with simply a touch.

"Ooooh." He now used both hands. One in front to rub whilst the other had slipped in from behind so that his finger now slid back and forth within the aching place. "Ooooh!"

She arched her hips to give him better access. Burning, she pleaded, "Yes, oh, yes. More."

Surely, she would perish with need. Oh, that his shaft with its moist tip should slide in where his fingers filled her.

She had to know. Had to know or lose her mind. She hiked her skirts and brushed his kilt aside. Ah, much better.

Kate wrapped her fingers around him, Ian groaned, and Kate's heart tripped. What she held in her palm was heavy, pulsing, and at the tip she found even more heat and a lovely, silky wetness. Yes, he is ready and able.

More, he wanted exactly what she sought.

The knowledge gave her courage and she threw her leg high over his hip, instinctively seeking contact with him. "Please, Ian, please."

Ian's breath caught when Kate shoved his kilt aside and his shaft was enveloped by velvet. Not the velvet he desperately wanted but as much as he could allow himself.

Then her fingers slid around him. Desperate to keep from getting ahead of her, he imagined MacGregor's flock of one hundred and six sheep and frantically started counting; one, two, three, four . . .

And then she did the unthinkable; she threw her leg over his hip and pressed forward, giving him complete access. Panting, grinding, she wanted to mate and God help him, he wanted to mate just as badly. Mayhap more, for he had never been this hard or in so much need in his life. Five, ten, fifteen, twenty . . .

Her tongue thrust into his mouth, in and out, in and out, in rhythm with her hips as she sought release.

Thirty, forty, fifty, sixty—

Oooh, just a taste, his wee self screamed. *Just one little thrust into all that hot sweetness. Ye needna linger. Ye are experienced. Ye ken what to do so ye willna spill yer seed in her, so that none are any the wiser. Just one thrust . . . well, mayhap two . . . just to be sure, so that ye will never forget. Ye love her, ye ken she wants it, and ye ken ye will hate yerself if ye dinna take it whilst ye have it in hand. Do it!*

Aye, oh, aye.

His hips lifted and he slid against delicious wet warmth. He pulled his finger out of her slick passageway to make room for his wee self.

And his big self shouted, *She is a virgin, ye bloody selfish arse!*

Ackkkk!

He went stone still. Deep breath in. Deep breath out.

Augh, he had never been in so much pain in his life.

What on earth had he been thinking—almost deflowering her? Shit, he hadna been thinking, just feeling, but laud, she felt so damn good.

Kate's hands came to rest on his cheeks. He opened his eyes to find her, brow furrowed, nibbling on her swollen lower lip. "What is amiss?" she asked.

Poor Kate. Poor him, for that matter. How to explain this. "I am so sorry, lass. I canna."

Still panting, she tipped her lovely head and silently studied him for a moment. Then, looking about to cry, she murmured, "So, it is true, then?"

"What is true, love?"

"That Scotsmen prefer sheep."

Chapter 20

"*Sheep!* Did ye just say *sheep?*"

Ian appeared totally aghast. Torment and then deny her, would he? Ha!

His countenance ruddy, his ears scarlet, he sputtered wordlessly as he stared at her, and she—keeping her face as placid as possible, given how funny he looked—waited, hoping.

His eyes narrowed. "Why ye, witch. Ye are having me on. I can see it in yer eyes."

Hoping for a wide-eyed innocence, she murmured, "*Moi?*"

Before she could squeal in alarm, his arm wrapped about her waist like a vise and he spun and landed on top of her, settling between her willingly wide-open thighs. Lovely. Mission accomplished.

Kate wrapped her arms about his neck and tried to pull him down for a kiss, to continue their love-making. To her consternation Ian resisted.

Keeping his weight on his arms, he shook his head and fingered a strand of her hair. "Katie, love, I want ye so much I can barely think, but I canna deflower ye. Someday ye may wish to wed and the man willna take kindly to kenning another has been here before him."

Augh! Moral men would be the bane of her existence.

"Ian, it's my virginity, my body. Do I have no say in the matter?"

"Aye, of course ye do, but passion can cause a body to want now and regret later."

She ran a shaking hand along his jaw. "I will never marry. More importantly, I will never regret our being together because I love you." He opened his mouth, no doubt to protest, and she silenced him with a finger. "Fear not. I understand that it would be suicidal for you to even consider taking me to wife. I am the enemy, a Sassenach, as far as your regent and people are concerned, but that doesn't mean I can't love you . . . and want you."

Ian groaned and rested his forehead on hers. "Oh, Katie, why hadna we met at another place and time?"

"Because fate is often cruel." God knows they'd both gone through or seen enough heartache to know.

She began rocking her hips ever so slowly beneath him as her fingers ran through the soft golden hairs on his chest. Dear God, she loved the look and feel of him. Even the way he *humphed* whenever he was exasperated with her. "We have only this moment in time, Ian." Feeling him growing, hardening against her, she rocked and said no more.

After a moment he raised his head and looked in her eyes. She saw renewed heat and need, but also struggle.

I will not squander this opportunity to love you, Ian MacKay.

Before he might sense her intention, Kate threw her legs about his hips, grabbed his muscled bottom with both hands and pushed from above and below.

"*Oh!*"

Oh . . . my. My, oh, my. How . . . wondrous.

Obviously shocked and mayhap even in pain, Ian turned to stone above her. "Good God, woman what have ye done?"

Holding tight else he tried to escape her, Kate licked her suddenly dry lips. "I have done what I have truly wanted to do for the very first time in my life."

His forehead again came to rest on hers. "Ack, lass."

Oh, no. His knightly code was, apparently, still warring with his nature. Hoping to tip the scales in her favor, she licked where his lips now formed a hard, straight line and slid a hand over the fine contours of his rounded arse and then to where his bullocks lay. Feeling him shudder, relishing the taut, controlled power beneath her hands, fire again bloomed where he filled her. Quite breathless, she whispered, "Will you deny me?"

He lifted his head. Smoldering gold now assessed her. Sounding hoarse, he whispered, "Oh nay, lass, ye are all mine now."

Not liking but having to accept the decision having been made for him, Ian grinned down at Kate in wolfish fashion.

She wanted him? Fine. She would have him until she couldna take any more. Toy with his emotions and good intentions, would she?

He captured her mouth and rode. In two thrusts he was as deep into a woman as he had ever been in his life, his balls pressing and sliding in her womanly dew.

God, there wasna question that she'd been made for him.

But made for him or nay, she'd upped the stakes, turned play into reality. For thwarting his honest resolve he would bring her to madness.

Reluctantly, he pulled his mouth from hers and rose on his elbows. "This gown has got to go." Thanks to their body heat and the lamp, the wee cabin was warm.

Without waiting for her agreement, he jerked the gown up and over her head and arms, then tossed it on the floor. He did the same with her undershirt, his shirt, sgian duhb and brass cuffs. Now both naked, wanting to feel the press of her breasts against his chest, he settled upon her again and threaded his fingers through hers. As she mewed in his mouth he mentally agreed that they did meld well together and raised her hands high above her head. Once caught in one hand, he snatched the excess rope that hung over the hook holding the hammock and looped it around her hands, effectively trapping them in place.

Taken by surprise, Kate jerked at her bonds. "What? Why have you—?"

He placed a gentle finger to her lips. "Shh. Ye want, ye will get, my love, but henceforth on my terms." Humph! She had nay idea who she was dealing with.

He took a firm hold of her waist—ensuring that they would stay fully engaged—and carefully dropped one of his legs and then the other over either side of the hammock so that he sat with her lovely long thighs falling open and over his thighs. Perfect.

With his hands on her hips, he studied her every curve and swell by the light of the lone oil lamp swinging above them. Good Lord, she was so very beautiful. He began to slide—slow and easy—within her. "Comfy?"

She mewed, her back slightly arched. Her breasts shimmered ever so slightly, their peaks tightening in the most delightful fashion. Oh, aye. Ye didna lie when ye said ye wanted this. Feeling her legs wrap about him, he grinned and moved his hands in wee circles over the gentle swell of her belly. "Katie, look at me."

When her eyes fluttered open—their sky blue depths now cobalt—he slid the fingers of his right hand into her damp curls and found her swollen bud. He started massaging. She gasped as her eyes rolled back and her back arched higher. "Feels good, does it not?"

"Ahh, ah, oh."

He just loved the way her breasts, now slick with sweat, trembled with every breath. Just the sight drove him to increase the pace. "Open those lovely eyes, Katie." He wanted to see them as she shattered.

Her eyes opened but just barely. Then her legs fell away from him and straightened, every muscle in her body growing tauter with each heartbeat, straining for something just beyond her reach. *Oh, aye. I have got ye now.*

His heart pounding as fast as her breathing, he increased the speed of his thumb and rocked his hips, driving deeper into her with every thrust. "That's the sweet lass," he whispered, "ye are almost there."

Her gaze locked on his as her panting increased tenfold. He slowly licked his lips as he stared at her breasts so she would not only feel but see how much he enjoyed watching her tremble, naked and exposed beneath his hands.

"Come to me, lass."

She shattered then, keening high and sweet, her every muscle violently quaking within and without.

Oh aye, 'tis definitely the way one does it.

He grinned, watching her relax, satiated. Next, to punish completely, drive her totally wode, but first she needed to recoup and they both needed meat.

Kate mewed as he slipped his hand beneath her lovely hurdies and lifted her higher in the hammock, allowing her arms to bend. He almost mewed himself when he slid out of her, still fully engorged while Kate looked all soft, floppy and content. Finally out of the hammock, he stood and looked about for the food and wine Iona had provided them.

As he bent for his blade, Kate whispered, "The storm has passed."

He straightened and found her looking out the window. "Aye, and the galleon held together just fine without ye fashing after it."

She nibbled on her lip, her gaze still on the portal. "Silly, I know, but my mind just gets to worrying about all that lurks beneath those waves."

"I noticed." Food and drink in hand, he straddled the hammock again and she drew her legs up to make room for him. "Hungry?"

She nodded. "And thirsty." She wiggled her wrists, trying to slip free. "Um . . . Can you please untie me?"

Grinning, he opened the pouch and found cheese, a loaf of fresh dark bread and a clay crock. "I will in a bit."

"But . . . ?" She huffed in obvious exasperation.

He drank her in, his gaze sliding slowly over her.

She immediately squirmed and blushed scarlet from crotch to forehead.

"My, my, I hadna kenned where a blush started before. Interesting." He flashed his dimples at her.

"Ian, this is not funny. Untie me so I might eat."

"Dinna fash. I will feed ye." He broke the bread into bite-sized pieces. After placing a piece in her mouth he lined the rest down the middle on her body, starting at her throat and ending just above her curly thatch. He reversed the process as he laid out the cheese. "I need tell ye I dinna ken yer father allowing ye to come so far alone."

Kate looked out the portal, tempted to lie, but then thought better of it. Ian had an uncanny way of sniffing out the truth. "He doesn't know."

"Pardon?"

She found him looking incredulous, his hands stilled mid-task. "He thinks I am in Salisbury with Nana." Kate looked away again. "He wouldn't understand." And if he did he would hate her.

"Does anyone ken ye are here?"

She nodded. "Sir Gregory does." But what Sir Gregory did not know was that he was not long for this world.

Ian resumed his task. "And how will yer father react when he learns what ye have been up to?"

Her attention jerked back to him. "He must never know!"

Shaking his head, Ian continued to lay out the cheese and then popped the final piece into her mouth. "Lass, he will learn of it, if he doesna ken already."

"You wouldn't tell him! You cannot. Please."

"I wouldna, but what if your grandmother writes

and asks after ye? Or Sir Gregory or James let slip something?"

Kate relaxed and shook her head. "Nana can't write and Sir Gregory's most tight lipped. Only James could prove worrisome." Under her breath she grumbled, "Too often, he speaks first and thinks later."

"But ye like him."

"I liked who he once was."

Frowning, Ian placed a piece of bread in her mouth and murmured, "Explain."

How did one explain what she had sensed and seen? Or who and what she was? And what if Ian thought as her father did? Their relationship was tentative at best as it was. She would not risk spoiling the last few hours she had with him by telling him she occasionally *knew* of events before they occurred. And why had she not foreseen this? Her lying naked, her hands tied and knees locked together, with the handsomest man ever created, who also sat naked but with his legs spread wide? Augh.

"Kate, ye havena answered me." He waggled the wine before her. "If ye want a drink, ye need respond."

She curled a corner of her lip, then huffed. "James was once a sweet child and now he's . . . angry and very full of himself."

"Hmmm." Ian pulled the stopper from the wine and took a drink.

"Hey, I answered. Not fair."

Grinning, he parted her legs, leaned over her and pressed his lips to hers. Instinctively her lips yielded to the pressure and wine, warm and rich, flowed slowly into her mouth. Ooooh. Her middle quivered. Oh, my. His feeding her was one thing but this . . . oh, my.

He straightened, a dark look in his eyes, his gaze on her lips. "So why do you care whether or not he's embittered, or for that matter whether or not he's ever ransomed?"

Hoping to change the direction of his thoughts, Kate muttered, "Why is it that women sit with their knees together while men sit with them apart?"

"If ye carried this"—he ran a hand up his swollen staff—"betwixt those lovely thighs of yers ye would be sitting with yer knees spread, too."

Feeling heat bloom in her cheeks, Kate pulled her gaze from his stroking hand. "I see."

He winked as he raised the wine to his lips. "Thought ye might." He swallowed, then asked, "So why do ye care about James?"

So much for diversion.

Realizing her thighs were still spread before him, she started to close them, but his hand forestalled her.

"Nay, I love looking at ye. Stay as ye are."

Oh, merciful mother in heaven. She huffed.

Well, she had started this, she wasn't uncomfortable and if it pleased him, why ever not? Although why he would want to look at that end of her she could not imagine. She relaxed her legs and let them rest against the canvas, her secrets no longer secrets.

"Ye were speaking of James."

Augh! The man had a steel trap for a mind.

"A bit of cheese if you please."

He grinned, flashing his dimples at her. "As my lady lusts." He leaned forward between her thighs, stroked his tongue over her right nipple, making her shiver and then, using his teeth, plucked up a bit of cheese lying on her breastbone and brought it to her mouth. Mesmerized, she opened her mouth and his lips brushed hers. After depositing the cheese, he gave her a quick peck and straightened. And all the while she'd been very aware of his swollen tip moving ever so slightly against her apex.

She closed her eyes and chewed, sure she would not survive an entire meal served in this manner. That thought had but formed when she felt his lips and tip again. She opened her eyes and to find him nibbling more bread and cheese from her flesh. He swallowed, then looked up at her. Watching her watching him, he slowly and laboriously licked up the crumbs.

Her nipples ached and her womb turned molten. There were still six more tiny piles of food on her belly.

Ooooh, lauds, I will not survive this.

He straightened and reached for the wine he had placed on the hammock behind him. "More wine?"

She was parched but shook her head. Out of self-defense she started to close her legs.

"Nay, love." He pressed her knees apart. "We have so little time left to us that I want to see as much of you as I can for as long as I can."

Uh oh, not good.

He raised the wineskin to his mouth. She watched as he drank, marveling at the way his throat moved. Done, he wiped the back of his hand across his beautifully shaped lips and smiled at her. Oh, those dimples would melt the heart of a crone.

"So what shall you do when you return to London?"

"London?"

"Aye, where ye are going."

"Oh, London." She gave herself a hard mental

shake. "First, I need check on Father." To be sure that he was safe, that her dream had simply been a nightmare and not a foreshadowing of what was to come. "Then I shall go to the Tower and tell James and Sir Gregory all that I learned."

Then I shall smite Sir Gregory for all he neglected to tell me.

Looking at the ceiling, her mind imagining Sir Gregory as she last saw him, all smiles and *Dinna ye fash, lass,* she asked, "Ian, when using a blade, where would you stab to get maximum painful effect?"

He cleared his throat. "From the look in yer eye, I dinna think 'twould be wise of me to tell ye."

She grinned. "No, I wouldn't hurt you for a pot of gold. No. It's just that I wander about, most often alone, and wondered what I should do should I be set upon."

He brought the wineskin to his mouth and leaned over her again. Unable to resist, she opened to him and drank thirstily. As he straightened she sighed.

Grinning, apparently aware of his effect on her, he said, "Best not use a blade. Even as strong and tall as ye are a working man could still wrench it from yer hand. Best use yer knee."

"My knee?"

"Aye, jam it up betwixt his thighs. When he folds—and, trust me, he will—grab him by the ears and ram yer knee into his jaw or nose. Either will set him down. Mayhap for good."

"Hmmm." *Sir Gregory, here I come.* "Thank ye."

"Ye are most welcome." He leaned forward again and licked up a piece of cheese, then bread as he had before and gave it to her. He licked the rest off her belly, leaving not so much as a crumb and sending fire everywhere within her.

Oh! Thank God that was done. She would have expired from want had any more remained.

Opening her eyes and finding him smiling down at her, she asked, "What has ye grinning now?"

"Naught." And everything.

God love a goose, the woman spread before him was a feast for the eyes. And he needed to get more wine into her. She wasna anywhere near tipsy enough for his purposes and was nay doubt still parched.

He brought the wine bag to her lips. "Drink, lass, before ye shrivel like a fall leaf."

Looking grateful, she did as he bid, drinking lustfully. He then reached into the satchel and pulled out the crock. "Now, what have we here?" He opened the lid and grinned. "Iona's strawberry jam." He scooped out a bit with his finger and brought it to her lips.

Her gaze never left his as she suckled, causing his poke of sweeties to ache and his shaft to throb. The saints preserve him. He couldna let her get the upper hand. He still had yet to ken the true motivation behind Katherine Margarita Templeton's journey. And he definitely needed to ken what she was referring to when she said Lady Beth would die and the bairns with her.

He pulled his finger from her mouth. As she licked her lips, he dipped his finger in the jar again. "Love, from whence comes yer Margarita?"

"My grandmother." She sighed, the wine apparently starting to take effect. "She is the daughter of a Romany princess, a fortune-teller. She was very beautiful, as was my mother."

Ah, that is where the golden skin comes from. He

offered her more wine. When she had her fill he asked, "Can ye tell fortunes as well?"

Her eyes widened with apparent alarm and then darted to the portal. "No."

Aha! She lied. Was she fey? 'Twould certainly go a long way in explaining how she repeatedly escaped him so readily. Humph!

He spread the jam about her right nipple.

Her eyes locked on his hands. "What on earth are ye doing?"

"Preparing dessert." He scooped up another dollop of jam and applied it lavishly to her left nipple, which he was pleased to see had puckered into a verra suckable peak.

She squirmed, trying to rise high and away from him. "This is not . . . I will get all sticky . . . And there is no water to wash with."

Ian grinned and used three fingers to scoop a large mound of jam out of the crock. He started between her heaving breasts and drew a line of jam down her belly and into the apex of her curls. Finished, he sucked his finger, tasting her essence for the first time and throbbed with need.

He then took her legs and, scooting forward, wrapped them around his back. "Dinna fash, love, I will lick ye as clean as a puss would a bowl of cream."

"Aaah!"

He leaned over her and circled her left nipple with his tongue. Sliding just a bit so she could feel his desire for her, he whispered, "Mmm . . . just as I imagined."

"Ian, *please.*" Her back arched and she again strained at the rope holding her hands.

He lifted the breast and drew the nipple into his

mouth, lavishing attention on the taut tip. God, she felt so good.

The jam gone, he licked his way to the second wee, jam-crested mountain. Licking his way up the full slope he whispered, "Love, why is it so important James have those names?"

"Aaah!"

"Hmmm." Kneading both breasts he sucked on the second peak, drawing it slowly into his mouth, and lathed off the jam. After a moment he raised his head and found her watching him. "I love the feel of ye in my mouth."

"Ah."

"Aye, and I canna wait to taste the rest." He immediately started down her breastbone, then on to her stomach, which quivered in the most delightful way. At her apex he blew a puff of air against her jet curls. Her hurdies—and voice—rose in alarm.

Ah, lass, I have been yearning to love ye in the most intimate of ways possible, but we must do it right.

His hands quickly slipped beneath her, bringing her hips up. Her legs, seeking purchase, immediately fell over his shoulders. He raised her hips and licked lightly through the curls. She nearly flew out of his hands.

"What . . . what?"

Taking a firmer hold, he blew against her. "Tell me a secret, Katie. Something ye havena uttered to another living soul, then I will share a secret." What they were about to do was so intimate that it had to be a melding of body and mind. "Do ye ken what I am about, Katie?"

"Nay!"

"Nay to secret sharing or nay to ye kenning what

we are about?" He allowed himself another wee taste and she rose higher still.

"I . . . I . . . don't . . ."

Oh, the poor lass, she is panting so hard her eyes are crossed. Enough.

He reached for the rope. "We canna do Kits in a Basket properly in this miserable hammock. Come."

When her hands came free, he wrapped her arms about his neck, wrapped her legs about his waist and stood. She immediately slid onto his shaft. Keening sweetly, she buried her face against his neck.

"Oh, God, ye feel so good, lass."

Holding her with one hand, he grabbed the furs off Bret's bed and tossed them onto the floor, then gently settled onto his back, she sitting upon him.

"'Tis time ye took control." He folded his hands behind his head and eased his legs apart. "Lean forward and stretch out yer legs betwixt mine."

Kate, her heart pounding so hard she was sure he could hear it, did as Ian requested. Stretched out so they were hip to hip, nose to nose. Oh, She rose up on her arms. Oh my. She rocked just a bit. She liked this.

Head resting in his hands, he watched her through barely opened eyes, dimples taking shape. Never had she imagined . . . Oh, and how wonderful he felt, they felt, together. That wonderful, throbbing need was building again. She began to rock faster.

"Tup me, lass. Take what ye need."

Tup him.

She rocked. She could. Oh, my! She slid forward and back on him, loving the way the hairs on his chest brushed and tickled her breasts, the way the muscles along his square jaw began flexing and how sweat broke out on his brow in response to what *she* was doing as she rode. Oh, yes. Such power.

His hands were suddenly at her hips. "Aaah, lass."

She picked up the pace, straining to find release. "Tell me yer secret."

His neck arched back. "Aaah!"

Oh, no you don't. He had tormented her for hours. "Tell me."

Panting, teeth clenched, he growled, "Ye first."

Her? Well, why not tell him? She had given her body, her heart. Why not her soul? It might prove a relief to have someone other than Nana know. Besides, how she could lose something she didn't hold? His love.

Angry at a primal level that she had the secret in the first place, that he would now reject her, she rocked harder. "I am fey, Ian. *Fey.* I see what has yet to be."

He looked at her, eyes sparking gold flames. Oh, what was he thinking? She rocked harder, so close, so close.

He pulled her down to him. Looking into her eyes, he whispered, "My secret, Katie, something I havena ever uttered . . . I love ye. I shouldna, I canna, but I do."

"Ye love?"

Grinning, he slipped his hands down to her buttocks and took control of their joining. "Oh, aye. I do."

How is this possible? He loved her . . . still? Whilst knowing? Oh! Oh! Oh! Oh!

As the world shattered into a million brilliant pieces, she keened.

"Aaaaaaaaaaaaaaah, Iannnnnn!"

Katie tumbled, as loose as a rag doll, onto his chest.

Ian laughed as he wrapped his arms around her and stroked her back. Aye. Never let it be said that he couldna drive a woman to madness should he set his heart and mind to it. And he had finally uttered those three special words he never thought he might. And it felt good. Something warm and strong now occupied his heart.

Hmmm, yet he still throbbed and was still most anxious to love her far more intimately. But to each there is a season . . . And Scotland came before his heart.

Chapter 21

Kate, on her side, a leg resting between his, nuzzled into his neck as her fingers toyed with the fine hairs on his chest. In a breathy whisper she asked, "Did you really mean it?"

He rubbed a fine hurdie. "That I loved ye?"

She nodded.

"Aye, I do mean it." God help him. "May I ask ye something?"

"Anything."

"What did ye mean when ye said Lady Beth and her bairns were to die?"

Kate rose up on her elbows and studied his face. He could see that something was at war within her. Love of country versus him? What? He could only pray she would finally speak the truth, for he hadna the heart to force it out of her.

Without saying a word, she sat up and reached for the wine. After pulling the plug she drank, long and deep, then handed him the bag. "You need promise that you will never . . . ever . . . breathe a word of what I am about to tell you to anyone . . . Albany included."

Ian mentally groaned. He had pledged his fealty to Albany, as James had yet to be crowned. Yet, his declaration of love had been a pledge to Katie. He was a man caught betwixt a rock and a boulder.

After a minute, hoping he had found a compromise, he murmured, "I vow never to divulge yer name should ye tell me something I need act upon."

As she thought on that he quenched his thirst and prayed.

She pointed a finger at him, her eyes hard and assessing. "You must promise never to laugh, nor ridicule or in any way denounce me as a person of worth should I make known to you what I see now or at any time in the future."

Good Lord, he would never consider degrading her in such fashion . . . Well, mayhap laugh should she say something preposterous, which she did tend to do, but . . .

He made a fist and crossed his arm over his chest. "Aye, I promise."

Kneeling before him, her hands in her lap, she took a shuddering breath. "Agreed. Well, where to begin? I have been like this all my life, as was my mother, her mother and her mother before her. Some being more . . . more sensitive than others."

Ian rolled onto his side and propped himself up on an elbow. "How do these visions come to ye?"

"Sometimes in dreams. Those may or may not come true. The worst, the most accurate, are the painful flashes I see when someone takes my hands or hugs me."

Curiosity got the better of him. "Have ye had such visions when I have held ye?"

She blushed to a pretty shade of rose. "Just one."

Hmmm. Must have had something to do with his

loving on her. "About Lady Beth." For that was most important.

"I dreamt about her awhile back, when I brought a present to James and he hugged—"

Bham! Bham! "MacKay!"

Kate nearly jumped out of her skin. He patted her leg. "Shhh, 'tis all right." To the door he yelled, "What is it, Home?"

"We are two hours out."

Shit. Only two hours. "Thank ye."

Home *humphed* and walked away. When the footsteps faded, Ian took Kate's hand and murmured, "Come, lay beside me."

Kate, still rattled, shivered as she cuddled up against him. He stroked her hip, reveling in her plush swells, and coaxed, "Ye were saying about Lady Beth."

"I gave James a present for his birthday and when he hugged me in thanks I saw blood everywhere. Flash after flash, different places, different seasons, death and dying, Lady Beth and her children—she is going to have another son, by the way—fire . . . And, in every one, James—grim-faced, gloating—holding a bloody sword." She started to cry. "He is not going to send a henchman, Ian. Oh, there will be an army at his back, but he's going to take great personal joy in slaying, killing at will."

He pulled her closer. "And when will this happen?"

"I don't know, but he appears more a man in the visions. Thicker-boned, long-haired. And his clothing bespeaks a man of wealth, Ian." She shuddered. "He will be set free and he will seek to punish those he believes betrayed him if he is not turned from his present course. I *had* no choice but to garner proof that not all had forgotten him. That many did care.

I have to prevent him from growing more embittered, to keep his hate from festering to the point of total madness, where no amount of reason will reach him."

Kate took his face in her hands and looked deep into his eyes. "Believe me, he is already well on the way."

"And I destroyed yer proof."

She nodded and settled against him once again. "I will think of something."

Dare he believe her? They had a cailleach in his clan but he kenned little of the man, and he had met two that were fey on his travels—Angus's Birdi to name one, and a more startling lass he had yet to meet—but none such as Katie claimed to be.

Well, naught that she had told him had altered his plans. Gregory Campbell would ken who received the ransom demand, who had betrayed Scotland.

He stroked Kate's hip. "I believe ye, love. I do."

She threw her arms about his neck and kissed him soundly. So soundly, in fact, that his waning interest in tupping flared to life with a painful vengeance.

He pushed the hair from her face and found a tear lurking near the bridge of her nose. "Ack, lass, has it been so hard?"

She nodded. "I have not had anyone to share my fears with for so long. I had only complained to Sir Gregory that James was changing and not for the best. When I offered to go to Scotland to try to learn why the ransom hadn't been paid, to learn who still supported James so I might hold out hope to him, Sir Gregory had jumped at the idea. Oh, I kenned he saw me only as a means of contacting his family and to garner coins to make his life easier whilst in prison, but he said that his wife knew all about Scotland's politics and would provide the answers I sought. He was the one to suggest I go as Robbie's widow. He provided the brooch."

Humph! Margaret Campbell had never been interested in anything but furthering her own station and wealth—as too many in Scotland were, unfortunately. And kenning that, Albany had made sure that she remained in isolation with her sister, where she would be lucky if she kenned who provided her eggs.

"Lass, I hear tell the Tower is really many towers."

"Yes, it's huge and has seventeen in total. James is in what they call the Bell Tower."

Ian grinned. "Because it has the belfry."

She blinked in surprise. "Why, yes. However did you know?"

He wiggled a brow. "I didna, but it made sense. How often do you visit James now?" Please say at least once a week.

"Once a month or so. As I said he's grown distant and to be truthful, I have a difficult time calling a brash child Your Majesty or Your Royal Highness."

Once a month. That would still work. She hasna been home for nearly a month. "And need you perform nonsense like secret handshakes and words to prove ye have a right to come in?"

She grinned, "They used to make me years ago. Now I just show up, and they let me in."

Verra good. One less thing to fash over. "I imagine 'tis a bit disconcerting at night?"

Kate nodded. "It is. Thankfully, I need not go after sunset too often and then usually I do only to meet Father. The evening guards are more . . . outspoken than those on day duty, although both can be rather crude." She shuddered. "Did you know they have clipped the wings of their ravens so they can't fly? Worse, they have trained them to fight for sport."

He had heard tell but shook his head and said, "Truly?"

"Yes, and they have a menagerie there. I feel so sorry for the poor animals. They even have a lion of all things. They keep it in a cage no bigger than seven feet by ten feet, and the poor thing is eight feet long. And they feed it live sheep and such. The gore—" She shuddered again.

He could empathize, not having a liking for slavery of any sort. Since the topic was causing her distress and she had already given him the information he needed, he murmured, "Enough of this sad business."

Ian fingered one of her loose tendrils. "Tell me a tale from yer past. A pleasant one."

"Hmmm." She thought for a moment, then asked, "Would you like to know how I came to be the youngest woman ever banished from court?"

"Ye?" Who in their right mind would ban such a luscious wench? The pudpocks were daft.

"Yes. It was May Day, and I was but ten or eleven years. The celebration was in full swing when Father, Mama and I arrived at Windsor. There were jugglers, puppet shows, acrobats, the maypole, of course, and food the likes of which I had never seen.

"Well, I drank more punch than was wise and needed to find the garderobe. En route I spied a handsome couple grinding in a dark corridor. I hadn't thought much of it. Children at court see all manner of things, and Mama had already explained that all the heaving and huffing was simply the way one made babies. Well, day became night, and we all went into the great hall. Father was going from person to person introducing us. When he stopped before the handsome man he made our introductions. I looked at the fat old woman at the handsome man's side and said in all innocence and in my best precocious voice, 'No, Father, you must be mistaken. That pretty lady in red is his lordship's ladywife. She is the one I saw him making a baby with.'"

Ian choked on his wine. "Ye didna."

"Oh, I most certainly did. Needless to say, all eyes turned our way. The duchess turned three shades of white, his lordship blustered, and I got hauled out the door by my ear. I later learned the duchess banished her handsome husband but not before he cleaned out her coffers. Worse, the woman in red was a favorite of Henry's, who just happened to be close by when I was doing my precocious best. I tell you, all was in wreck and ruin within court for weeks, and I was never allowed back."

Ian kissed her nose. "Poor Katie, routed and at so tender an age." He ran a hand over her hurdies and asked the question that had been nibbling at the back of his mind for days. "Lass, have ye ever been in love before?"

Grinning, she blushed and shook her head. "Apparently I intimidate *wee* men."

Ian thanked heaven for wee favors. He would have hated to ken that there was a man out there who had stolen a kiss or who could look at Kate—even from a distance—and ken that he had mayhap run a hand over what his hand now grazed.

"What about you?" she asked. "Do you ever lust to be liege of the clan MacKay?"

He grinned. "Aye, I do lust verra much, but I will need to develop a clan of my own for we—the MacKays—already have Black Angus and he has a son. When Seabhagnead is finished—becomes a worthy stronghold—many years from now, I will return to the Highlands and hopefully with many a strong knight in need of someone to serve. 'Tis my long-held dream."

He pulled her closer and fondled a breast, bringing the nipple to a taut nub. As he rolled it between his thumb, he asked, "Would ye like more to eat?"

With her gaze on his lips, she shook her head. "Not food."

Good God, I love this woman.

Mindful of her recent deflowering yet feeling her body heat rise, he ran his hand lower still. "Are ye sore down here?"

She licked her lips and again she shook her head. Grand! She was proving to be as lusty as he.

As if to prove his conclusion Kate's hand glided ever so slowly over his middle, making his muscles contract, and then brushed his swollen shaft. "How is it," she began, "that I have umm . . ."

"Come?"

"Yes, if that is the word, yet you have not?"

He smiled and placed his hand over hers, closing her fingers around him. "I have been waiting for us to come together in a most special manner, one that would ensure I didna get ye with child, yet allowed us a verra special pleasure." His hand guided hers, teaching her how to stoke his passion. "Are ye willing to let me lead ye?"

Her tongue darted nervously across her lower lip.

Hmmm. Hoping she would realize he had nay intention of making her do anything she wasna comfortable with, he pressed his lips to hers and opened to her, inviting her to explore as she would. She did, and he groaned, thoroughly enjoying her tentative manner.

When she ended the kiss he whispered, "'There is no fear in love; but perfect love casteth out fear.'"

She sighed into his mouth, "John, 4." Rubbing her leg along his thigh, she began a tentative exploration of his poke of sweeties, which were about to explode. "'Many waters cannot quench love, neither can the floods drown it . . .'"

Ah, he did so love her mind. "Song of Solomon, verse eight." She was telling him to bring it on.

Throbbing and heart soaring, he rolled onto her and captured her mouth, delving for her soul.

At which point the *Sea Witch* mysteriously heaved to, and the cabin pitched nearly sideways.

"*Ayyyyyy!*"

Kate screeched and nearly strangled him whilst the fur beneath them slid at breakneck speed across the floor. Ian rolled, curling around Kate a heartbeat before his back slammed into Home's bed. He grabbed the bedrail, thinking they might be tossed in the opposite direction but relaxed as the ship settled to an even keel.

He brushed the tears from Kate's cheeks. "Shhhh, ye are fine. All's well." He was going to kill Home. "Shhh. Not to fash, Shhh."

Bham! Bham! Bham! "MacKay!"

Ian covered Kate's ears and bellowed, "God's teeth, Home! Where in the hell did ye learn to sail? In a *friggin' piss pot*? Ye damn near killed us!" Not to mention ruining a perfect moment.

Home chuckled. "Sorry. New man at the wheel." He cleared his throat in an obvious effort to mask laughter. "We had a good tailwind and will be dropping anchor momentarily. Distant sails on the horizon. Best don yer breeches, friend."

Ian ground his teeth as he heard Home laughing his way up the gangway steps. He uncovered Kate's ears and lifted her chin. "Are ye all right, love?"

Wiping her eyes with the heels of her hands, she nodded. "Just startled me . . . whales, you know. They tip ships all the time and I thought . . ." She shuddered and dragged in a hitching breath.

Ian helped her rise. "Nay whales, love, just an errant seaman." *Who doesna ken his butt from a hole in the ground, but he would ken it soon enough if it meant my having to pound the man's former into the latter.*

Christ's blood! Kate could have been seriously injured.

He looked about for their clothing. "We had best dress. We are about to disembark."

Arms crossed protectively over her breasts, Kate peeked out the portal. "So soon?"

Wondering why she bothered to cover her breasts as he admired her bare hurdies, Ian shook his head and knelt to pull out the basket from under Home's bed. Women.

When Kate turned she found Ian donned in black breeches and matching long-toed boots. As he held out her gown and slippers, she asked, "Where did you get those?"

"My stash, under Home's bed. I canna go about London dressed in my *breachen feile,* now can I, lass? Shouts Highlander."

"But—"

"I am coming with ye."

Kate's throat clogged with panic. "*No!* You will not put yourself at such risk for me. I will not allow it!"

He shrugged into his leather jerkin and reached for his sporran. "Ye canna stop me, love."

She wrenched her gown over her head. "But you'll be courting disaster."

He donned a knee-length black tunic, covering his sporran and six-inch sgian duhb, and pulled a short mail tunic out of the basket. After giving it a shake, he tossed it into the air to straighten out the links. "My lady Templeton, I will have you know that I can and will pass any muster, any question, you and yours should put to me, a knight of the realm."

Kate's mouth gaped. He had spoken just as she or her father did—his Highland burr completely gone.

"Oh." She could not have effectively mimicked his accent had she been threatened with hanging. "But still."

"Dinna argue, woman. Time isna on our side."

Realizing that no matter how she argued he would do as he pleased, Kate huffed and ran agitated fingers through her hair. "Have you a brush?"

Ian had one in hand. "Here."

Suspecting it was not his she checked it for lice, just in case, before running it through her hair.

Her hair braided, she opened her mouth to ask if he had seen her lace, and he handed it to her. Ah, exactly how many women had he helped dress that he could anticipate so easily? Or undress, for that matter? *Grrrrrr.*

He looked her over, nodded his apparent approval and draped her cape over her shoulders. He nuzzled her neck. "Ye look lovely."

She didn't feel the least lovely. She felt achy and lonely and miserable, and he had yet to leave her side . . . forever. If she felt this miserable now, there was simply no telling what kind of pain the morrow would bring.

And brokenhearted, she would still have to deal with her father, James and Sir Gregory. How easy it would be to simply drop to the cabin floor and wail as her heart wanted, but should she, Ian would doubtless insist on bringing her right up to the Tower gates, which would not do at all.

Ian led her on deck where they found a dinghy bobbing beside the galleon and, at some distance, acres of marsh and beach. Kate went to the rail. Her England, her land, yet nothing looked the least familiar. She nibbled her lower lip as she looked from left to right. She had absolutely no idea where she was, or how far from London they were. Odder still, she would have to trust that Ian did.

When Home came to stand beside her, she murmured, "Thank you."

He took her hand and kissed her fingertips. "My pleasure, m'lady. Any friend of Ian's is a friend of mine."

"May I ask where we are?"

"Just north of Blackwater."

"Oh, lovely." Wherever that was.

Realizing Ian had left her side she looked over her shoulder and found him next to the helmsman. Whatever he said caused the man—a boy, really—to blanch to the color of the reefed sails above their heads.

Ian returned to her side and held his hand out to Home. "Be careful."

Home muttered, "Aye, and Godspeed to ye."

As Ian threw his leg over the rail, Home placed a hand on Ian's arm, halting him. Keeping his voice low, he grumbled, "And, MacKay, given what I heard below, if ye ever so much as glance at my Iona I will cut yer heart out."

Ian grinned at Kate. "Dinna fash, friend."

Kate, feeling heat rush up her neck, groaned and caught several of the sailors grinning at her. Lauds, *everyone* apparently knew what she and Ian had been doing in the cabin. Augh!

So where were those damn whales when a woman needed one?

London. Ian hated the place. It stank, it was crowded, and it held his king. Five years back he had spent the height of summer here, posing as a mercenary knight and had never been so miserable in his life. Moreover he'd sworn never to return, yet here he was again.

Standing in the shadow of Greyfriar's Christ Church, a massive edifice of gaily glittering glass, Ian pulled Kate to his side, so that a near-to-buckling ale wagon being pulled by two oxen could ease past. Once clear, he took Kate's elbow and pointed to a pile of steaming dung. "Watch where ye step."

They continued south, heading toward the Thames and Kate's apartment. Passing a multistalled stable, Ian murmured, "Lass, wait here. I'll be right back."

He slipped past the dozing stable lad and began inspecting the cattle in each stall. Finding an aged black destrier with hair as dark as Katie's, he slipped his sgian duhb from his forearm and ran a hand down the once-mighty charger's side. "My apologies, laddie, I wouldna be doing this to ye if I hadna a real need." He lifted the destrier's massive tail, felt for the bone, and just below it, started sawing.

Two minutes later he stood before Kate. "Ready, my dear?"

At the area she called the Strand, Kate pointed left. "This way."

Ahead stood massive homes of brick and he pondered how much her father must earn to live in such a fashionable place. He was surprised when they turned right and entered a narrow lane of buttressing buildings of caulk and brick with thatched roofs. She continued on, passing three churches and came to an even narrower, twisting way. She took his hand. "We are here. The third house. Come."

Not the least anxious to meet Hugh Dupree Templeton after deflowering his daughter, Ian asked, "Will yer father be here?"

She shrugged. "Given the hour, I'm not sure. He may be at board at a public house."

As if on cue, bells atop a dozen churches let loose, all bonging at different pitches, making it difficult to count the hour. He settled on the deepest. Six. So, three more to go before he could enter the Tower.

Kate climbed the narrow stairs ahead of him, stopping at the second landing. She pushed on the door latch and frowned. "Father's not home." She reached above the door. Key in hand, she turned the lock.

The moment Kate closed the door, she took one look at the narrow, darkly paneled room that apparently served as their living area, and gasped.

Books and pamphlets were everywhere, a man's tunic had been thrown on the floor, the table was littered with moldy trenchers and a tipped tankard, and in a bowl sat shriveled and rotting fruit. Kate threw open the shutters and looked about, hands on her hips. "It's not normally like this." She placed her hand on a kettle sitting on a shelf and heaved a sigh. "It's still warm. He must have just left."

She pulled out a stool. "Make yourself at ease while I see if Mr. Boots is still around."

"We can meet another time." Focused as he was on how he could possibly say good-bye, he had absolutely nay interest in exchanging banal remarks with her gray-headed admirer.

Kate entered the doorway to his left. When she returned she was grinning and holding a huge, scruffy gray cat with half an ear, four white paws and a wide white blaze down its muzzle. She rubbed her face against its fur. "Ian, please make the acquaintance of Mr. Boots."

"A cat?" Ian laughed, couldna believe he had wasted hours fashing over a friggin' cat. "How do you do, Mr. Boots."

Kate dropped the furry beast into his lap. "You two get acquainted, and I'll find something for us to eat."

Whilst Kate routed around and sniffed this and that for freshness, Ian sat straight, his hands on his knees, and stared at the yellow eyes glaring up at him. When the cat started kneading his leg with its claws extended, Ian snatched him up by the scruff and whispered, "I was being nice for her sake."

The cat hit the floor with a yowl, and Kate turned to see what was amiss. Ian muttered, "I think he's hungry."

"I don't doubt it. Father often forgets to feed himself, much less Mr. Boots. At least there is a fresh loaf so Father has been up and about as usual."

Ian frowned. "Did ye have reason to think he might not have been?"

Kate placed the bread, along with a crock of honey

and a flask of wine, before him. "I have had a frightening dream. I didn't see a face but somehow knew it was Father." She shrugged and took the seat opposite him. "Thank heaven a dream is often just a dream."

Ian reached for her hands. "Love, I need—"

Kate's stomach heaved and she pressed a hand to his lips.

Not yet, please, dear God, not yet. I do not think I can bear it.

He kissed her fingertips and grinned. "I was merely wondering if ye had some twine."

Kate blinked. "Oh. Of course."

Merciful saints, she had to get a handle on herself and her fear. But how? The moment when he would kiss her good-bye forever was almost upon her.

She rose on shaking legs and reached above the wooden pantry for her whatnot basket. Twine in hand she turned and found Ian standing, a pained look on his countenance. Oh, no, he had asked for twine to distract her. It fell from her hand as blinding pain seared her chest and tears flooded her eyes. *"No."*

"Aye, lass." He came to her then and wrapped his arms about her. His lips pressed her forehead as his hands swept over her back. In a hoarse tone, he whispered, "I do love ye so verra much, Katie. I never thought I would love, had nay hope of it until ye came."

She couldn't breathe. Oh, dear God, how was she to live now without him? She certainly did not want to. She slid her arms about his neck and clung tight, wishing she could get inside his very skin so that when he left he would have no choice but to take her with him.

"I, too," she whispered. "I do so love you . . . more than you'll ever know."

He took in a shuddering breath and gently removed her arms from his neck.

Seeing tears glazing his eyes, knowing he was vulnerable, the urgent desire to drop to her knees and beg him to remain nearly overwhelmed her. But understanding only too well why he could not, she began to sob.

"Oh, lass." He clutched her to him again. "I dinna want to leave ye, either." He lifted her chin so he could look in her eyes. "Someday there will be peace and when that day comes, I promise I will come for ye." He kissed her, hard and deep, imparting some of the anguish he was feeling.

Kate responded in kind for it was all she had left to her. This one final kiss that would have to last them a lifetime for, as hopeful as his promise was, she knew in her heart that the conflict betwixt their countries would never end. England and Scotland would never be at peace. Never had, never would be.

Too soon, he took a deep, shuddering breath and gently eased her away. After clearing his throat he murmured, "There is something I would like ye to have." His hand slipped beneath the top of his wide brass belt.

Kate swallowed convulsively in an effort to silence her sobs and clutched her hands before her, else she throw them about his neck again. She would not make this more difficult for him. Ian could ill afford the distraction of knowing he had left her shattered and wailing her heart out. He had too great a distance to travel before he'd be safe at home again.

Tugging the strings on a small leather pouch, he murmured, "I hope ye like it."

Kate gasped, seeing a large sterling-and-amethyst

cross and chain in Ian's palm. "Oh, my word . . . It's magnificent, but when, how?"

He grinned, flashing his dimples at her, mayhap for the last time. "Would ye believe I have been carrying this, intending to give it to ye since before ye conked me over the head?"

"Oooh, Ian." Despite her resolve, tears started streaming down her cheeks again. He had cared for her deeply even then. And they'd wasted so many hours, days . . .

He opened the clasp and put it around her neck. "It belonged to my mother and her mother before her." He took her shaking hands in his and brought them to his lips. "As the eldest son 'tis mine to give to my intended."

Kate leaned into him, taking the time to savor his warm, musky scent and strength for the last time. "I shall wait, if need be, forever."

He let loose her hands and wrapped his arms about her and squeezed. "And I for ye."

Fire burned beneath Ian's breastbone as he brushed the flood from Kate's cheeks. He *would* find his way back to her. As soon as he kenned who had deceived his people and set the matter to rights, he would return. "One last kiss, love, and then I must go."

He found solace in the way Kate melted against him as their lips met, matching him ragged breath for ragged breath. He threaded his fingers through her hair, memorizing the feel, unable to let go of her just yet.

The door suddenly swung open.

Kate squealed, "Father!"

Hugh Dupree Templeton—tall, thin and bald—stood in the doorway, looking from his red-eyed daughter to Ian. "What is the meaning of this? And who are *you?*"

Kate dashed the tears from her cheeks. "Fa-Father, may I present—" She looked at Ian with horror in her eyes.

Ian bowed. "Sir John Goodman of Hawks Nest, sir."

Templeton, his brow furrowed, eyed Ian from head to toe. "Hawks Nest. Never heard of it." He looked at Kate. "I thought you were staying in Salisbury for three months. And why are you crying?"

Ian slipped an arm about Kate's waist. "She is crying because I put the cart before the horse, sir. I have just asked Kate for her hand and she said yes, pending your approval."

"Well now." Templeton, his surprise evident, looked at Kate. "Did you in truth say yes?"

Kate nodded, her fingers wrapping about the cross. Templeton tossed his cape in the general direction of the wall hooks. As the cape fell to the floor he muttered, "I see. And what have you there?" He pointed to Kate's hands.

Nibbling at the corner of her mouth she murmured, "A gift . . . from Sir John."

Templeton closed the distance between them to better examine the cross. "Humph." He then turned to Ian. "You're a knight?"

"Yes, sir. Earned my spurs at the age of twelve."

"So you have the wherewithal to care properly for her? A roof to put over her head?"

"Yes, sir, I do." In truth, not exactly, but before he returned he would see to it that Seabhagnead did indeed have a roof.

"All right, then. You can have her." To Kate he said, "I am starved."

Ian had all he could do to keep from decking the man. Nay hello, nay *Good to have ye home, Kate,* much less a kiss for his daughter who had been fashing over him for the last week. Ack!

Heart aching for her, now kenning why she hadna bothered to tell her father anything prior to heading for Scotland, Ian pulled Kate close after Templeton vanished into a back room. "I hate that I need leave ye now, but I must."

Kate, her lips and hands trembling, patted his chest. "I will see you to the door."

Before she could take a step, her father shouted, "Katie! When will we sup?"

Ye had best leave before ye kill him.

"Nay, lass, 'twill be hard enough as it is. Tend to yer father. Just remember that I love ye beyond measure."

He kissed Kate a final time, then turned her by the shoulders. Giving her a pat on the arse, he sent her forward to do her father's bidding. His heart heavy in his chest, Ian slipped out the door, taking Kate's cape with him.

Chapter 22

Despite it being gloaming, the lanes and roadways were still crowded as Ian, Kate's cape balled under his arm, made his way toward the Tower of London. Eyes scanning for livery, soldiers in the Henry's service, he made his way east on High Street to Emms Lane, where he turned left and entered a mercantile. He passed a dozen market stalls selling all manner of foodstuffs, from fish to grains, and as many enclosed shops of thatch, clay and brick offering all manner of cloth, house goods and baubles. At a fruit vendor's he purchased a wee woven-reed cone full of raspberries and farther on a wedge of farmer's cheese.

He had eaten all but one raspberry by the time he reached the Thames, where he turned east and walked down the wharf, passing hundreds of ships and boats tethered to quay after quay. Despite a slight breeze the air felt heavy, carrying the scents of sewage, spices, leather, wine, sweating bodies and mildew.

The dock men and seamen, consumed with moving and counting cargo, paid him nay heed as he weaved his way around the mountains of bales and casks. Seeing a bale of cotton with a flapping rope, he remembered his need for twine and slipped his sgian duhb from his forearm. Without breaking stride he sliced a goodly length of rope free from the bale and continued on.

When the Tower of London finally came into view ahead and to his left, Ian slowed, again struck by the very size of the place. Surrounded by a moat and fronted by the Thames on the south, enclosing hectares, the Tower was a most impressive sight. Built on a Roman fortification, he'd heard the walls were fifty feet thick and didna doubt it. Before him—in the center of the river-facing wall—stood the formidable Traitors Gate.

Walking a few yards farther he found the roadway that went past the west wall where he kenned another, less-formidable gatehouse to be.

As he turned into the lane, he took his time examining the Bell Tower on the southwest corner. To the best of his knowledge he need only enter the west gatehouse, cross the moat on a footbridge, pass through another guardhouse, go over another wee bridge and *tra-la,* he would be at the Bell Tower, which would also be guarded.

'Twas doable. Had to be.

The only uplifting aspect was seeing that a goodly distance lay betwixt the Bell Tower and the massive keep the pockpuds called the White Tower, the royal residence, where most of the guards should be concentrated. Ack.

He continued on, looking for a hidey-hole until such time as the bells struck nine.

Finding a carriage shed, he eased open the right side of the double doors and slipped into the close interior. Leaning against a wheel he pulled the balled-up destrier's tail from inside his sleeve, wrapped a short length of the rope that he'd pilfered about the clubbed end and then made a loop. After combing out the bits of straw with his fingers, he began to braid the coarse hair, so unlike Kate's except in length and color.

His preparations done, he settled on the ground, his back to the footman's box. He would try and catch what sleep he could. 'Twould likely be a verra long night.

At Benochie, near Aberdeen, Shamus sat seething upon his roan destrier high above the flat moor of Harlaw beside the wee river Drie, looking at what many a Highlander thought of as the gateway to the Lowlands through the Grampian range.

Behind the ridge at his back awaited 10,000 furious Highlanders. All were anxious for blood after Donald, Lord of the Isles, had fired their blood with tales of how his original forces—which included Donald Dubhs and the Camerons—had charged, brandishing fire and sword, through the Stewart-held Inverness and Dingwall, only to be soundly routed by Albany's forces after Albany had announced that the earldom of Ross wouldna go to Donald but to *his* son John.

The fact that the raging liege lords were all cousins mattered naught.

Land and power were at stake. Mayhap even the crown. Which meant none behind him would leave this field until those before them were routed, or they themselves couldna raise an arm.

And Shamus had nay doubt that the opposition was of the same mind.

Mounted on the opposite side of the field sat Albany's son John, earl of Buchan, and his cousin Alexander Stewart, earl of Mar. Selfish bastards both, in Shamus's opinion. With them sat Irvine, Davidson and Sir Andrew de Leslie and his six battle-hardened sons. Beside them stood or rode every burgher of Aberdeen.

Yet that wasna the worst of it.

Having studied long and hard, kenning the area and more importantly what Ian would advise, Shamus had spent the better part of last night arguing with the Highland command in his brother's stead for a three-pronged attack, but being outranked, he'd been overruled. They would go forth at dawn, he was told, in a straight frontal attack. Donald and Cameron were dead set on plowing through the enemy, using their larger numbers in a wave-after-wave fashion. Worse, kenning Mar's battle strategies of the past, kenning their steeds would be well armored, Shamus felt certain the enemy would be closely packed with long spears aplenty.

'Twould be a friggin' bloodbath.

Shamus cursed and looked to the sky. His gaze on the North Star, he prayed for Ian's safety wherever he might be and for the lass who had captured his brother's heart should Ian ever catch up with her. As for himself and those at his back, he murmured, "Thy will be done."

The bells rousted Ian out of a fitful slumber as they had repeatedly over the last two hours. He rose and stretched. 'Twas time.

He shook out Kate's hooded cloak with its embroidered front placket and brought it to his nose, inhaling the scent of roses and woman. How many moons would have to pass before he'd next lay eyes on her? Feeling pain bloom in his chest at the very thought, he gave himself a shake, threw the cloak over his shoulders and threaded the bone button through the loop. Gathering his shoulder-length hair into a queue, he caught it in the remaining bit of rope, and then settled the loop attached to the horsehair braid on his right ear. Using the last raspberry he darkened his lower lip to what he hoped would approximate Kate's rosier hue. He then pulled the braid forward so that it hung down the front of the cloak, giving ample testament to his supposed sex, and pulled the hood forward, masking his upper countenance.

Ian silently thanked Kate for her long stride so he had no need to mince as he approached the west gatehouse and the spike-toting guards.

"Well, if it ain't the Templeton cow," the guard muttered at Ian's approach. "Come to pay his lordship a call, have ye?"

Praying he didna sound like a squeaking door, Ian murmured, "Yes."

The guards guffawed and uncrossed their spikes. As Ian passed, the guard on the right pumped his hips in lascivious manner and said, "When you're through servicing his lordship I will be waiting, sweets."

Ian's hands clenched, wondering how many times Kate had had to endure this kind of abuse. Deep breath in, deep breath out. Now isna the time. On the way out, he'd have ample time to drive his fist into the bastard's balls.

It took willpower to keep to a sedate pace and to keep his temper in check as more guards verbally abused him at the next gate. God's teeth! He'd kill them all if one said another disparaging word.

At the Bell Tower door, the single guard grinned as he lifted his spike and reached for his key. "Hey, you're back. How was Salisbury?"

Ack! Now this one wanted to chat him up. Relying on Kate's favorite word, he squeaked, "Fine."

"Good to hear it. By the way, they brought in a bear cub yesterday. Cute bugger."

"Ah." Please shut up and open the damn door!

The door finally opened on silent hinges—a blessing—and Ian entered and waited to hear the key turn. It did. On silent feet he took the winding stairs two at a time. On the first two landings he saw no light beneath the doors and no guards and continued on to the third. There he found a guard dozing and gold lamplight oozing from beneath a door.

He tapped the guard on the shoulder. The man immediately jolted and rose. "Good eve, mistress." Without another word, he inserted a key and shoved the door wide.

Ian nodded his thanks, stepped into what was now James's royal apartment, and the door closed behind him.

A slender lad sat at a desk on the opposite side of the circular room, his back to him, apparently reading. In slow fashion, James I turned to face him, and Ian saw that he was pale to the extreme.

"Oh, 'tis only ye." He turned his back and pointed to a ewer at his elbow. "Pour me some wine."

Ian threw back his hood and pocketed the braid. "Pour it yerself."

James spun, mouth agape. "Who . . . Who are

you?" Since the lad had sucked in a lungful of air and looked about to bellow for the guard, Ian crossed the room in three quick strides, grabbed James by the scruff and slapped a firm hand across the lad's mouth.

Verra quietly Ian hissed, "Ian MacKay, my liege, and I would much appreciate it if ye'd keep yer bloody voice down else the lot of us rot in here for all eternity."

Bug-eyed, James, near death-white, nodded.

"Good lad." Ian released his hold and looked about—taking in the cold fireplace, the worn carpet, the barren stone walls, the multiple books on the desk and the few tallow candles.

Humph. Nay fragrant beeswax for our laddie.

Keeping his voice low, Ian asked, "Where is Sir Campbell?"

James silently pointed to an adjacent room.

Ian smiled at the lad who so looked like his father. "Please be so kind as to fetch him, Your Majesty. We have much to discuss and precious wee time to do it in."

James ran. A moment later Sir Gregory Campbell, his faded green robe askew, came through the doorway, and Ian was taken aback despite Kate's warning. The man had aged terribly.

Ian held out his hand. "Dinna look so shocked, Campbell."

Gregory Campbell came forward and took his hand. "Ye are the last man on earth I expected to see."

The right corner of Ian's lip lifted. "So I ken." Without waiting to be asked if he was thirsty, Ian poured wine into what he assumed was Campbell's tankard and drank his fill. He then faced them. "I have come in the hopes of exchanging vital information. My goals being to see James and ye set free and Scotland safe . . . and not necessarily in that order."

Sir Gregory nodded but skepticism was written all over his countenance as he settled on a stool. James stood at Campbell's shoulder, his hands behind his back.

Ian looked James in the eye. "Ye havena been forgotten. We want ye back. Many a chieftain has been sacrificing, hording coins for yer ransom." He rattled them off, starting with his own liege lord and ending with Duncan MacDougall of Drasmoor. "These men have let much-needed repairs slide, kenning the demand will be high."

Campbell held up a hand. "What do ye mean *will be?* It *was* made."

Ian looked at Campbell. "To whom was the ransom demand sent?"

Campbell, his color rising, sputtered, "Ye damn well ken who. To Albany."

So it was true, all that Kate had told him. Ian collapsed onto a nearby stool. His head in his hands, he asked, "When?"

"Four years ago. Exactly a year after we were hauled in chains into this godforsaken place."

Bile rose in Ian's throat. For almost a decade he'd served Albany faithfully and to what end?

More importantly Scotland and her people had been betrayed. They were already on the brink of civil war—just a heartbeat and a lie away—because no one was "officially" on the throne. If Albany's duplicity became public . . . ?

He shuddered, kenning too well what would happen.

God, he was going to be ill.

Campbell rested a hand on his shoulder. "My God, man, ye really didna ken, did ye? Does anyone?"

Ian shook his head, not yet ready to speak.

After a minute, having decided he would confront Albany and kill him if need be, Ian straightened and rubbed his hands across his face. "How much is the ransom?"

"The document His Majesty affixed his signature to, as proof that he still lived, said 60,000 in silver."

A king's ransom and unfortunately not to be had in Scotland's coffers. Ian kenned that for a fact, having seen the registers.

To James he said, "We—those I named—will get ye out, my lord. Of that ye can be sure."

But *when* would prove the problem.

Campbell asked, "How did ye come to be here?"

Ian rose, needing to pace. "Ye have a good friend in Kate Templeton."

Campbell blew out a breath. "So she got to Scotland."

And no thanks to ye, she nearly got killed. "Aye, she did, and she is back, safe and sound where she had best remain." Since James had no inkling of what Campbell had set into motion, Ian left the rest unsaid but his tone told Campbell that Ian would brook no disagreement.

"And my ladywife?" Campbell asked. "Is she faring well?"

Oh, shit. "Campbell . . . Greg, I am so sorry to be the bearer of—"

"Nay!" Campbell, suddenly the color of whey, began to waver, and Ian reached for his arm.

After settling Campbell on a stool Ian murmured,

"She passed peacefully in her sleep, Greg." Thinking a lie might prove more comforting than saying naught, he murmured, "At her funeral, I was told that her last words were prayers for your safekeeping and return."

In a broken sob Campbell asked, "Ye were there?"

"Of course. Margaret was a respected lady of the realm, Greg. How could I not be?"

"Thank ye."

He patted Campbell's shoulder. In truth, Ian had been there only to recover any documents Margaret might have left in her wake.

Ack.

Suddenly the room was reverberating with the sound of bells. Ian slapped his hands over his ears. To his amazement James and Campbell didna appear to notice. When the ringing finally stopped both within and without his head, Ian grumbled, "God's teeth, how in hell do ye stand it?"

James shrugged. "Ye get used to it after a few years."

"Ah." 'Twas nearly time for the changing of the guard and he needed to leave. He hauled up his mail shirt, reached into his sporran and pulled out a few gold coins. He handed them to James. "'Tisna much, but they might buy ye a few boons whilst ye wait. More will be on the way." To Campbell he said, "I need go."

Ian donned his braid, pulled up his hood and bowed to James. "Never lose hope and never forget who yer friends are, my liege."

Nodding, James said, "I willna forget, and God-speed, MacKay."

Ten minutes later Ian was again at the west gatehouse. The foul-mouthed guard, seeing his approach, hooted and grabbed his groin. "Hey, how 'bout a suck before you take leave, sweets?"

Ian, head down, was hard-pressed to ignore the man, but ignore him he did. Unfortunately, the bastard made a grab for what he perceived to be Kate's breasts.

Chapter 23

"Aaaaaaaay!"

The scream ripped from Kate's throat. *Ian! It was he who was being tortured on the rack. Stretched out naked, hands and feet bound by rope. She could see his face, the sweat, see and smell his blood.*

A scream ripped from his throat and she screamed with him.

"Katie! For God's sake, wake up!"

Someone held her close and she flung her arms, trying to get free.

"Kate, open your eyes. Child, you're all right. Open your eyes."

Still screaming and heart bounding, Kate did and was shocked to see that she was in her room and in her father's arms.

Panting, she managed, "Papa?"

"Oh, Katie. Thank God." He wiped the sweat from her brow and continued to hold her close. "You frightened me near to death. You have had some bad ones, but this has got to be the worst."

"Ian!" She struggled to get free.

Her father held firm. "Ian who? You kept screaming the name."

She shook her head and fought harder, her mind consumed with the images and sounds of Ian's pain. She had to get to the Tower. She'd seen her cloak, his boots in the corner of the cell, knew what he had done. How he had been captured was still a mystery but the fact remained that he was in the Tower and desperately needed her help.

Her father grabbed her by the arms and shook her. "Answer me!"

She shook her head, renewing her struggle to leave the bed. "I can't. I can't."

He pulled her to him again, surprising her with his strength. Running his hand over her head he murmured, "My child, my poor child."

Blinding pain bloomed behind her eyes. Oh, no, not now! I do not have time for this now.

She was suddenly looking at her mother, a girl of sixteen through her father's eyes. Black glossy hair being blown out behind her, smiling at him shyly yet knowingly. Kate could feel her father's joy in just looking at her, then a rising apprehension.

"Will you?" he asked.

Her mother twisted back and forth at the waist, her hands behind her back. They were surrounded by fields of wheat. The sense of apprehension grew to near pain, and then her mother's face broke into a broad smile.

"Yes, I will marry you."

Overwhelming joy, so strong it nearly took her breath away, flooded her.

The image subsided and with it the pain lodged behind her eyes. She shook her head and found her father, tears in his eyes, staring at the cross Ian had given her. "Why are you crying?"

He cleared his throat. "I know you're fey, child. Just like your mother. I have known for a long time."

It was on the tip of her tongue to deny it, but then Kate saw little point. She had lived with this lie for close to twenty years and was bone weary of it. "So now what? Will you now hate me as well?"

A tear slipped down her father's cheek and he took her hands in his. "Never. As long as I breathe, Katie, I shall always love you."

He loved her? She dare not believe it. "You stopped loving Mama."

"No, I let her die without admitting my mistake or letting her know that I had never stopped loving her." He squeezed Kate's hands. "I was frightened, Katie, but not of her and what she knew. I feared that she would say the wrong thing to the wrong person and we would all hang for heresy. My fear manifested as anger with her when in truth I was angry with myself, for I lacked the courage to walk away from an important post, the court, my king. I thought if I made her knuckle under my will, I could have it all: keep my prestigious position and income, and keep us safe." He took a deep shuddering breath. "I was foolish and prideful and cruel."

Kate's heart and mind churned. "So why are you telling me this now?" She had to go and quickly.

"Because I am about to lose you, and I did not want you to go without your knowing that I do know and still love you."

She desperately wanted to believe him, but experience had taught her caution and she refused to risk Ian's life in the hopes of salvaging what little was left of her own.

"Father, do you have any coins?"

He nodded and reached for the pouch he always carried unless in bed. "How much do you need?"

"As much as you have."

He took a deep breath and emptied the pouch into her palm. "Will you tell me what you need this for?"

"I wish I could, truly, but I do thank you from the bottom of my heart."

Scrambling out of bed in her cotton night dress, she threw on over it the filthy gown she had worn for the last week and then donned the last clean gown she had to her name over that. Her father silently watched as she gathered her few ribbons, her extra undersleeves and underskirt. Tossing them in a basket, she looked about the room. "You will take good care of Mr. Boots?"

He nodded and rose. "I will miss you."

"I will miss you, too, Fa—Papa."

He managed a brittle grin, his eyes again filling with tears.

"Oh, Papa." She wrapped her arms about him and gave him a kiss on the cheek.

Her heart as heavy as it had ever been, she tore around the living room, throwing the wine budget, some bread and her shears into the basket. She then grabbed her father's cloak from the floor and raced out the door.

Hugh, tears streaming down his face, swore lividly as his daughter disappeared. He ran to his room, lifted a floorboard and pulled out a small leather pouch. Kate had screamed far more than just *Ian* while trapped in her nightmare. He knew she was on her way to the Tower where this Ian was apparently being held. Fearing he might have already lost her forever, he raced down the stairs and into the night.

* * *

Jogging along the wharf, ignoring the catcalls of sailors weaving their way back to their berths, Kate had eyes only for public houses. She had to find doxies, a handful at least. Hearing shouts she peered down a short mews and saw lamplight splashing onto the hard-packed ground. Mayhap. Keeping to the wall, she peered in the window and found two ladies with painted faces, leaning or sitting on men's laps. Perfect. Now to get them out where she could speak with them.

She waved before the glass. No one noticed. She went to the partially open door and waved, hoping to catch one of the ladies' eyes. Nothing. Ugh! Time was fleeing. Kate threw the door wide. All eyes turned to her.

She forced a smile and crooked a finger at the doxie closest to her.

A scruffy buffoon in rags bellowed, "Watch it, Rosie, else ye end up in the cloisters."

For some reason that set all within the low-ceilinged room to howling like braying asses.

The one named Rosie, a short woman of mayhap Irish descent, ambled up to Kate, one hand on her hip. "My, my, what have we 'ere?"

"I need a private word."

Rosie turned back to the crowd and, jiggling her breasts, hooted, "She needs a private word."

The room exploded with laughter.

Kate, her fear mounting and her patience at an end, took hold of the woman's elbow and hauled her into the mews. "Mistress, I do not have the time for foolishness. Would you like to earn a fast pound or not?"

The woman's eyes narrowed suspiciously. "A *pound*? And what need I do to earn it, fuck the king?" She threw back her head and laughed.

Kate crossed her arms over her chest. "Fine. If not you, then give me the name of one who will."

The woman sobered immediately. "What *exactly* need I do? I am not into beatings, mind ye."

Beatings? Kate shuddered. "I need you to find three more ladies and come with me."

"The *ladies* ain't a problem. But come where and do what?"

Merciful mother, give me patience. "I need you and the ladies to entertain—keep happily occupied, if you will—several of His Majesty's guards so I might . . . do what I need do."

Rosie cocked her head. "At the Tower, ye mean? Whilst ye *entertain* someone else being held within?"

Kate felt hard-pressed not to scream in frustration. "Yes, if you must know."

The woman grinned. "Well, ducks, never let it be said ol' Rosie has a hard heart, but it will cost ye two pounds. One for me and one for the ladies to split. We are gonna need seven ladies. They have doubled the guard yon, for some reason. And we will need wine. Lots of it." She held out her palm. "Half now . . . for the wine and the girls."

Praying the woman was honest, Kate counted out the coins and put them in the woman's soiled palm. "Doubled the guard?" She had no idea in which tower Ian was being held, much less how she would get him out.

Rosie pocketed the coins and took her by the arm. "Not to worry. One of the guards is a reg . . . friend. I will say we have come to celebrate some good fortune with him and his mates. Get 'em drunk and *entertained* in no time 'tall and then ye can slip in."

At the corner Rosie murmured, "But don't ye dally more than an hour. They will be changing the guard and we had best be away."

My word, was it so late already? No, it couldn't be. Kate looked about for a clock.

"Come, m'lady, in here."

Rosie led Kate into a dark alley with yet another public house. "Wait." A moment later she returned with two young women in tow. They went to three more establishments before the garishly dressed doxies numbered eight. All carried flagons of wine.

At the southwest corner of the Tower, Rosie pulled Kate aside. "Ye wait there in the shadows as close to the moat as ye can. Give us a bit, then come look. If ye see naught by the gate, then all is well. We made it into the gatehouses. If we are still at the gates, then ye have lost yer coins for naught."

Kate nodded and handed the woman the rest of the coins she had promised. "Godspeed."

Rosie chuckled. "Ain't no God here, ducks. 'Tis the Devil's work we do, but I thank ye for the thought . . . and the coins."

As Kate moved into the Tower's shadow, Roxie collected her friends and, arms about each other, they started laughing and weaving, heading for the gates.

Minutes felt like hours. Kate wrung her hands and strained to hear what went on just yards away. The women's voices finally grew distant, then faded completely.

Oh, please, please let them be in.

Her basket looped over her arm, Kate edged toward the torch-lit gatehouse. At the unglazed slit

aperture she peeked in and saw Rosie, her back to
the wall. Before Rosie stood a guard, his hose down
around his knees. Next to her another girl had a
guard fully occupied, but from behind.

Hurrying around the portal on silent feet Kate
silently blessed Rosie. At the middle guardhouse,
Kate found the same scenario. Four girls, four
guards rutting. Two couples in either side of the
moat guardhouse.

She slowed as she entered the bailey. The guard
before the Bell Tower frowned as she approached.
She pushed her hood back and his features relaxed. "Ah, it is you for sure. Kind of late for you,
though."

Her dream was proving too accurate. "Good
evening, Mr. Potts. Yes, it is late, but Father has come
down with fever and wanted me to fetch the Latin
books for him."

Mr. Potts unlocked the door and muttered, "But
be quick about it."

Kate's heart suddenly plunged. She'd given no
thought to how she would get Ian out should he be
too injured to walk. She looked toward the stable.
Guards sat three deep playing with dice. Praying she
sounded calm, she replied, "I shall."

At the first landing she checked to be sure no one
observed her, then ran down the long corridor
toward Beauchamp Tower. If any questioned her
she would lie and say she was looking for her father
who had come this way. He often wandered about,
enthralled with the history of the place. She, on the
other hand, loathed the Tower's dark passages and
cold stones.

Finding Beauchamp empty, Kate searched on.
Panting, she cursed at the top level of Deveraux

Tower. Empty. To the next, then. She flew down the stairs, coming close to falling twice. At the lowest level she peeked out the door, and finding the north corridor empty, she ran toward Flint Tower.

Just as she reached the portal someone reached out and grabbed her. Her scream became trapped in her throat as a strong hand covered her mouth, and she was pulled backward into shadows.

"*Hush,* Kate. It's only me."

Kate's legs nearly gave out. "*Father?*" What on earth was he doing here?

"I have been praying I was wrong but your presence here obviously proves me right." He hauled her deeper into the shadows. "I found him. He's in the Salt Tower. You may give him food and water and then you need say good-bye. I forbid you to risk your life like this."

He took her arm and led her forward. Kate, still not believing her eyes, sputtered, "But how? Why?"

"Later. Just prepare yourself. He's hurt and badly."

As they passed Constable Tower a guard stepped out of Broad Arrow Tower some distance ahead of them. "Easy, daughter. We are just walking about. Nothing more."

As the guard approached, her father murmured, "Good eve, Mr. Tooley."

Not until after the guard answered in kind and continued on down the long east corridor did Kate release her breath.

At Salt Tower her father paused. He checked the hallway and then peered through an open aperture to view the courtyard before pulling on the door and whispering, "The next level. Hurry."

Kate grabbed her skirts and took the winding stairs two at a time. On the first level she lifted a

rush torch from its wrought iron holder and carried
it to the nearest cell door and peered through the
narrow grill portal. Empty. She went to the next cell,
held the light high again and nearly screamed.

Chapter 24

Naked and covered in blood, Ian lay at an odd angle on filthy straw. His face was swollen near to being unrecognizable. Her beautiful Ian had been brutalized . . . by her own kind and for no reason.

"Oh, Ian."

Sobbing, Kate grabbed the door handle and pulled. It didn't budge.

Her father came to her side. "Shhh. Hold the light near the lock."

From a leather pouch he retrieved several large black keys. He tried to fit the first and then swore. "Must be Newgate's." He tried another key.

Kate's mouth dropped open. "You have keys to Newgate?"

"Katie, I have keys to every prison in the city." He tried a third key. "I have lived in mortal fear that either you or your mother would say the wrong thing at the wrong time and be taken away."

Kate's world turned completely upside down. "Surely they weren't given to you."

Grumbling, "This has to be it," he worked the next key. "A cask of wine, a friendly chat until the bailiff passed out, and a block of warm wax ensured that if I ever had need of it, I would have the means for your escape." The lock tumbled; her father blew through his teeth and pulled the door open.

Kate rushed past her father, fell to her knees beside Ian and ran a shaking hand along his swollen jaw. "Oh, my sweet, look what they have done to you." She looked up to her father. "We have to get him out of here."

"Katie?"

Kate's attention snapped back to Ian. "Oh, love, whatever were you thinking coming here? Never mind. Where do you hurt?"

In Gael he said, as if to himself, "I am dreaming, aye."

She answered in kind, "Nay, love, I truly am here, in the Tower, and we are getting you out of here." She had no idea how but would die trying if need be. "Papa is here. He'll help us." She looked up and found her father staring at Ian. "You will, Papa, won't you?"

"He's Scot." He looked at Kate in total disbelief. "Woman, what the hell have you been doing?"

Knowing she couldn't lift Ian's weight on her own, she hissed, "Later, Papa! Right now we need get him out of here."

Ian stirred, then groaned in obvious agony. "Katie, go. Go before they come."

She would spend eternity in hell first. "I *will not* go without you."

Thinking she had best hurry, Kate grabbed Ian's arm. He cried out and her father pushed her away with such force she toppled.

"Kate, for Christ's sake, his arms are dislocated. Mayhap even his legs. We can do nothing but offer a moment's comfort and then get out before we're discovered."

"No!" Sick at heart, having difficulty believing what her countrymen had done, she stroked Ian's fevered brow. "I will not leave without him."

Her father swore lividly. "Child, you must listen. We cannot get him out. Worse, if you're caught in here you will hang for treason."

Kate, tears burning the back of her throat, rocked back on her heels. "Father, help me or leave. My future is with him. Be it at the end of a rope or elsewhere. On this I will not waver."

"Katie." Ian's voice was hoarse, barely above a whisper.

She leaned over him to better hear. In Gael she murmured, "Aye, love. What?"

"Can he understand us?"

She looked at her father and whispered, "I dinna think so."

"Listen to him. He kens the truth, dautie. I canna move, and ye are putting yourself at risk for nay reason. I need to ken that ye're safe. I canna endure what I must if I fear ye are at risk. They need only mention your name, threaten to harm ye, and I would spill all I ken. Leave!"

"No." There had to be a way.

"Katie," her father hissed, "do you realize in helping him you will be giving up your king and country, all you hold dear, mayhap even your life?"

She looked up at the man who had sired her, but who had been too afraid to love in the face of adversity. Never more sure of anything in her life she whispered, "Yes, Papa. I love him that much."

Her father nodded. "Then get your basket and tear your undercoatie into strips and be quick about it." To Ian he grumbled, "You know what needs to be done."

Ian grunted since it was all he could manage, furious that Kate was in the Tower, furious that he had put her in such danger, and furious that she had brought her father, who could mayhap prove a danger to them both.

Templeton whispered to Kate, "Quick, give him some wine and then kneel at his head."

Kate settled a knee on either side of his head. "Can you open your mouth?"

Ian did with a minimum of discomfort which he found reassuring. He was either almost dead or his jaw wasna broken. Good news either way. He drank deeply, kenning what Templeton was about. Closing his eyes Ian started preparing himself. Kate, on the other hand, protested when Templeton put a cotton gag between his teeth. He would have told her not to fash but speech was impossible.

Her father ordered, "Kate, slide forward and put your knees on his shoulders—as close to his neck as possible—and hold on for dear life."

Templeton grabbed Ian's right wrist with both hands and placed a firm foot on his shoulder. As Ian groaned Kate hissed, "Papa?"

Templeton jerked, and Ian saw stars, brilliant as any in a winter sky, as pain shot through him in all directions. Unable to breathe, he took consolation in realizing he hadna shamed himself by screaming in Kate's presence.

He wasna able to suck in a deep, shuddering breath until Templeton placed his arm across his naked chest. Yet it wasna over and both men kenned it.

Kate, whimpering, stroked his cheek and re-moved the gag.

He managed to croak, "More wine, lass."

Kate brought the wine bag to his lips and he opened his eyes. God, she is lovely even with her face streaked with blood and awash in tears. He drank, never taking his gaze off her, still not fully convinced her presence wasna a dream. That she really was at his side, that he might again walk out-side these walls.

"Kate, again."

'Twas Templeton and he had taken hold of Ian's left wrist. Sobbing, Kate placed the gag between his teeth and settled her knees on his shoulders and her hands on either side of his head once more.

Ian tried to relax, to breathe deeply through his nose and hold tight to the image of her lovely face as Templeton's boot landed next to Kate's knee. He felt the jerk clear to his toes, and then the world turned black.

"Kate, quick. We need bind his arms to his chest. His left forearm is also broken."

Weeping, Kate did as she was told. Ian had yet to awake despite her slapping his cheek. "Oh, God, Papa! Is he going to die?" Oh, please no, please.

"Not if we can get him on his feet and out of here. Hurry, child. Your tears can wait for later."

Kate's hands shook like an old woman's, but Ian's arms were finally secured to his chest.

Her father wrapped his arms about Ian's waist. "He will be in a good deal of pain, but at least his shoulders are now as they should be. Come, we need make haste and get him dressed."

Together they managed to get his bloodstained clothing on, drag him out of the cell and prop him up against the corridor wall. Her father ran back into the cell, collected her basket and relocked the door.

"Papa, I can carry him if you can get him on my back."

Her father snorted. "Child, *think*. He weighs sixteen stone."

How could he possibly know she could not carry him if they didn't at least give it a try! Fearing the doxies would be gone soon, Kate pleaded, "Please, Papa. We cannot drag him with any speed and will only hurt him if we try."

"Kate." Ian opened his eyes. "I can walk. I just need a wee bit of help."

Kate started kissing him, cooing at him as if he was a bairn.

"Lass, just help me." God, women could be so . . .

Templeton grabbed his waist. Ian wavered, bile clawing its way up his throat as his ankles and hips screamed in protest from their time on the rack. Deep breath in, deep breath out.

They shuffled, wavered, groaned and slid their way like sots toward Traitors Gate.

Templeton slowed, peered out an aperture, then pulled Kate's silk cloak from her basket. "You put this on. Put mine on him. Wrap your arm about him as if he were I and do not let go of him until you get to the road."

Kate muttered, "But the guards?" She told him how she had entered through the west gate with the help of the doxies. "We need leave the same way."

Her father shook his head. "You can't get him that far and then onto the roadway. Not in his condition."

"Yes, we can. You and I together, we can get him out and then leave, forever."

Ian suspected that anguish made Templeton's voice hoarse as he told her, "I am not leaving with you, Kate. My life is here. I am too old to start over. Besides, if we both disappear we will draw suspicion."

"But—"

"No buts, daughter. Once you go through the gate you become an enemy of the crown. I will go to Campbell and James now, so should they be asked, they will repeat that you came to get my book. I will tell anyone who asks that I felt better, came as well, and you left immediately with me. Stay to the shadows and take the first wagon you come to. Head west. The soldiers will likely search north. I will leave through the west gate in only a few minutes, but do not dally. You do not have the luxury of time."

Seeing Kate was ready to protest, Templeton murmured, "We have no choice, Kate. Should I catch sight of you when I come out, I will help you, but again, do not dally or you'll find yourself back in here." His piece said, Templeton took a firm hold of Ian again.

By the time they hauled him through the inner Traitors Gate, Ian was ready to fall on his face. Seeing a shallow stone recess, he whispered. "I need rest."

Deep breath in. Deep breath out.

From his seat he could see the shadows of four guards chatting among themselves beneath huge oil lamps only yards away. Shit. To Kate he said, "Nay fashing. We will make it."

Already exhausted and terrified, Kate pressed a hand to her forehead. "Ian, your hubris speaks. I doubt you can get through to the gate, much less walk along the wharf without Father's help."

"Lass, 'Nothing is too high for the daring of mortals . . .'"

She took his face in her hands and kissed his bruised lips. "Horace: 'We storm heaven itself in our folly.'" Despite her tears, despite all she was about to lose and a very questionable future ahead, she somehow found the strength to smile. "As ye lust."

God, he loved her so, and his heart ached for her as she wrapped her arms about her father.

Against Templeton's cheek she whispered, "I shall write as soon as I can. And I do love you, Papa."

Templeton hugged her back in awkward fashion. "Do so as soon as possible for I shall worry until I know you are safe." Using the heels of one hand to clear his eyes, he whispered, "I love you, daughter. Godspeed."

Ian cleared the thickness in his throat. "My thanks, sir. I shall cherish her."

Templeton, his anguish in losing his daughter evident, only nodded, and shoulders hunched, turned and walked away.

Unable to fathom the amount of trust and love it must have taken for the man to do such, not sure he would have been able to do it had their roles been reversed, Ian muttered, "Katie, I forbid ye . . . to have daughters."

She brushed the tears from her cheeks. "You do, do you?"

"Aye." He had nay desire to ever walk in Hugh Dupree Templeton's shoes.

Kate took a tight hold on the fabric at his waist. "Lean on me as much as ye dare. Once we're past the gates we're turning right and going west along the wharf. There we'll be more likely to find a horse and mayhap a wagon." She kissed his lips. "Ready?"

He wasna, but it was now or never. "Aye."

She positioned the hood over his head so that it covered most of his face, and he grit his teeth and stood as straight as the bandages, a broken arm and his broken ribs would allow.

As they approached the guards Kate said in a chastising tone, "Father, if I've told you once I have told you a dozen times not to eat those oysters at Pickwicks. What need you do? Die? Ah, I see you are going to heave again, aren't you? Well, not on my slippers. So help me, if you vomit on me one more time, I will toss you into the river."

Ian groaned mightily as if he was about to heave, which, given his pain, could well happen and saw boots scamper backward.

After saying good night to the guards Kate took more of his weight and half-carried, half-dragged him out of the Tower of London.

When the pain grew to near blinding and he wavered, Kate whispered, "If you don't last long enough to teach me Kits in a Basket, I will never forgive you."

God, he loved this woman. "If I dinna . . . I will never forgive *myself.*"

What transpired over the next few minutes he couldna have said, so acute was his pain, and then next he was falling. Helpless to stop it, Ian grit his teeth and prayed he woulda scream when he landed.

Only four steps along the dark wharf and Kate knew in her bones that Ian couldn't walk to the nearest stable, much less ride out of London. Their only choice for a speedy escape sat rocking at their moorings in an oily river just a yard to her left.

Coming abreast of a row boat of a size that she

thought she might manage, Kate glanced over her shoulder. Seeing that no one was paying them any particular heed, she tossed her basket into the boat and then, holding tight to Ian, stepped off the wharf and into the little boat's bow.

With a groan, Ian fell as lifeless and heavy as a rolled carpet, knocking her backward and knocking the breath out of her. The boat rolled and thankfully Ian with it, so she could breathe again.

When the boat settled, Kate, praying she had not done him more harm, asked, "Are you all right?" She couldn't tell, given the poor light.

"Uh." He grimaced as she tugged on him and set the boat to rocking again. "Katie, sit. Please, before ye drown us."

"But you're so—"

"*Please* just get us away."

Kate looked toward the Tower clock. Almost midnight. The guards would be making their rounds and raising the alarm at any moment. "Do not move."

Ian muttered as she crawled over his legs and untied the rope holding them to the wharf. One hard push and they were floating backward between two large, single-masted vessels. A moment later the current grabbed them and they were floating backward down the Thames in the direction of the sea . . . and directly toward a looming four-masted galleon the size of Madrid.

"Augh!" Kate scrambled for the oars.

From his position on the damp floorboards Ian grunted, "What is amiss?"

"Naught. Not to worry." Kate's hands shook as she frantically shoved the first oar into an oarlock and reached for the second. Never having rowed before in her life, she prayed as she dug the oars into the water and paddled.

"Turn around."

In no mood for criticism since she had made almost no progress and they were now drifting at breakneck speed toward the galleon's Cyclops-like bow lamp, she hissed, "I am doing the best I can."

"Ye are facing . . . the wrong way."

How the hell did he know which way they were going? He was lying below the boat's walls. She slung the oars forward and pulled again for all she was worth and suddenly sailors were above her shouting, "*Heave to!*"

Heave to where? The saints preserve her.

"God's teeth, woman!" a sailor yelled. "Ye are sitting backward. *Turn around!*"

Oh! No wonder the rowing was impossible. She scrambled around and picked up the oars as more shouting came from the galleon's crew on watch. Two pulls and the boat surged . . . toward the ship! Oh no. No, no!

"Oh, shit!"

Kate looked down to see Ian staring up. She looked up and found the ship's bowsprit hovering above her.

"Use only yer left oar, woman!" someone shouted from the ship's rail.

She dropped the right oar and grabbed the left with both hands. Using her back and legs she pulled over and over again, not daring to look over her shoulder.

And suddenly they were sliding past the ship's side, staring up at dozens of open portals, miles of rigging and long yardarms. Her arms, back and thighs aching, Kate collapsed over the oar.

"Ye did well."

Kate wiped the stinging sweat from her eyes. "What idiot decided one must face backward to row forward?"

Not expecting an answer she glanced over her shoulder and found a dozen more ships at anchor waiting for the outbound tide to turn before they could make their moorings and unload their wares. "Augh."

Ian, grimacing, rolled to face her. "Love . . . the oar ye dropped . . . before we lose it."

"Oh, of course." She reached over him, making the boat rock and Ian groan yet again. "Sorry."

Hours later, having passed the snaking curves that marked Greenwich and now into a straighter, wider stretch of the Thames, Kate pulled in the oars and rested her stinging hands in her lap. The long blisters across her palms would burst the next time she grabbed the oars.

"Ian?" Kate stroked his cheek with the back of her hand and found his skin hot and dry. "Oh, no." She gave him a gentle shake. "Ian, please open your eyes."

When he did not respond in any fashion, Kate looked about helplessly. She could not pull to shore. They were still within an easy ride of London and might be confronted by soldiers.

The current was fast but her rowing doubled their speed and the sooner they reached the coastal marshes, the sooner she could seek help. Or at least find a horse and wagon.

Kate picked up the oars again.

Feeling heat on her face, sensing a bright sun on her eyelids, Kate yawned and stretched, only to feel her back muscles revolting. "Ooow."

Good Lord above. She then noticed she was rocking.

Kate bolted upright. Rolling silver and green sea surrounded her in every direction. "Oh, no! Merciful mother in heaven."

The Thames had carried them out to sea.

Chapter 25

Ian!

He had not moved since she had last looked at him. Laying a hand on his face, feeling the heat, Kate's panic tripled. He was burning with fever. She shook him. "Ian. Wake up. Oh, please, you need to wake up!"

Oh, dear God. She had to get help, had to get to shore. But in what direction? Grasping both sides of the boat, Kate carefully rose up on one knee, intent on gaining a higher perch by kneeling on the seat, and in doing so set the boat to rocking.

Do not think about whales and sharks. Do not think about the squid. Just do it, one knee up and then another.

Slowly she let go of one side and straightened.

At the top of the swell she saw land to her right. To her left she saw white splashes of various sizes dotting the horizon. Ships. But whose?

She scrambled for the oars that were dragging in the water and made the mistake of looking into the waves. "Ooooh." Bile rose in her throat. Oh, God.

Do not look, just row. You'll be fine. Just row.

Having no idea of the time of day but thinking it

still had to be morning, she angled the boat's bow toward what she hoped was the northwest and pulled back on the oars. Every muscle in her body screamed in protest.

You can do this. Just row.

With her gaze locked on the closest set of white sails, she pulled for all she was worth for land, disheartened to realize the water felt heavier, which made pulling back on the oars more difficult—or mayhap it was simply her aching muscles. The boat also sat higher in the water, which in her estimation could not be a good thing, would make it more likely to tip. Worse, the waves made judging her progress next to impossible.

Just row. Do not think about the waves, the distance or the ship. It appeared to be angling slightly, taking a more head-on tack, directly toward them.

When she realized the oncoming ship was twice the size, was in fact gaining on her, she didn't take the time to rise on the bench and assess her distance from land, she simply doubled her efforts.

Too soon and too far from land, the ship loomed large before her. Black as pitch, its sharp bow easily sliced through the waves that she had been fighting with body and soul, a flag flapping at the stern. But the sun's glare made it impossible for her to tell the colors, much less the nationality.

As it drew closer still, she could hear the slapping of sails, hear voices and creaking.

Please, Lord, let it be anything but an English man-of-war. Please, I am begging you, please.

After all Ian had been through, being rescued by an English ship would be the cruelest of ironies.

Barely able to lift her arms, she pulled the oars in. It was too much to hope that the ship would simply pass them by. As if reading her mind, sailors were suddenly scrambling up rope ladders and onto the yardarms. Sails suddenly collapsed and were gathered in. The ship loomed larger but at a much slower pace. It was going to stop.

All was lost.

Kate reached for the wineskin behind her, then slipped off the seat and sat next to Ian.

"I am so sorry I failed you." She lifted Ian's head and dribbled a little wine into the corner of his mouth. He coughed, swallowed convulsively and groaned but still didn't open his eyes. It took what little strength she had left to lift his head and shoulders onto her lap, to hold him a final time.

Running her fingers along his jaw, feeling the soft brush of golden whiskers, her heart folded in on itself. "I love you so very much. So very much."

He was dying and there was nothing she could do to stop it. Nothing anyone could do. "I never meant for any of this to happen. Never, I swear.

"Had I foreseen . . ." She pressed her lips to his hair. "God forgive me. I would give my life to see you whole again, to see you home, safe and sound." Her tears splashed onto his cheeks, making streaks through the blood and dirt, coating his once-handsome countenance. "Did I ever tell you how beautiful I find you?" She nodded. "Or how impossible I find your caring for me to be?" Tracing a finger along one gold-winged eyebrow, she whispered, "I shall never love another, never. You own my heart and soul, what there is left of it."

Sobbing, squeezing him to her breast, knowing she could not hurt him further for he was well beyond it, she rocked him. "Dear God, what have I done?"

Too soon their little boat went into a violent

side-to-side pitch, and she felt a great shadow loom over them. Eyes closed, she tightened her hold on Ian. Metal screeched on metal and then something— mayhap an anchor—splashed into the sea. Wood groaned, protesting its halting, and a deflated sail snapped and cracked in the breeze only yards above her. Voices, the words indiscernible, were carried away on the wind, yet still she held tight to Ian, not daring to look up. Not wanting to know what awaited them.

"Ahoy!"

She heard what sounded like cursing, and a ladder being dropped over the side and someone scrambling down.

Oh, God, not yet. Please. They'll take him away, and I'll never see him again. Please, God, no.

Something banged on their small hull, and she felt the boat lurch, then thud against the ship's hull.

Above her a man shouted, "'Tis MacKay and the wode lady, Madame Campbell, Home!"

Kate's head snapped up, her eyes wide. "Home? *Home!*" The *Sea Witch* rocked beside her in all her leaking-and-squeaking glory. "Oh, thank God! Home! Come quick, he's dying!"

The man with the grappling hook dropped into the boat. "Let go, mistress, so I can see." Kate leaned back so the man could run his hands over Ian. A moment later he was swearing and issuing instructions too fast for her to discern. Ropes dropped over the side, one falling loose into the boat.

On deck Captain Home shouted, "Get Mr. Bones!" He then scrambled down the ladder and into their boat. Together he and the sailor made a makeshift sling out of the rope and Ian was hauled, hand over hand, onto the ship. Home then turned his attention to Kate. "Can you climb the ladder?"

Kate nodded and stood. Either the boat rocked or her legs wobbled, but in any case she lost her balance and grabbed Home's arm. When she let go and reached for the ladder, Home growled, "God's teeth, woman."

Kate looked at the arm he held out. Blood smeared the sleeve of Captain Home's otherwise pristine white shirt. "I'm so sorry."

She turned her hands palms up and was surprised to see they looked like something she might find hanging in Butchers' Lane.

Home grumbled, "Christ's blood, they look like raw haggis." He bellowed up to the men on deck, "We have need for another sling!"

"No, really, don't bother." Her hands no longer hurt. They were numb.

"Lady Campbell, as long as I am master ye follow my orders."

Too tired to argue, Kate muttered, "As you lust."

"Damn right."

In short order Home had the length of rope looped around Kate's waist and bottom and then she was airborne, being bumped and scraped up the side of the *Sea Witch*. The moment her feet hit the swaying deck she asked, "Where is Ian? Is he alive? I must see him."

Leading her down the narrow companionway stairs, Home growled, "What the hell happened to him?"

"He was captured trying to enter the Tower." Kate explained as much as she knew, then added, "We didn't have time to make a splint for his left arm. It's broken. He can barely walk, so something else must be broken or dislocated."

"We will find out soon enough."

Before Kate's eyes could adjust to the *Sea Witch*'s darkened interior, the men at the capstan had hauled in the anchor, wenches and yardarms squeaked, and the ship began moaning its way north.

"Over here." Home walked to a long plank dining table. On it lay Ian, naked, discolored from his brow to the soles of his feet.

Hands over her mouth, Kate's gaze ran over the huge welts, his swollen joints and the massive bruising covering him. *Merciful mother in heaven,* how could any sane person inflict so much damage on another?

Home, his gaze also raking Ian, asked the wiry sailor at Ian's side, "Well?"

"Broken left forearm, several broken bones in his left foot, two—mayhap three—broken ribs, and a swollen liver. His shoulders had been dislocated but were reset properly and should mend. I'll work on his fever after I set his bones. His head injury"—he shrugged—"is in God's hands."

Kate, light-headed and nauseous, slowly slid to the floor. Ian, beautiful and gregarious, the man she loved with every ounce of her being, lay battered and broken . . . and all for naught. James was still fuming in ignorance in the Tower.

"Madame Campbell?"

Kate blinked the tears from her eyes to find Home squatting before her. Ian apparently had not told him her real name. "Yes, Captain?"

"Come, lass, we need to tend to yer wounds and feed ye."

Kate shook her head. "Tend Ian."

"Mr. Bones will tend to Ian." He took her arm and helped her to her feet.

Eyes locked on Ian, Kate murmured, "I will not leave him."

"I will not ask ye to. Sit there." He pointed to a bench tucked between two cannon carriages.

While Mr. Bones waited on the ship's carpenter to make splints, he cleaned Ian's wounds, and Captain Home directed another man to clean and apply salve to her palms, and wrap her hands in cotton sheeting. He handed her a lead tankard and ordered her to drink. She did and immediately choked. Augh. *Visgebaugh.* What Fraser had called the water of life.

Home stood over her, his hands on his hips. "Keep drinking."

Eyes watering, throat still burning, Kate eyed the remaining foul liquid. "But—"

Home tapped the tankard. "Drink or I will pour it down ye."

Not doubting he would, Kate took a tentative sip and shuddered as another dose of liquid fire ran down her gullet.

Home growled, "More."

Augh!

He stood over her until the drink was gone—which, after the fifth or sixth sip, wasn't so bad—then nodded to a sailor who handed her a wooden bowl of mutton stew.

Knowing she would be ill if so much as a joint touched her lips, Kate merely held the bowl and watched as Mr. Bones manipulated Ian's forearm, wrapped it in cotton sheeting, braced it fore and back with wooden slats, and secured all with leather strips. He then moved to Ian's foot and did the same while Kate prayed Ian would flinch, groan, *do something* to indicate that he was still aware, if only marginally. But her only reassurance came with the rise and fall of his massive chest—the sole indication that he was still alive and she could still hope.

Once Ian's bones were set Mr. Bones called for his medicine box. When the foot-long wooden crate arrived, he took out two glass vials and sprinkled the black powders into a bowl of piping water. "'Tis black willow and black currant. Should help reduce his fever." After straining the concoction through a scrap of linen, he held out the bowl and a thin hollow reed to her. "Would ye like to give it to him?"

Kate nodded, grateful to be of some use.

"Just a drop at a time. No more, or he will choke."

Having already managed to get Ian nearly killed, fearing she would now be his final undoing, beads of sweat broke out on Kate's forehead and her hands began to shake.

Mr. Bones patted her shoulder. "He's still swallowing his spit so he should do fine so long as ye take yer time."

He watched as she parted Ian's dry lips with a shaking finger and deposited a drop of the herb tea into his mouth. When Ian didn't choke, Mr. Bones grinned at her. "See, ye will do fine. I'll be back in a wee bit."

Harlaw Moor, once green and lush, ran red with the blood of Scotland's finest. Thousands lay dead or maimed as Shamus, soaked in blood and sweat, sheathed his claymore and grabbed his fallen liege under the arms. Dragging the MacKay backward, Shamus kept a wary eye on those few who remained from both sides as they checked their dead and dying.

"Ye will be all right, Angus," Shamus panted. "Just a wee bit more, and we'll be in the wood. Hang on."

The wood was still a good hundred yards behind them and at the rate Angus was bleeding—he had been struck down by a poleax—Shamus was none too sure that the man would make it there alive but he had to try, if for no other reason than to have him die in peace.

Finally in the relative safety of the wood, he lowered Angus to the ground and wrenched his own shirtsleeve free and slipped it beneath Angus's rent chain mail, pressing it to the man's open chest wound. From his liege's coloring and thready pulse, Shamus strongly suspected that Angus held on to life only by sheer willpower.

As Shamus craned his neck in hopes of seeing some of his clansmen about, Angus clasped his hand and hissed, "Promise . . . to take care of wee John."

Kyle, a powerful clansman and Angus's master at arms, suddenly materialized at his side as Shamus reassured his liege, "Aye, I promise, but dinna fash, Angus. We will get ye home."

"Aye," Kyle murmured, "just hang on, Angus."

Their liege looked from Shamus to Kyle. As his tears took shape, he whispered, "Bring Ian home . . . laird until the laddie comes of age. Kyle . . . Keep them safe."

As they watched, helpless to stop it, Angus took a final shuddering breath, his head lolled to the side, and all went still.

Heartsick, Shamus closed his liege lord's eyes and with head in hands cursed. His brother-by-marriage had been as querulous as they come, but he had always proved a good husband to their sister and a fair man when dealing with clan matters.

Aware that they couldna take time to grieve just

yet, Shamus gave himself a shake and rose. "How many have we left?"

"Seven hundred, mayhap a few more."

They both looked down on the blood-soaked moor—now, in gloaming, much of it a rusty brown, cluttered with their dead and dying. The MacKays had come there three-thousand strong.

Kyle scrubbed his eyes with the heels of his hands as Shamus cleared his tear-clotted throat. Kyle clapped Shamus on the back. "We had best get to it. I will take some of the men and check the field for survivors if ye will collect what horses ye can. Take Robbie and Alex with ye." He pointed to a collection of boulders close to the ridge. "They are all up there. Should ye spy any unscathed stragglers, set them to cutting saplings so we can haul our wounded home."

As Shamus turned, Kyle said, "In case ye were wondering, Donald is sorely injured but managed to ride away."

His blood still hot with fear and the fury of battle, still seething with the loss of so many, Shamus stopped and faced Kyle. "Truthfully, I dinna give a shit what happened or happens to that man, and ye damn well ken why.

"Right now my only concerns are for what will become of my clan because of *this*"—he waved back toward the Killing Field—"and how I am going to break the news to my sister that her husband of four years—the father of her three wee bairns—is dead."

Chapter 26

Howling wind and the faint but familiar thud and whoosh of waves crashing on shore rousted Ian from sleep. He opened his eyes, wondering why they should feel so gritty and his mouth feel so dry and coated, and blinked at the familiar stenciled-and-beam ceiling directly above him. He turned his head to look at the plaster-and-stone walls and shuttered window, recognizing the elaborate tapestry flanking it.

Now how the hell had he come to be in Siar Dochas's round solar?

Intent on finding out, he rolled to get out of bed and came to a groaning halt. Not because Katie lay slumbering and fully clothed at his side, but because his chest, shoulders and back hurt like hell.

Humph. Something was verra wrong. Kate, his lovely . . .

Ack! It all came rushing back; leaving Kate, going to the Tower, speaking with James and Campbell, the guard grabbing him and the ensuing fight, the brutal beating he received with a pike at the hands of the Tower guards, the rack and the agony of his joints coming apart, his limbs being slowly torn from his body, the agony of Kate's father putting his arms back in place, their escape into a dingy, and then . . . nothing.

His left shoulder protesting, he reached for Katie and found his left arm wrapped from bicep to palm. Humph! He threw back the furs covering him and found his left foot in similar shape. Deciding he had best take a careful inventory of his body, he rolled his shoulders, took deep breaths, wiggled toes—and came away from the experiment none too happy but without grievous complaints. He was sore to be sure but whole and alive.

He gave Kate's shoulder a gentle shake. "Katie?"

She jolted awake. "Ian!" Her hands clasped his cheeks and she kissed him soundly, then pulled back as if not believing her eyes. "Oh, thank God. Talk to me. Are you in pain?"

Seeing her eyes grow glassy he managed a grin. "Just sore, but glad to see ye." Verra glad in fact. "How did we come to be here? Last I recall ye dropped me without warning into a dinghy."

Kate blushed to a pretty pink. "Yes, that I did." As she started rushing through the tale of their rescue he slowed her down, anxious to ken every detail.

"So Home still believes ye to be a French widow that I was dallying with?"

Kate huffed, "Apparently."

Good news to be sure. The fewer that kenned Kate was English the safer she would be, particularly with his clan.

Overwhelmed by love, gratitude and regret that she had had to go through all that she had—emotions that he had nay words to express—he kissed her forehead and then tried to pull her close but his ribs protested. He had to settle for simply stroking her arm. "Thank ye. If not for yer bravery and"—he tapped her nose—"yer blessed stubbornness, I'd be dead."

She tapped his nose in turn and wiggled closer. "You are most welcome."

Would he ever ken this woman fully? Deciding it wasna likely, and still wanting to know how they had come to be in the far Highlands, he said, "Tell me why we are here."

"Captain Home took us into Edinburgh, but hearing what had happened at Harlaw, he decided ye'd be safest here."

The hairs at the back of his neck bristled. "What happened at Harlaw?"

Katie took his right hand in hers. "War, Ian. I don't know the details, just that it was a large and bloody confrontation and that your liege, Angus, is dead, as are many others. Your poor sister . . . So many are grieving here."

Ian's heart, already racing with the news of war, began to hammer with fear. "Shamus?"

Kate placed her hand on his cheek. "He's fine. Just bruised and weary."

Incredulous and sick that the fragile, spiderweb peace he had been diligently spinning and nurturing for years had been rent, Ian asked, "When was this?"

"A fortnight ago."

God's teeth! A *fortnight?* "Help me up."

Kate caught her lower lip between her teeth and shook her head. "I don't think so. I'm not sure you're ready."

"I am!" Ignoring the pain, he rolled onto his left

side and Kate scrambled off the bed. "Just stand firm, love, and let me use ye for leverage."

Looking none too sure that he was sane, much less ready to go about, Kate held out her arms.

He managed to sit but the room began to spin. Ack.

Keeping him balanced, Kate handed him a tankard. "Drink. Mr. Bones swears by it."

Kenning Bones had a magical way with herbs, Ian drained the tankard. Waiting for the bitter drink to take whatever effect it might, Ian's mind raced through the possibilities that could have initiated the strife. Most pressing was learning who was involved and if it was ongoing. Should it be, he needed to get to the fractious liege lords as soon as possible. His confrontation with Albany would just have to wait.

Feeling a bit better, Ian took hold of both Kate's arms and rose. The moment his feet hit the floor searing pain shot up his left leg. "Ack."

"Please, Ian, let me fetch Shamus here."

Ian shook his head. He needed to get to the long house where he would hear multiple versions of the battle, where his sister no doubt sat nursing her broken heart instead of being in this chamber where she belonged. Which was another confusion he had yet to fathom.

"Kate, stand to my right." When she did, grumbling all the way, he draped his arm over her shoulder and took a tentative step, putting as little weight on his left foot as possible.

He blew through his teeth. 'Twas doable.

Halfway across the room, he mustered a grin. "Like ol' times, huh, Katie?"

Carrying a good bit of his weight, Kate mumbled,

"Not the least humorous, MacKay. You should be abed until your bones knit."

"Trust me, I would be and with ye naked beside me had I the luxury, Katie, but I dinna."

Kate pulled open the door and they were immediately hit with a damp, buffeting wind, heavy with the scent of salt and rain. He took a deep breath. Home.

By sheer will they managed to cross the grassy spot separating the liege house from the long house, beneath which the MacKays wintered their cattle, above which lived many of their clan.

After taking the first of the four stairs fronting the whitewashed long house, Ian began having second thoughts about not allowing Kate to fetch Shamus. By the top, he seriously regretted it.

As Kate reached for the elaborately carved door, Ian removed his arm from her shoulder and straightened. Wouldna do, after all, to have the clan see him leaning on a lass.

Stepping inside he was assaulted by the scents of roasting mutton, fresh sea grass mats and warm bodies. All turned, growing quiet as they looked, realizing who stood in their midst. Then the voices rose in welcome and everyone rushed forward to greet him, his sister and Shamus in the fore.

"Ian!" His sister, a good foot shorter than he, wrapped her arms about his waist and pressed her face against his chest. "We have been so fashed."

He lifted Mary Kelsea's chin with a finger so he might look into her dark chestnut eyes and found dark circles and creases, stark evidence of her grief. "I am so very sorry for yer loss, dautie, so verra sorry."

She took a shuddering breath, her tears pooling but remaining trapped within the confines of her thick, blond lashes. "He died as he had lusted with sword in hand."

Aye, better by the sword than dying auld, lonely and riddled with pain, he supposed, yet still . . .

Shamus murmured, "Come, sit. We have much to tell ye."

Ian leaned on Shamus as they made their way to the long table at the center of the opposite wall. Shamus pulled out the center bench and Ian sat, his sister to his immediate left and Shamus settling to his right. Frowning, Ian nudged his brother. "Slide down and make room for Kate."

Shamus looked at him as if he was daft. "Since when does a coigreach sit next to the laird?"

Ian gaped at his brother. "Not I."

"Aye, I . . . ye. Angus wanted it. Ye ken the lairdship passed to John, but being too wee, ye, as his eldest maternal uncle, take stewardship, and they"—he waved to the assembled clan—"have already voted their unanimous agreement."

Oh, shit.

He was now the laird of the clan MacKay. Aye, he had always wanted a lairdship, had hopes that Seabhagnead would be the foundation for building his own sept, but that was to be years into the future when Scotland was stable and secure.

He looked about and found anxious faces from one end of the long house to the other. All expected him to immediately take the helm, make life not only livable but as secure and pleasant as nature, opportunity and his ingenuity would allow.

Not wanting to say the words but honor bound he murmured, "'Tis my honor."

The room erupted with the clamor of applause and banging fists on tables. Too soon for Ian's comfort the men, many wounded, rose and came forth to pledge their fealty. As he acknowledged each one he couldna help but notice all that were missing: Big Red, Connor, Kendrick, Hamish, Tyree, Glen, Tavish, Johnny, Clem, Wee Robbie, Erik the Tall, Drum and so many more. As the last came before him he looked about for Katie and found her standing by the door looking at the floor, her expression inscrutable.

When the last man returned to his seat, Ian levered himself to his feet. "Kate, please come here."

Heads turned in her direction to watch her approach. When she stood before him, he told his clan, "This woman saved my life twice in as many days. I hope she will pay me the honor of dining at this table."

There was a surprised *Oh* here and there but most just smiled. He waggled his fingers at her to come and she did, her cheeks rosy with embarrassment.

As the wine was poured, Ian slid down to make room for Kate betwixt himself and Shamus rather than push his sister to the side. 'Twas bad enough that he was now expected to lay in the bed that Mary Kelsea had called hers for the past four years.

To Shamus he said, "Tell me what happened at Harlaw and how it started."

As Shamus related what he had seen and heard at Stirling immediately after Ian's disappearance, Ian's temper began to rise. By the time his brother finished telling him about his confrontation with the Donald, every profanity Ian kenned sat perched at the tip of his tongue.

"Then what?"

"I told Angus, the MacDougall chieftains and then Albany, and we rode for home. By the time we got back here, word had already spread far and wide that Donald had torched Inverness and was heading for Dingwall. There, he ran into trouble and had to hie off."

"That doesna surprise me. Then?"

"He sent word for the clans to unite behind him. He was heading for Aberdeen."

Ian's patience, already frayed, strained to the breaking point. Praying he wasna about to hear what he kenned in his heart he would hear, he asked, "And the MacKays went where to join whom?"

"We joined the Donald just north of Aberdeen."

"God's teeth, Shamus!" Ian was on his feet. "Ye joined a friggin' uprising?"

Shamus rose, his hands balled into fists. "Angus said we ride with our own. Ye ken how it is!"

"But Donald was in the wrong. He's a selfish prick and well ye kenned it! Good men died for naught! Albany will win in the end!"

Shamus stuck a finger in Ian's face. "Right or not I couldna join Albany and Mar and kill my own clansmen."

"*Albainn bheadarrach*—beloved Scotland—before all!"

"Are ye calling me a *traitor?*"

"If the boot fits—"

They lunged for each other. Before either could land a blow, Kate bolted to her feet and pressed her hands against their chests. Her elbows locked, she shouted, "Enough! The pair of you! These good people are in mourning. Who the hell cares who is right or wrong? It's over!"

The room went deathly quiet.

All eyes swung from the combatants to Kate. One

by one the clan began murmuring, "English? Pock-pud. English?" Then someone shouted, "Aye, Sassenach!"

"Ah, *shit.*" Ian swept Kate behind him with his good arm and then jerked Shamus's dirk from his belt.

As his clansmen—their anger apparent in their red faces—rose, benches fell backward and women keened, Ian hissed. "Brother, I need yer help here."

Shamus's claymore sang as it came free of its sheath. Broadsword pointed at the advancing crowd, Shamus hissed out of the side of his mouth, "What the hell goes on here, Ian?"

Sensing he had only a heartbeat to explain, Ian shouted, "Clan MacKay, hear me out!" As the room quieted marginally, he continued. "I have told ye this woman saved my life not once but twice. Her name is Katherine Margarita Templeton, not Camp-bell. Aye, she is English, but has been in service to our King James I of Scotia for some five years."

The shouting dropped to a murmur at the men-tion of their king. After silently thanking God and his people's good sense, Ian continued. "She came to Scotland because she kenned a ransom had been issued and couldna understand—any more than our king can—why we hadna ransomed him."

Shouts of "Nay!" and "'Tisna true, there hasna been a ransom demand!" rang about the long house.

"'Tis true!" Ian shouted back. He took a deep breath. "Please sit and listen and I shall tell ye the whole sordid tale."

With much grumbling and banging, the clan fi-nally took their seats, all facing forward.

"I heard tell the English had demanded a

ransom," Ian told them, "but not believing it either I went to the Tower to speak to James. To hear it with my own ears."

Someone shouted, "How is that possible? The Tower is a massive, armed fort."

Ian smiled sheepishly. "I went in dressed as a woman."

Hoots followed the embarrassing admission. Even his brother looked at him strangely.

"I cut a destrier's tail off, braided it, stole this fine lady's cape, reddened my lips with raspberry and then dressed as her"—he indicated Kate—"made my way into the Tower."

Kate's head poked out from behind him. Her eyes as big as an owl's, she said, "You *did not!*"

"I most certainly did." As she scooted out from behind him, he told the now-enthralled crowd who thrived on details, "James is nearly a man now. Too thin and pale for my liking, but solid of bone and of medium height. He is being well educated, thanks to Kate here and her father. Campbell, on the other hand, has aged terribly."

"What is it like? The cell he's kept in?" someone shouted.

"He and Campbell are kept a suite of three rooms, not one, in what the pock—umm . . . English call the Bell Tower, for 'tis round and has a belfry." He described the barren stone, the worn carpet and narrow, unglazed windows. "There is furniture enough—more than most of ye have—and an inglenook opposite the door, outside which sits a guard day and night. James is taken out for walks within a walled bailey on good days." He didna ken this to be true but reasoned it would ease his clansmen's worried minds. "He's dressed well enough but not as he would be were he home. But the saddest part: he has grown angry thinking we have forgotten him."

Voices immediately rose in denial, and Ian raised his good arm to silence them. "Aye, I told him as much. Told him we are saving coins, keeping him in our prayers. I then asked if it were true that a ransom demand had been made. He told me that aye, he had signed the bottom himself as proof that he was still alive. That the ransom demand had been sent to Stirling four years past."

The room exploded, and Ian waited, kenning their anger. When the room finally quieted, he continued. "I swore before leaving him that I would find out who received the Henry's demand and see that all within the realm kenned it."

He took a deep breath, his memories of his incarceration still vivid. "'Twas on the way out that they nabbed me. I was beaten, put on the rack and then thrown into a cell. That is where Kate found me and took me out under the cover of darkness." He looked at her and smiled. "She saved my life and in doing so became a traitor to her own king and country."

"Why did she do it?" someone in the corner shouted.

His clansmen were acting as if he were telling some bard's fairy tale.

"I dinna ken. Why dinna ye ask her?"

Shouts erupted for Kate to come forth and speak.

Clutching her hands before her, Kate asked in Gael, "What do ye need ken?"

"Why do ye care about our king?"

Deciding on a half truth, she said, "I have watched him grow as an auntie might and ken him well."

They thought on that. And then someone asked, "And Ian? Ye didna watch him grow."

Actually she had. But just one part. "Ummm . . . He has a lovely smile and a way with words."

"What words, mistress?" a dark-eyed young miss asked, her wistful gaze on Ian.

"Let me see . . . 'shit,' 'damn' and 'I am going to kill ye, Katie' immediately come to mind."

The room erupted into laughter, and she looked over her shoulder to find Ian scarlet and shaking his finger at her.

"Do ye deny it?"

"Nay."

Kate faced the crowd again and shrugged, as if to say *I told ye so*. "Truthfully, he has been most kind."

A man shouted, "So how and when did ye meet?"

"The MacDougall's ladywife introduced us about a month ago." A month was stretching the truth but Kate felt like she'd known and loved him since birth.

One woman suddenly pointed to the pendant about her neck. "Lauds, she wears his mother's cross!"

Not liking the woman's accusatory tone, Kate looked at Ian just as he stepped forward and wrapped his free arm about her. The room erupted again.

Someone shouted, "Nay! Ye canna!"

Another shouted, "But she's a Sassenach!"

Soon the words just ran together in one violent, shouting melee.

The man she'd come to know in the past week as Kyle thumped his tankard on the table and bellowed, "Silence!" When the crowd hushed, he turned to Ian and said, "'Tis true, my liege. Ye canna take the Sassenach, an Englishwoman, to wife now that ye are laird. 'Twouldna be right."

Ian glared at Kyle and then at all those before them. "I can. The MacDougall married a coigreach. The Davidson married an Englishwoman. Even one of our kings has married one."

"And look where that got us!" someone roared from the back.

A frail old man at the far end of the table stood and banged his tankard on the table and suddenly the room quieted. To Kate he said, "Lass, ye are bonnie, there is nay denying it, so we can readily see what our laird finds so appealing in ye. Ye're also quick-witted and nay doubt as brave as any of us could ever hope to be if all that MacKay has said is true, but the fact remains that Ian is our liege now and needs to marry within his own kind . . . for the security of the clan and our way of life."

He looked deep into her eyes, and Kate felt a momentary jolt, recognizing a kindred spirit. My God, he's fey! Just as she, but powerful. And he was telling her to go, if she loved Ian. *To just go.*

Her throat, already tight, closed with the knowledge that the old man in tattered plaid—with a rispie, a bulrush, pinned to his crookedly donned cap—was right. Tears burning their way to the fore, she silently agreed.

"Nay!" Ian shouted. "I take ye, Katherine Templeton, to wife. I take ye, Katherine Templeton, to wife. I take—"

Kate spun. Left hand behind his neck, she slapped her right over Ian's mouth, preventing him from finishing the pledge. Said three times before three clansmen they would be handfast for a year and a day, or so James had told her.

When he reached up to pull her hand away, Shamus grabbed his wrist with both hands. "She is right, Ian, and well ye ken it."

As he struggled against his brother, Kate's tears spilled. "Shhh, Ian, *listen*. I will not take your destiny from you. I did not give up all that I hold dear to see *you* throw your life away. Aye, I love you and will no doubt die loving you, but love is not enough to sustain a man with naught else. A man needs work, he needs purpose, the respect of his peers, he needs the love of his people and you will not have that if I stay at your side."

Heart shattering, Kate lifted the cross from her neck, kissed it and hooked it onto the bit of wood sticking out of the dressing on his left arm. "I love you too much to destroy you, Ian MacKay."

She then turned and walked the length of the table. The people, silent, parted as she, tears streaming unchecked, headed for the door and an uncertain future.

"*Kate!*" Ian's shout echoed off the rafters. "If ye dare set foot out that door I swear I will hunt ye down if it takes me a lifetime!"

She stopped. Why did he not just cut out her heart and eat it? Her back still to him, she said, "You'll never find me."

"Ye are running, tail betwixt yer legs, to yer Nana's, Kate."

She had been thinking of doing that very thing. Nana would hold her, rock her, reassure her that everything would be all right—if only she could remember who Kate was. "Nay, Ian, you're wrong. I am heading for Cove to steal your horse . . . again."

"God damn it, Kate! Dinna ye even think on it!"

"You cannot stop me, Ian. Not in your condition."

She had only a dozen more steps and she'd be cloaked in night, where she could fall apart in privacy. "Good-bye and God be with you, my love."

She took those twelve steps and pulled the door open and suddenly it was jerked from her hand and slammed back into its frame.

She looked at the hand, the one that had touched her so intimately, and whispered hoarsely, "Why are you doing this to me? Leave me my pride, Ian, for God's sake, leave me my pride."

Panting from the effort it had taken for him to come to her side, he rested his head against hers. "I willna let ye go. Not now, not ever." He raised his head and asked, "Is there any among ye who still believes this woman isna worthy of the name MacKay?"

Consumed by pain, Kate wanted nothing more than escape, would have welcomed death if only it would stand before her. Already knowing their answer, she pulled frantically on the door latch. "If this is some ghastly test you need to know—"

In a taut whisper, Ian responded, "Nay. 'Tis life and death. Yers and mine. For they now ken I willna be liege without ye."

Kate's blood, once sluggish with grief, roared to life. "But you're their laird. They cannot—"

"They can and have in the past."

"Merciful saints pre—"

"Katie, shhh. Listen. Listen to the silence."

She searched Ian's eyes, not understanding. She turned. Everyone was smiling at her, including the old man in tattered plaid. Why?

They rose and started clapping and cheering.

Her insides quaking, she grabbed Ian's sleeve. "What is happening?"

His finger hooked beneath her chin. Totally

confused she looked at him and found him grinning like a golden god, deep dimples softening his normally chiseled countenance.

"I take ye, Katherine Margarita Templeton, to wife. That makes three." Ian's lips came down on hers in most possessive fashion. Once he had successfully drained her of any and all sense, he lifted his mouth from hers and whispered, "Did ye honestly think I would let ye go, Lady MacKay, without ye kenning Kits in a Basket?"

Heart soaring in understanding, still not believing the joyful smiles and hugs suddenly being thrust upon her, Kate clutched Ian's hand as someone brought him a stool to sit on and his people came forward to welcome her into the clan MacKay.

All were wishing them a joyful life and several of the men winked when they wished them many bairns. When the old man in tattered plaid finally stood before her, Kate took his dry, gnarled hands in hers. Knowing he was ever so much more powerful a fey than she, she silently asked, *Did ye do this?*

He smiled at her. *Nay, I canna bend any to my will any more than you can. We who see too much can only advise and hope. Only ye and he, by showing them the true depth of yer love, could erase their fears.*

Despite his denial in helping them, she gave his hands a gentle squeeze. *Thank you.*

At her side Ian grinned. "Ah, ye ken a kindred soul. Katie, please make the acquaintance of our draoi, our wise man, Belfour MacKay. I have never had need to call on him but most swear he works magic."

Belfour, his eyes sparkling with merriment, brought her right hand to his lips. *Ah, lass, how often their ignorance is bliss.*

Belfour, but what of James and Albany?

He nodded and took Ian's hand. "My heartiest well wishes for the pair of ye, my liege. May ye prosper and multiply like the hares on our grassy plains."

Ian laughed. "Belfour, ye are in obvious need of a ladywife."

Letting go of Ian's hand, Belfour grinned. "Nay, this rowdy clan is more than enough wife and family for this auld man."

He kissed Kate's cheek. *Much heartache and disappointment awaits him, lass, but he has ye now to balance the evil he has yet to face.*

He walked away and Kate, her gaze following him, asked, *But that isna what—*

Sweet dreams, lass, and go forth and multiply for Scotia will be in sore need one day.

Ian tugged on her hand and she leaned over. "Love, I am growing weary. Let us hie off to bed, shall we?"

Realizing she would not be getting the answers she sought out of Belfour this day, Kate heaved a resigned sigh and smiled at Ian. "For Kits in a Basket, my lord?"

He flashed his glorious dimples at her. "Woman, have I ever told ye that I truly love yer mind?"

Epilogue

Seabhagnead Castle, Scotland
1424

"Shamus, there she is."

Seabhagnead Castle, Ian's four-storied edifice carved out of sandstone and granite, surrounded by concave, ten-foot-thick battlements and a lovely ditch, stood proud against a heather and flame sunset, overlooking Loch Eriboll. To the south of it a rather impressive village was taking shape.

Oh, the keep wasna as grand as he had first envisioned it but then, times had gotten a good bit harder after he had confronted Albany and resigned his position. His clan was now dependent on what they could garner from the sea, be it fish or plunder, but that was life. And then there was the ransom.

The moment he returned from Stirling he had sent missives to every chieftain in the land, telling them what he kenned about their king. It had taken the chieftains thirteen years to collect the necessary coins which twelve chieftains, Ian among them, had just brought to London, where they secured the release of their king. Finally.

Now, after three arduous months, he was home. He could sit by his hearth dressed in naught but his *breachen feile*, play with his bairns, and tup the bloody stuffing out of his beautiful ladywife. Kits in a Basket, here he comes.

Tupping on his mind as it had been for the last week, Ian asked his brother, "So, will ye be seeing Maggie now that ye're home?"

His brother huffed. "Ye ken what Maggie is, Ian."

"Aye, a winsome wench in need of a husband, a father for her three bairns."

Shamus snorted. "Nay, she is a death wish. The woman has had three husbands in as many years. Nay thank ye."

"But the bairns?"

Shamus swung a fist and caught Ian's upper arm. "Ye're so concerned about the bairns, take them in under yer roof. None, least of all Katie, will ever notice."

Ian grinned as a distant trumpet announced their imminent arrival. He was rather prolific. Thirteen years married and eight bonnie bairns.

God, life was good.

As the portcullis rose in welcome, he cuffed his brother back. "Maggie is still winsome, brother, and once they have had a taste of loving . . ."

"Ack, I would be safer bedding down with yon flock."

Grinning, Ian waved to those lined up before Seabhagnead's stout front door, every inch of it cut from MacKay land.

In the bailey he slid from the saddle as bairn after

bairn came running across the square bailey, shouting, "Da, Da!"

Squatting down on his haunches, he hugged each and every one. Tow-headed, dark-headed, flame-headed. All his and Katie's and all beautiful but more importantly, perfectly sound and normal. Not a fey among them.

Mhaire, just three—and in his opinion the loveliest of the lot for she so favored her mother—held out a bouquet of wilted wildflowers to him. "These are for ye, Dada!"

"They are droopy, Mar," his eldest, Wee Ian—who wasna so wee any longer—grumbled. "I told ye not to pick 'em yesterday."

"But I saw him coming yester morn!"

"Enough, you two," Kate said as she approached, grinning from ear to ear. "Da loves them. Now everyone give him a kiss and then be gone so Mama has her chance."

After his bairns did as they were told—intelligent, wee dauties the lot of them, if he did say so himself—Ian grabbed Kate by her fine hurdies and kissed her senseless. 'Twasna until after she sighed contentedly that he thought about precisely what Mhaire had said. "Katie, what did Mar mean by she saw me coming yester morn?"

Kate, looking far too innocent, waved to the door. "Come, love. Ye and Shamus must be starved."

Suspicious, he opened his mouth to ask again, but Kate squealed in alarm and took off at a run in the opposite direction. 'Twas then Ian spotted wee Brion—all of a year and a bit, and still on Kate's teat—chasing after their gamely rooster, which nay doubt meant Brion needed to give up said aforementioned teat, in

Ian's none-too-humble opinion. Humph! 'Twas a wonder the place functioned without him.

After his squire took Thor's reins, Ian—with a giggling bairn hanging off each leg—shouted to Shamus, "I really think ye need give some thought to the widow."

Shamus looked at him as if he was totally wode, then called to wee Robbie, "Want a ride?"

Bairn on his back and with a few more trailing behind, Shamus, laughing, disappeared into the keep.

Seeing Katie round the corner with Brion in her arms, Ian slowed to admire her still-lush shape and long, youthful stride. "Ye grow lovelier with each passing season, Katie."

She blushed. "Go on with ye. Sup is waiting as are your bairns. They have missed you and are most anxious to hear about your journey."

What they were really interested in were the surprises he had for each of them in his saddle bags, but then he had been the same at their ages. He waggled an eyebrow at her. "And their mama?"

She blushed prettily. "Aye, my lord." Once everyone was fed and the wee ones were abed, the adults settled on benches and pillows before the sandstone hearth, anxious for news of his journey and of their king.

"So he's truly home?" Erik asked.

"Aye, truly, in Perth."

"What did Murdoch have to say?" Travis asked.

Their regent had high-tailed it like a deer. "He and his family were gone by the time we arrived."

Kate asked, "When will he go to Scone to be crowned?"

Ian suspected it wouldna be long in coming, given the current tensions. "We will hear as soon as arrangement can be made. The man has waited a long time to be crowned, and I'm sure he wants the event to be worthy of a king."

An hour later he had finished his tale to everyone's satisfaction and looked at Kate. She stretched and yawned in grand fashion. "Will you be joining me, my lord?"

Grinning, he scooped her into his arms. His poor Katie. She still fashed about James, her reasoning being that despite all he had endured James was still a Stewart to the bone, and lastly she still had nightmares about him although less specific than in the past.

Sequestered in their comfortable solar he found a hot, fragrant bath awaiting him. An hour later they lay satiated in each other's arms.

"Kate?"

"Hmmm?"

He brushed her hair—now shot with silver at her temples—off her face. "What did Mar mean when she said she had seen me coming yesterday morn?"

Kate ran her fingers through the once-gold, now sandy, curls on his chest. "You ken how you are always saying Mar favors me? Well, she *really* favors me."

Ian frowned. "Ye mean . . . ?"

"Aye, love, she is *fey*."

"Ack." After a moment he dared ask, "How so?"

Kate grinned. "Yesterday she awoke, climbed into our bed and gave me a kiss. A moment later she said, 'Mama, Dada's coming home tomorrow and he's bringing oranges and kittens in a basket.'"

While this is a work of romantic fiction, the Battle of Harlaw or "Red Harlaw" was, in fact, one of the bloodiest battles in all of Scotland's long, turbulent history.

The result was indecisive, for the casualties were so heavy on both sides that the fighting simply came to an end at dusk, with both sides claiming victory. Among the dead on the Highlander side were the chieftains Macintosh and MacLean and with them eighteen hundred of their clansmen. While Albany's forces remained on the field to collect their dead and dying (the earl of Mar lost nine hundred men and Sir Andrew de Leslie lost his six sons), what remained of the Donald's forces retired from the field and returned to their Highland homes.

In the end the Stewarts retained control. Albany had the satisfaction of seeing the Donald humbled and his son Murdoch ransomed. On his deathbed Albany named Murdoch his successor and the general assembly voted him regent. At age twenty-nine, James I of Scotland was finally ransomed for the reduced price of L10,000 sterling plus an additional L700 per year for bed and board. He was given an English bride, Jane, great-granddaughter of John of Gaunt. Crowned at Perth within a year, he settled on Perth as the royal seat and took his revenge with sword in hand.

After a trial, Murdoch was beheaded along with his two sons, the Douglas was imprisoned along with Graham, and the many earldoms and dukedoms of Scotland were reduced to just eight, the families affected being turned out without means or titles. A year later James called the Highlanders to Inverness. As the fifty chieftains arrived they were seized and imprisoned. Some were executed or exiled. Others were spared.

About the Author

Award-winning author Sandy Blair was raised in a small New England town and graduated from Northeastern University, Boston.

Winner of the Romance Writers of America 2003, Golden Heart and the 2004 National Readers' Choice Award for Best Paranormal Romance, and a 2005 RITA finalist, Sandy has traveled extensively, and fell in love with Scotland's history and beautiful, diverse landscape.

A Thief in a Kilt is Sandy's fourth Highland novel.

She currently resides in Texas with her husband and children.

For more information or to contact Sandy, please visit her website at www.sandyblair.net.